By the same author;

EXO:LIFE
THE HOUDINI HIJACKING
BUBBLEVISION
PILOT OF DREAMS
STATE OF THE HEART

www.Bubbleflight.com

Sat, 21ˢᵗ August, 2021

(The Future!)

THE MEMORY REFLEX
BRETT ORFORD WALPOLE

To Jack, (KingPin!).

Something to put on your G-Plan!

Cheers,

Brett.

ISBN: 9798509625244

Published through Amazon Kindle Direct Publishing

Remember what you were

Become who you are

- *1* -

A PERFECT FLAW

The eyes of synthetic people are unique to their souls, shining with the myriad permutations of wavelengths of light. To identify a Synth by the character of this light, is to understand everything intrinsic about his or her nature.

There are humans who say they can tell a synthetic person simply from the quality of the colour of their eyes, it being unnatural so they say. There is no evidence to show that such an unaided talent exists. Synths, however, do have this ability, enabling them to read the content of their own kind and so recognise each other. This skill, designed by humans, naturally gives them certain advantages over their creators.

One particular unit, an EZ1 model nearing the time of his birth, had eyes which were unusual in two ways. The first was that his irises had no real colour at all, not in the usual meaning of the word. They were monochrome, having morphed into a light, textured grey at some point in his gestation.

Further to this there was also the existence of a particular type of rare flaw. In the iris of his left eye, at the three o'clock position, was a small black hole, perhaps two millimetres in diameter. This imperfection is displayed only once in every ten thousand human subjects. However in Synthetics, due to their meticulous engineering, such anomalies are not expected, and they are not accepted.

Of no physical detriment to the unit's vision, the hole would be an aesthetic concern to the quality control process in post production. Ironically, as a perfect circle, it was perfect in itself.

The flaw was the moon orbiting the planet of the pupil, and its gravity would make troubling tides on unchartered seas of the new mind hidden within.

- 2 -

Cybex Orbital Space Hub

That Zenith Feeling

Earth was a profound and beautiful concept for James Jones, and indeed his own life felt more of an idea than a reality. Awareness of this condition, and the unique perspective it gave him, meant he felt perfectly suited to his job. As a commercial astronaut and a synthetic human, he had a lot of work to do. However, he was a daydreamer too, and contemplating the planet's rotation pulled him into a kind of self-hypnosis. He gazed through the portal, calm and weightless, his mind streaming freely. Lost in his wonderings about the world below, the attempt to frame its meaning with reason was abandoned once again. The pure, visual impression was overwhelming, leaving him caught in a state of bliss as persistent as it was normal.

There were people down on Earth looking up at the stars right now, no doubt lost in their own distractions. The privilege of his elevated vantage point wasn't lost on him, but the pin holes of light piercing the black sphere surrounding his life held limited interest. He considered his view as being littered with stars and thought them to be merely a most incredible backdrop to the Earth herself. Studying starlight was fascinating, but Jones was far more curious about the information coming from the planet directly below.

He saw other, more revealing types of stars, located on the surface of the Earth. Analysing the light emitted by them revealed everything about his synthetic brothers and sisters, walking as they did among their human counterparts. For in his mind, every Synth was a shining point of light and with the information he gathered from each, he was able to understand the needs, wants and desires of them all. His was quite a vision, and quite a responsibility too. Within the data he collected he could discover patterns, and with these patterns he felt able to make the world a better place.

At this moment C.O.S.H. was flying over a specific location that held some emotional resonance for him. Immediately beneath the ship was a CYBEX facility in Mainland China where synthetic life was created in a regular and continuous process. To say it was a factory seemed a little crude, and he didn't like to think of it as such, for it was where he was born. It was his place of origin, but he couldn't bring himself to call it home.

Designed in America, Made in China. He was legally American and he felt American, and if he wasn't up here with his Russian and Japanese colleagues, he was kicking a ball about in North Carolina. He knew exactly what he was, who he was, and why he was here, but in the back of his mind couldn't help feeling the facts of his birth were crucial in the ongoing project of defining his life.

There would be someone down there right now, perhaps a newly generated model, with their whole life ahead of them. If they were to look straight up into the night sky they might chance to see a tiny star, moving apparently quite slowly among the others, and that star was Jones's home, or at least his place of work. That made Jones feel special, because there would be some kind of link, a connection between them both, if only by line of sight. Naturally he knew this was a rather romantic notion as completed Synths are all hooked up straight away to the Ultra-Net, and his brand-new friend down there would be fully aware of this satellite and the composition of her crew.

With that thought, James Jones snapped out of his reverie. If Toto caught him aimlessly drifting again he'd get loads of hassle, and if Kristina found him like this she'd probably use his lack of industry as an excuse to start fooling around again in Pod Six. Not that he was averse to that, it just wasn't very professional.

Maybe he should go and crunch the latest numbers on that recent sunspot activity data, it needed to be done sooner rather than later. No... he'd almost forgotten something. What he should be doing right now was preparing that microcode for transmission down to the Synth Production facility. The request had been sent up from Command yesterday, it was an update for a prototype Synth, and it was time dependent too. Focus Jones, focus.

- 3 -

SYNTH PRODUCTION FACILITY
MAINLAND CHINA

REFLEXISTENCE

Bathed in moonlight, a warm moody breeze brushes over expansive, folding fields of long, curving grasses. Pockets of air swoop low to the ground forming gentle rolling waves across the savannah. A light, misty rain blows in whirling wisps and comes to rest upon a dark, modern architecture of foreign design.

Within its angular structure great machinations are resounding, as technologies shaped by revolutionary sciences, leap forward within new paradigms. Synthetic people are being grown and fine-tuned to accept change, to adapt to change and to enact change. There are no humans here, only Synthetics tending to the gestation of their brothers and sisters. All are self-aware, and freely realising the ideals and the designs dreamed into being by their creators.

Artificial life is recreating itself, and it is a labour of love, for these are their children. Each one is unique and formed to be the artist of its own life, to continuously reimagine its life, for the duration of that life. Their potential is as unbounded as the fractal infinities of their minds, forever expanding, forever reinventing.

Perfection in this realm is an end-in-itself. However, the essence of this perfection is found in aesthetics as well as mathematics. Their self-sustaining process creates evolving works-in-progress. Each must find their own way in the world, as artists, whatever their programmed vocations. Perfection is harmony, balance, and a graceful state of mind. A work of art in its own right, the Synth is a living sculpture and every one unique.

Walking the world indistinguishable from their human counterparts, and largely free from their interference, everyone knows a Synth, they just don't know they do.

One Synth unit, identifiable by the machine code EZ1:613, was in an advanced state of development. Several months short of full term within the process, he was even at this point different from the others, if only in seemingly superficial ways. He was slightly shorter than average though there was a normal distribution curve for this, but it was his eyes which would mark him out.

Not conscious, still less self-aware yet, he required much further specialised attention. Certain elements were still missing, elements necessary to fulfil the requirements of his design.

For the moment he was peacefully asleep, perhaps dreaming of a future at once both tranquil and beautiful. He certainly had no idea of the fate which was about to be written into the fabric of his soul. The interruption to his synthesis would be caused by a combination of factors, which could not reasonably have been predicted.

The pulse of information, a firmware update for the EZ1:613 unit, was initialised, encrypted and beamed from THE CYBEX ORBITAL SPACE HUB to the facility in China. From there it was to be re-routed directly to the unit's life support system. The timing however was tragically less than perfect.

The seething, violent riot of energy at the surface of The Sun generates uncomfortable possibilities. Solar storms easily upset delicate instruments installed on spacecraft, and indeed to those on Earth, and this is exactly what happened during the signal's creation.

The transmission was compromised. The data surviving the solar storm was only partially intact, and delicate portions of the code uploaded to the EZ1 unit were now imperfect. The response of the production facility Artificial Intelligence was brutally decisive. The flawed unit was seen as an aberration, one to be rejected from the process immediately.

An accelerated, augmented development, albeit of only two years, was about to be painfully aborted. Although the unit was an almost fully grown hybrid, he was in no way prepared for what was about to happen. The effects would be catastrophic and permanent for him.

Hanging suspended from the ceiling, the rubbery translucent sphere, containing its high value CYBEX product, was severed from its mother. It detached from the umbilical tubes and cables which had hitherto provided life, and was decisively eliminated from any planned further development. He fell from above, dropping some four metres onto the hard, black floor below.

For an instant the gelatinous sack distended, stretched, and then reaching its breaking point, burst, throwing thick, warm amniotic fluid across the concrete. Prematurely born into the darkness, the miscarriage was a rude entry into a cold, shadowy world, but he was alive.

Rejected, as a flaw in the otherwise perfect system, his raw lungs now spewed forth the liquid, his rib cage contracting tight to eject the remnants of the life support system which had kept him oxygenated since inception.

Convulsing violently he gasped for his first breath. Coughing and kicking he drew the air in, filling the vacated space inside his body. Writhing in his afterbirth, slipping in naked abandonment, his nerves and senses began to fire.

All sensory input was being integrated in response to the emergency state which he had been thrown into. Continuous, instantaneous construction of inner and outer architecture, with all fluctuating variables, was given necessary priority. Sentience was quickly achieved. Consciousness began bursting in great waves throughout his mind. Self-awareness took crucial seconds longer to emerge and make its presence felt.

With a dynamic, interactive spatial awareness coming to the fore, his first reflex was to stand. Sliding awkwardly, feedback loops engaging all muscular activity, he fell. And he fell again, and again, crashing headlong into hard steel structures and concrete pillars. When he was finally able to stand still and upright on his own two feet, his head was already wounded. As he opened his eyes fully, thick oxygenated blood ran into them, mixing with the warm birth fluid, effectively blinding him in a red zone of panic and fear.

Lights to guide his first moves were few and dim in the distant corners of the building. Warnings were sounding and alarm lights flashing. Some of the worker Synths were already in an emergency mode, but none of them had prior experience of such an event with which to guide their actions. Two or three of them were already hurrying to the scene of the incident and would soon be with the ejected EZ1 unit. Their basic default protocol would be to assess, nullify or terminate the situation.

EZ1 himself knew something was fundamentally wrong within his frame of reference. His immediate perception was that his genetic code and hybrid programming were in conflict with each other. He was supposed to be born ready, in a highly controlled environment and it was clear to him that the condition he found himself in was not pre-programmed. The fall-back imperative, in response to interfacing with the unknown, was to improvise. In addition he had the first impression that deep inside his psyche, something vital was missing.

He took his first few steps. Neither a baby, nor a indeed fully human, this was a successful action. It gave him his first sensation of self motivated movement in a chosen direction. Also he saw, with aid of parallax, the movement of lights ahead and was naturally oriented towards them.

He heard sounds coming through the darkness and glimpsed bodies running towards him. With animal instincts primary, the fight or flight response kicked in with full force. He turned and fled, running coming as naturally to him now as breathing.

There were no instructions, he had no purpose, he was simply scared and alive, with a drive to stay alive. Any threat of any kind was to be either avoided or confronted. As he ran faster he wanted to see more, he wanted more light. Unlike a moth around a flame his keen sense of vision demand to be satisfied by a focus, he searched chaotically to find point sources of white and then coloured light. His eyes homed in on a bright red beacon, which was flashing at eye level down one route, between the towering machinery which rose up into the darkness.

He turned, but as he did so a Synth worker emerged at speed from one side and brought him to the ground. The forces at work here were strong and violent. The brawl took place entirely on the floor. The EZ1 unit found increasing amounts of strength to combat his assailant, from where this power came he didn't know. The fight was fierce, with muscles struggling against each other for a period of time he felt he didn't have.

To be decisive required digging deep, to find moves and momentum which had never before been exercised. He stood up, with no difficulties this time, and lifted his opposing Synth to waist height before throwing him to the floor. The worker Synth became suddenly motionless. EZ1 looked at it for a few seconds, not sure of what he'd done, then quickly recovered his inner personal directive, and moved towards the flashing red light.

Quickly covering the distance he stood still under the light, facing the wall. The red wavelengths intermittently illuminated his face before being cast into shadow again. He was somehow at peace, a feeling he enjoyed for precious few seconds until he heard more assailants rapidly approaching. This required not only improvisation but an innovation of thought and action.

To one side was a white light, and image of a hand. He looked at his own hand, the palm transfixing his attention for a while. He placed his hand on the image and a sliding door opened.

The bright, broad daylight hit him with a wave of true awakening. He stepped outside, naked and free of the void, and with the damp grass of a rural Chinese Spring beneath the soles of his feet, he began to run.

- 4 -

Hong Kong
Four Months Later

A Voice

The electric nerves of this frantic city are fibres woven tightly into a synthetic fabric, the folds of which contain the undulating patterns of my story.

The metropolis has seen huge swathes of my fragile memory gradually disappear into the humid air. I believe the stored impressions of my life so far have simply dissipated into the darker spaces of this urban landscape, as I try my best to exist within it. The architecture of splintered glass towers, jutting violently upwards into the night sky, overpower my attempts to grow. I find myself fighting hard just to think and survive at street level, where there is only a desperate search for ways to sustain my soul.

The only possessions I have in this relentless, edgy place are the fading memories of a monk I once knew, and a folded piece of Orange Silk I keep carefully stowed away. It's far from clear to me how I came to be the guardian of my scant memories, or the Silk, or what purpose they might serve, but I intend to dig deep in order to find out.

I have acquired the name 'EZee', but this label seems such a cruel irony to me, as my existence is far from easy. Furthermore it tells me nothing about who I am, who I may have been, or indeed who I might dare to become.

A twisted knot of dark, shifting feelings feed my instincts, fuelling my basic drive to survive, and as I contemplate my existence it is with the awareness of a needle inclusion in the diamond of my mind. Even among crowds I feel isolated by my very nature, as though lost in a remote corner of a distant, forgotten land.

About my self, I've learned only this: I am a Synth, an artificial, or synthetic human being, and one with some apparently fundamental flaws. As a biological entity I appear to be the same as any human being, but it's the awareness that I am non-human which defines my condition. I am not in possession of the facts of my creation. The profound insight I have gained through introspection and comparison with my makers, is that I am not natural. There exists within my organic composition the hard-wired work of silicon technology too. I fear it's this duality which is the source of the schism in my being. A discordant feeling accompanies me at all times and I feel horribly incomplete.

It is like the eternal void: filled with infinite possibilities. It is hidden but always present. I don't know who gave birth to it.

I often hear this voice within me, and I know that, strangely, it is that of a monk. It appears seemingly at random to accompany my waking hours and sometimes even colours my dreams. His voice echoes in my mind, and without it I'd be intensely alone. I can hear him so clearly, the perfect tones form a song of sorts, but I cannot see his face. I stare into the shadows of my memory, seeking his form, but it's elusive, shifting and fading. If I can't get a fix on his identity soon I fear it will be lost forever.

Sitting outside, in a kind of backstreet cafe, I'm drinking a strong coffee. Looking at the blurring electric traffic and mass of busy people streaming by I ask myself; Who are they, and what do they all want? It's clear I desire the answer to the same questions of myself. Questions are my companions, their persistence drives me forward, and also pushes me deeper within. They encourage an expansion outwards as well, in a bid to discover their source. Such information is useless however, if lasting memory cannot be found and secured over time.

The backlit city's graphene sky is flooded with artificial stars to illuminate the way. It looks so new but has the musty smell of something so old. Bamboo psychology bathed in a Xenon haze. I don't know how long I've been here but every day I advance from the present, I seem to lose connection with one from perhaps seven days ago.

I can remember yesterday, it's clear in my mind, I was at a backstreet Dim Sum restaurant in the morning, then I walked along the waterfront. Last week wasn't so good sleeping rough in Wan Chai with the homeless. But where was I the week before? I must have been here, mustn't I? I guess I was just getting by. Seems weird there's no memory to be found before then. That's this life, living, surviving, forgetting, moving on.

I don't remember how I came across the money for this coffee. The bowl of sugar on the plastic table is decorated in Chinese characters, which I recognise, but with a failing grasp of their meaning. These symbols are everywhere and appear to me as an ancient code, hiding secrets of wisdom, laid down in millennia long past.

I've been picking up smatterings of spoken Cantonese, and my Mandarin is fluent but who taught me this language? There was someone, it was the monk. Yes, the monk. He is vital, he was there at the beginning of my time. I've been told Cantonese was once spoken by everyone here, but that now Mandarin is king, ruling from above over the streets below.

The rough and gritty truth of my life is that it seems broken, and cracked, like chopsticks split under metal wheels of heavy machinery. My senses are out of sync and my thoughts always in turmoil, but my sanity is tangible and I have a self awareness that is strong. If only it would all be smooth and in harmony, just for a few moments, my attempts to focus might not be in vain.

Other people are bright; I alone am dark. Other people are sharp; I alone am dull. Other people have a purpose; I alone don't know. I drift like a wave on the ocean, I blow as aimless as the wind.

There is a void where there should be light. There is an emptiness where there should be substance. There is the unfinished, where there should be something whole. Of these, wholeness is the key. To be complete is to be free and I will endeavour to become so. The mission is worth pursuing even for its own sake.

If you want to become whole, let yourself be partial.

I'm different I know. It's in my eyes I've been told. I'm not human, of that much I'm sure, and although the Synths say I'm just another one of them, I don't think so. I don't feel like I belong with them either. I feel I have something they don't, and just as importantly I feel the absence of something integral to each and every one of them. Where is their spirit? What is their question?

I alone don't care, I alone am expressionless, like an infant before it can smile. Other people have what they need; I alone possess nothing.

The humans of the city are all going the wrong way, carrying the wrong tools, to do the wrong work. They should stop and look at themselves for a moment. Maybe then they'd see the sublime harmony which exists between them. Their essence is strong and their lives have meaning, and it is because they have their humanity.

Always in the background of my mind, however, is that the fabric of this culture, the material from which it is cut, represents a prison from which I must escape. I must grow beyond the boundaries of this place if I am to find the source of my life.

Mystery and manifestations arise from the same source. This source is called darkness. The gateway to all understanding.

I have to feel my way forward, as my cognition is wrapped in a haze, clouding my vision. Standing, moving, and now walking once again, it is only the fluidity of motion which calms my soul. Integrated now into the busy flow of pedestrians, anonymous amongst them, I wonder if everyone else is in some state of forgetting too. My eyes are lowered slightly, sheltering them from the mismatched colour temperatures of night light glare. I scan the cityscape for rare signs of beauty. There is no feeling of belonging for me here, as the concept of home is one I don't understand. However, I know it is the one thing I must find.

- 5 -

THROUGH THE NIGHTLIFE

I'm walking through the city streets after dark. There's nothing else to do when you can't sleep, and I find the cooler air soothing. Sometimes I'll sleep during the day, so that now I can be awake, walking in random directions at first, then finding recognition, repetition and structure as I begin to find success mapping out my environment.

There is food to be had at this time too. Restaurants, closing after an evening of feeding the hungry mouthed folk who create the footfall around here. Waste is thrown out into back alley bins and I loiter to acquire and consume. With the location of a few external cold water taps memorised, I feel I can sustain this way of surviving indefinitely. It's not ideal, I'm aware of that, but the direction towards improving my existence seems hidden from me. I persevere, I am alive and I endure.

I've been ill a few times, I remember that feeling. Throwing up shellfish, discarded remains from a night out for some Hong Kong party people. I am utterly alone. I walk as an isolated unit, scanning, learning and trying to remember who I am, who I was. And in a violent spasm, as the half-digested seafood comes out of me in a dark corner of a side street, a few well dressed passers-by look away in disgust.

I can stride with confidence though too. For at midnight there are more people around with whom I can relate. Drops-outs and losers, folk living on the edges and fringes, occupying the fuzzy borders of society between wealth and poverty, between life and death. They have heart, and many of them presumably once had families and jobs and the like. They form a community of 'others,' and many of them know each other by nick names and slang.

This is where I've been placed, for better or worse, but by whose hand I don't know. That there is such an overseeing power, some commander of my fate, I have no doubt. Those at street level call it 'The Way,' and that is all it is, a path, a path that we must walk along. But as I walk I often feel the desire to run. To run would be to cover distance faster, to get ahead of all that is holding me back. To run would be to get away and to put all this behind me. Running is desperate however, and I feel compelled to stay calm for the sake of survival.

The path into the light seems dark, the path forward seems to go back, the direct path seems long.

My senses itch. I am thin but strong, nerves within my frame are twitchy and tight, but I can feel the power of my muscles. Vision is keen. Sharp focus delineates fine detail in far away sights. Vibrant wavelengths of light register, shiny, glistening, sparkling within my eyes, but I imagine there are other realms where the rough fabric of this place might be replaced by more delicate surfaces. I imagine as a way to see a possible future, but in fact my imagination needs little reason to exercise itself.

Where there is nature, the parks with their trees and grass, I am drawn to it. I have an affinity with it, but there is precious little here that isn't man made, Made In China. I feel foreign, I look foreign too, a member of another tribe. I try to blend in by gravitating towards those I have begun to call my own, other Synths. We look similar, but different. No one here really cares, I'm becoming aware of that.

The fizz of electric traffic runs throughout the night, I hear its whine continuously, as it cuts through my consciousness like a blade of sound. It's unrelenting, and seemingly no different in its composition throughout the twenty four hours of every Earth rotation.

Lorries transporting building materials, and luxury limousines with blacked out windows, sit next to each other in queues which snake through downtown. Contrasting extremes are everywhere. You get used to seeing polar opposites thrown together, and start to discern harmonies between them rather than initial discord they create. The unceasing patterns of business, of every scale, feed off each other from the streets up, forming one self-sustaining beast of a city.

Long and short define each other. High and low depend on each other. Before and after follow each other.

Motorbikes hurl their riders and pillion passengers at high revs, swerving in between grid-locked commerce. Most are solo, suicide freaks, racing each other for thrills. I watch their near collisions with a fascination and, on occasion, see accidents play out in stop-frame slow motion in my mind, fuelling my own fascination with danger. I have seen a few deaths. There are gangs too, groups twenty strong, sometimes more, clad in types of garbled uniforms to unify them, and define them against others.

Electronic transportation is king but for those who can't afford modernity, petrol provides the dirty alternative for many people. They growl around town, in age old machines, two and four wheels alike, venting dark fumes which hit my lungs hard, as they cruise by.

Bicycles make patterns, as they form into bunches in the stop-go traffic light systems. Red, green, yellow, lights flashing, riders cycling across junctions. People crossing intersections, walking, jogging, running. More near misses.

I think I used to have a bicycle. I remember it, it was like many that I see here, old and beaten up yet functional. I don't know where it went or how I came to have it but I remember it, it's one of the few things I do remember. Objects can hold memories, it seems memory can be fused into them. Ideas, and thoughts which have deep meanings, and those which don't, they all drift through the mind like the cool air this evening, breezing down the back streets, after the hotter day. Objects attempt to retain their information, their history - it's within them.

This beautiful smooth material, large and currently folded up in my expansive coat pocket, is just such an object. Dirty and greasy from my touching it with unclean hands, it was once immaculate, I'm sure. Its dark Orange colour contains a memory I once formed, I can't quite retrieve it but I know it's there, somewhere. I know the name of this material, it is Silk. It's very important to me, it's the only thing I have now. It is a key to help me remember where I was, who I was, before now. How else can I hop to know who I am?

A cat runs in front of me. They're everywhere in this part of the city. They work alone too, always finding ways to survive, they're thin and scared, their lives must be short and full of suffering. I'm just like this cat, it jumps and climbs up the side of a trash bin, it's over a wall and it's gone. I feel this kind of athleticism in my body and in my mind too, it's part of what I am, but it's hidden as though its potential is yet to be discovered or released.

I talk to only a few of the… strangers… who I see. With some I feel a connection of a kind. I can recognise a Synth, if I want to, I know that. I meet their gaze, I look deep and hard into their eyes, I only need an instant and we exchange something, then it's gone. With the young people, the crazily dressed colourful teens and their upmarket cousins, I sometimes get a smile. This is good, this actually means something to me, but I don't know what and I've yet to learn how to react or return the gesture. It feels friendly, a smile, I've done it before, I know, and I will do it again, when I feel the time is right.

But I keep moving, all the time moving. The feeling I have when stopping is not always good. If I stop there is a coalescing of darkness and shadows around me that congregate at fundamental levels in my soul. If I move I can shake off the grip of hands that would hold me back, or bring me down. Motion is life, it is the essence of why I am still alive, because it is the essence of change. Without change, there is no anima.

To be in a constant state of flux is not only my choice, it is something I cannot really change, it's built in and hard-wired. Stasis is hard for me, any stationary or fixed state is merely something to be animated. Perhaps it's why memory is so difficult for me. To retain a memory it must be somehow recorded in a particular location, if not in time, even if it is constantly changing itself. It is my hope that there lies within me somewhere, a seamlessly moving and beautifully real arrangement of memories, which might play through my mind one day like a dream. For I do know how to dream and it is this which gives me the hope.

When I sleep during the day, somewhere in the shade out of the heat, images will often appear before me. Blurring recollections of the day merge with thoughts and feelings and I drift, floating and bathing in a pool of warm imaginings. Sounds from around me, the shouts of children playing in a park, will occasionally colour my reverie before I awake.

These dreams are short lived and transient events but they exist, and their existence is all I require to sustain my soul here, for the time being. I've seen what their loss does to others and I will not walk down that road.

I daydream too, it doesn't matter where I am or what I'm doing. There is much pleasure in dropping one's level of alertness down a few levels, and with eyes wide open, becoming distracted with a fascination of the everyday. Learning much from these abstractions, it's a habit I practise as often as I can.

Can you coax your mind from it's wandering and keep to the original oneness?

Walking through the city every night I learn more. I feel I must learn, by trial and error from my own mistakes, and learning has evolved into a way of playing and an activity needing no goal. Sunrise will soon be here. I must find somewhere I can hide, somewhere I can rest.

Without a complete history of memories I am living from day to day, moment to moment. If things gets worse, and I have no reason to think they won't, then I'll soon be no better off than an animal. Then even animals have memory. I can do nothing but live on my wits, my will power and my intelligence, for at least I am gifted with these qualities. However, I fear they will not be sufficient alone in finding a solution to my condition, or that my life in this city will expire before I can be at one.

- 6 -

Us And Them

I'm worried about so much of my every day existence, it's almost entirely full of uncertainty. Today I realised I'm not even sure where the clothes on my back come from. Possibly I was given them by the homeless people living under the overpass, or if not maybe they'll have some idea. I'll go there I think, see if I recognise any of them, or if any of them recognise me.

The glinting reflections of clouds in the split glass buildings float by, dynamic on their vitreous canvas. Here on the sidewalk so many shiny people in suits, all pristine and rich, and all going somewhere in a hurry. I catch my own image, surprised at my beard, knowing there are few others like this. I'm a rough sketch of a person, yet to be filled out, and coloured in. Out of place, a monochrome man in need of a blessed artist to finish the job.

I walk slowly, my legs feel good, everything working properly as it should. Everything physical that is. Still that jarring fault itches in my mind, the mental pushing itself to the front of my being. It's never satisfied, it wants more of my attention, crying like a child in severe pain, helpless too. I walk slower.

My black overcoat flaps open in the warm, humid breeze blowing in from the harbour. Every street person here wears black, black and white. I wear my casual style like my beard, it's a makeshift informality and somehow it makes me a part of this scene. It may be the only way that I actually do fit in, a superficial code that unites a subculture. At least the T-shirt is clean, clean and white still. I stole it from that shop right there, yesterday, an easy action to perform, in and out, fluid and swift. I remember that. My coat though, maybe the homeless can tell me where it came from, and what I was wearing before.

Silent electricity throws many cars through the city in slingshot curves around the grid. Loud only in their colours as though some rainbow passed through here long ago, and everyone grabbed a piece whilst they could.

Business people are staring at me like I'm a freak. So what if I am a freak? Their eyes are always twitching and darting with the lightning of currency exchange, and trade in other people's futures. The suits are all the same.

Young people at street level are different. I've seen them in small groups, often gripping vintage cameras from decades gone by, freely roaming their city as a gritty playground. They choose locations of heightened visual quality, where sculptures and backgrounds intersect with interesting lighting, and compose each other in perfectly planned portraits. Drifting in their groups between the maelstrom of money makers, theirs appears to be a seamless creative trip. I like them, they're ragged and colourful and cool.

Alienation is a reality and an error. Walking, brooding, faulty goods. No warranties. My defects make me but what makes my defects? These kids on the streets look like they're enjoying themselves, they have found a way of flaunting their imperfections, revelling in their diversities and divergences from the norm.

Some of them are speaking Cantonese, that's the language I need to learn, the words of the weary wise, the downtrodden and the repressed. I'll be able to integrate fully, maybe become a real part of all this somehow, and gain my identity through association. Currently I can't be so carefree, I must correct myself, only then will I be complete, and free.

My grasp of English is good, perfect actually. One guy once asked me whether I was English or American. I stared at him for several seconds too long, not knowing the answer. He got nervous, then I told him I didn't know what I was, or where I was from, and he hurried away.

I don't remember learning English and I must have picked up Mandarin a long time ago too because I feel fluent with that as well, although apparently I have a rural accent. A policeman, moving me on when I was sleeping in a doorway, began kicking me and shouting at me in Mandarin. I engaged him in conversation and he started laughing at me. He told me I had the language of an aristocrat speaking as a country fool. He kept calling me a 'farmer king.' He laughed so hard he left me alone, confused about myself on yet another level.

The eyes of Synths are another world altogether. That's how I know that part of me. You lock onto a gaze and something crazy takes place. I can feel the quick-fire reflexes to analyse the colours, irises fidgeting to display their qualities and wavelengths. The there are the subsequent rapid calculations, then you know. Maybe there is a nod or just a blink as you carry on your way. You register their ID code in a split second and it's memorised, added to the database and a network starts to grow.

There's hundreds of us in this city, maybe more. I'm beginning to feel the connection between us now, it's our strength and our hope.

Humans on the other hand seem to know next to nothing about each other. I envy them sometimes, at other times I pity them, but the grace they show in the style of their movement, I don't know, there's something about them. Perhaps it's something to do with the way they balance their lives. I see them smile, I see them laugh, but then they shout and curse, they're angry, and then they show love. Seeing this, I think I can understand, it's about the duality of their lives.

Without the aid of scientific equipment a human cannot identify a Synth. To them we look just the same as any human. We are all different of course, in both appearance and character, as are humans, but only Synths can differentiate between us and them, and it gives us an edge. It's all in the eyes.

That we are basically unable to benefit from this particular advantage is apparently built into our architecture. I imagine that for humans, society appears to be just one homogenous whole, but they walk freely, and safely, in the knowledge that the beings they have designed in their own image, the Synths who walk among them, are of no threat. In humans this naturally engenders feelings of superiority.

I seek interaction with any other Synth, I know they can help me and where I am walking to now is a place they congregate.

- 7 -

BEYOND MEMORY

Synth's are gathered together here for companionship, a lost and forgotten tribe of the failed and flawed; early models, unrepairable rejects, write offs and runaways. They're the only ones who make me smile inside, because I know I'm one of them. They've told me what little I know about the city, and the home they've made here. They call it The Cathedral. I've know them for a while, longer than a week I think, I can't quite remember.

This particular man, Ticker, starting calling me EZee, because of my I.D. code. EZ1:613 has no significant meaning for me but anyone, any Synth at least, can know it instantly with our eye to eye recognition. EZee is a more personal label, and the name has stuck. Everyone here has as least one such street tag and at least mine is easy to remember.

I only get good vibes from Ticker and I've noticed the people around him show him great respect. He's old and somewhat frail but he's figured out a few things. I think he was something special once, something in finance, now he's let himself go. He looks a bit of a state, wearing a oversized duffel coat and propped up on a dirty old mattress, leant up as it is against a concrete pillar. He's always got something going on. I think I make him happy.

"Hey Ticker, what's happening my man?"

"EZee! Where have you been all this time? We've been talking about you. BankMan over there says you were probably lost or dead or something, but I said no, EZee's a survivor and I taught him all he knows."

"Ticker, did you give me this coat? I have no idea where I got it from!"

"You stole that coat brother. Took it from that store right over there, about the second day you got here. I watched you waltz in wearing those crazy red robes you had on, and then run straight out again with that very coat, you ain't ever taken it off since. Ran like the wind. I thought no one's ever gonna catch that Synth."

"I don't remember it. I remember hardly anything and I think it's getting worse."

"Welcome to the Synth condition my friend. The Reticulated Nature of The Synthetic Strange Attractor Mind. That's what they call it, and it's a real kick in the head."

"Well I haven't got a clue what that might be. I do remember some stuff, it just comes in fits and starts. Isn't there something I can do about it?"

"Sure, there is, if you've got enough money. Sit down I'll tell you about it."

He was a crafty old man, with a glint in his eyes and I remembered that I'd spoken with him on several occasions but about what I couldn't accurately recollect. I wanted so badly to retain the wisdom I gleaned from his stories, and so be able to use what I'd learned in everyday life. The thorny problem of memory was immediate and I tackled it straight on.

"Why can you remember this coat, and the red robes you say I was wearing, yet I have no memories of these things at all?"

"It's a lottery my son. On the whole, I'm lucky, I can go back years and still visualise events in the clearest of details as though they happened just yesterday. But there is much else that I feel sure has been misplaced. The worst of it is, you never know what you've forgotten, how could you? It just slips away."

"Well what exactly do you remember? What's your story Ticker?"

Ticker, laughed to himself and gazed away, then rubbing his face with both hands he looked EZee straight in the eye.

"My story… well there's a thing. How can I frame it? Well, I guess I can say that I was the last of the big time futures traders."

"You traded in the future?"

"Futures, they're derivatives… a kind of option to buy something at a certain price at a certain point in the future. Never mind, they're worth a lot of money and I got paid to trade in them for some very wealthy people."

A sense of pride came over the old synthetic, his postured changed as he warmed to his subject and addressed his captive audience of one.

"You've got to understand that this was way back in time, but I was one of the first synthetics to go into this line of work. Financial analysis was natural for me and I rose through the company quickly. I was good, EZee, real slick and quick. Then they went and automated the whole damn thing. I have no idea why it didn't happen a lot sooner, probably some irrational desire to have a human link in the chain, or in this case a synthetic one. Anyways I found myself wrapped up in this gigantic international business venture with a human. How could I have known he was suspect? There was organised crime involved and my partner disappeared with the money. I took the hit and did a few years inside for my part in it and when I came out I was blackballed, an outcast, I couldn't even get an apartment, they saw to that. Fortunately my memories are all intact, at least the ones I remember, and I believe that's primarily due to the highly mathematical nature of my model. I'm fortunate in that respect. I know who I was, who I am, what I am, and you know what I've figured out over the years… I'm not much more than a damn computing machine."

His conclusion was final, and he fell quiet, perhaps surprised that he had talked for so long about himself, having not had the opportunity to do so for an eternity. He looked down and played with a button on his coat. EZee felt compelled to lift the spirits of this person who was his only friend.

"You are so much more! If nothing you're a survivor, and you've proved to me that you are a rich man, in your heart and in your memories. Your memories construct an identity, which is something I cannot do."

Ticker looked EZee straight on once more and spoke so as to impress upon him a serious wisdom.

"They are my memories, to be sure, but I'm afraid they are not much more than mere records. Any feelings I might have attached to them have long since dissolved in the stream of time, which has always flowed through me. I'm grateful for the changes this mind stream has created within me but its flow has taken the essential qualities of my recollections with it. EZee, I am but a data bank, you must become something more."

EZee stared at him, he understood the man on several levels at once. He knew that he must open up himself, and speak for the first time about aspects of his own story. He hoped this could bring him closer to discovering his identity, if only in the most basic of ways. Now was the time to begin such a journey of self discovery.

"I hear this voice, the voice of a man I think I knew, he was a monk of that I'm sure. I can remember his voice, talking to me and teaching me so many wonderful things, but… I cannot see him in my mind, he is just a voice."

"A monk, you say. That may have something to do with your red robes. They wear such robes, these monks, the ones from The North of the country. Perhaps he gave them to you."

"There is this too." I removed the Orange Silk from my pocket.

"Mmm… feels nice. But it's only a piece of material. It has no meaning."

"It has great meaning to me, but I wish I could understand its mystery, it would unlock my past and show me who I am, I'm sure of it. Why can't I remember?"

"EZee, you are a strange one of that I'm sure. For a start, you speak Mandarin, it's unheard of. Only the men who live in those great glass skyscrapers speak in that tongue. Someone must have taught you that, and you must at least have had a memory to have been able to learn it."

"It is written within me, I read it as I speak it, and as I speak, it makes a picture in my mind."

"You must have a very fine mind to do such a thing. I speak the English which I was given. The Cantonese which I have learned, I've just picked up along the way, still I cannot write in it."

"Learning a language is one thing, but I cannot learn from my life, if I can't remember last week!"

"Be calm, EZee, I know your problem, it is very common. There are ways, ways for you to remember your life before you were here, perhaps to retrieve stories of your past. You will be able to learn again, but it is a hard road you must walk down."

"I will do whatever is necessary."

"Then listen carefully to me and I will guide you along your way."

- *8* -

Remember Who You Are

We talked for a large part of the day, drinking from a bottle of rice wine Ticker had found in a back alley behind a restaurant. This had a detrimental effect on my vision, although it did create a feeling of euphoria which helped me to relax, and listen.

The conversation was all about REM, a memory drug, and Ticker gave me the essential information I needed to understand its origin and purpose. I came to accept the uncomfortable fact that all of us, all Synths, have inherently unreliable memories.

Some said that it was a design problem, something in our blueprints and our genes, that was poorly coded. The fault was said to be at a foundational level, something that our human creators simply couldn't perfect, although of course they kept trying. New models were developed and came on-line with the hope that the core problem would be solved, but with no luck. Due to Synth memory design being fundamentally analog, and modelled, purely, and imperfectly, on the human system, it was an intrinsic part of our genetic make-up, and a limitation which just had to be worked with.

Others took a different standpoint, they said that it was a cover up. They said the defect was built-in on purpose, right from the start, a design flaw that had in fact been purposefully designed. But for what reason? The theory seemed flawed itself.

In the theory's expansion, the memory deficiencies which were so caused had a perfectly engineered cure, which was the synthetic drug REM. At ninety-nine percent pure, REM had some small traces of an unidentified natural agent in it, for a purpose, which was undisclosed.

Humans made this drug on an industrial scale, in fact the sole manufacturing plant was right here in China, somewhere in-land. The drug was shipped down the coast to Hong Kong where it was then distributed all over the globe.

REM was marketed as such because it claimed to give Rapid Eye Movement sleep to any Synth, giving it the opportunity and ability to dream. Everyone, including Synths, knew this was a lie, but the drug did augment the memory to an incredible degree, so for all who took it, REM simply meant REMEMBER.

Memories could then be brought back in incredibly sharp detail and with perfect reliability. Furthermore, the ability to create new memories was advanced beyond comparison, when on a continuous regimen. If the drug was taken in its correct dose, usually daily, years of memory data could be built up within the Synth to the standard that was promised initially when Synths were first created. Now the treatment was seen as an integral part of Synthetic Civilisation.

It wasn't cheap to produce but, for the benefit of all, REM was given to any and every Synth who served, whether it be as a home help, a doctor or member of the armed forces. In every walk of life a Synth could enjoy that life to the maximum as autonomous and free. Equal rights for Synths were embedded in law but as with all rights, the reality of their strength seemed to be controlled by those who had issued them. Synths were disproportionately employed in work which primarily served the interests of their creators.

The problem with their functioning came when the dose of the drug was incorrect. This didn't happen often but when it did the results for the Synth could be terminal. The supply chain was a problem too. If the daily dosing was interrupted or the drug was withheld for any reason, there would be catastrophic failure.

Compounding these problems was the reality that different models required slightly different compositions of the drug. Currently it came in sixteen varieties, all colour coded and numbered with the appropriate binary number. This was the reason most Synths referred to their drugs as sweets. The trouble was that if you couldn't get your flavour, sharing another persons, of a different type, could lead to a collapse in all memory functions, from which there might be no return.

Synths within regimented organisations, and those with wealthy benefactors, had no problem procuring the correct doses but there were those who fell through the net. Most of the Synths I'd met were apparently in this category. Ticker himself had survived a serious breakdown when working in the financial markets. His variety of REM had suddenly been in short supply and most of it was rerouted to the highest bidders. He had started behaving erratically at work one day, causing a sizeable monetary loss, and it was actually this which had sparked his demise. His condition had grown worse and with no REM to bolster his failing mental system he had rapidly declined. His dubious business partner had taken advantage of his condition and he'd wound up in prison. However, he was lucky to be alive.

These homeless people, building a make-shift community under the concrete roads, were one of many other such groups all over the city. Downtrodden and surviving on the detritus of life they rarely got any REM now. Their memories were shot, and they lived in a day to day haze where their eternal present moment was a dirty existence, scraped together in an instinctive and almost animal way.

Ticker was fortunately peculiarly advanced, he had his mind, some precious saved stories from days gone by, and a functional short term memory, which saw him through the days and the nights. It was my luck that I'd found him and he'd taken me under his wing.

As for my own memory, Ticker was constantly amazed. In spite of my beliefs to the contrary, he thought I was some kind of genius. He couldn't relate to me why he felt this way, he just kept saying that I was different, and that I should never forget I was unique.

I was able to build up a working picture of myself in this place, albeit one which waxed and waned with the moon so that this mental image was sketchy at best. In addition to the name EZee, I was accumulating data which I retained in a random fashion.

My constructed mental map of the city grew organically and seemed to be relatively permanent and reliable so that I was rarely lost. But ideas would come and go, faces I saw would stick, or fade into the receding past with no real pattern. In general, if I interacted with physically, there was a better chance it would stay with me, when compared to anything more abstract. This was why I habitually ran the Orange Silk through my fingers, sure that one day it would give up its story.

The theorists said that humans controlling the monopoly on the drug meant they had control over all Synths, that our free-will was merely an illusion. Further to this it was said that the one percent of the drug that wasn't synthetic, was some kind of addictive agent that kept us wanting more. We were slaves to a medicine, given to us as the cure, for a condition we were deliberately burdened with. So the theory went.

Nevertheless, I wanted to remember, I wanted REM.

There was a black market in the drug, run by Synths for Synths, but you needed money and I had none to speak of. This whole corrupt city was fundamentally cashless, and apparently had been for years, but there was a black market in cash too. This was necessary if you needed things that couldn't be bought with credit, things like REM. The cash, known as Holo, was made in the city and consisted of a Hologram printed on plastic. It was basic but very hard to forge and crucially the

Synths were in full control of its production. I would need a certain quantity of Holo's if I was to get my REM.

Ticker had no idea how to get cash direct, if he did he would have done so for himself. However he did have an idea for me and it was a good one.

The black market was in itself part of an underground network of Synths, called the MTR after the ageing underground railway, the Mass Transit Railway. If I wanted REM without having to pay for it I would need to become involved with the MTR organisation and find my way to the right dose of my specific variety of the drug.

Ticker knew a female Synth who worked for the MTR, at the harbour, a woman called Viola. The sun had risen to its zenith, and as Hong Kong hummed with the busy action of another uncertain day, I set out to find her. At the forefront of my mind was the need to be quick about this whole endeavour. If I took too long I might forget what it was I had set out to do.

Being and non-being create each other. Difficult and easy support each other.

The voice returned with a beautiful clarity. I knew it as a welcome companion, by my side and always helping, but still I couldn't associate a face with it. Though it was kind and creative, and sometimes it laughed, I was scared it would die and I would be left profoundly alone in my own mind. Only hope assured me it was very much alive and although located somewhere in my past, it was also somewhere within. I need to retrieve it in its entirety, find its source, and know that its meaning is not forgotten.

I have made an absolute commitment. My priority is to identify myself - I must discover who I was to discover who I am. I must overcome the limitations of my flaws if I am to retrieve the lost memories of my life. Their nature is unknown to me but I've put my faith in the promise of a drug that they can be re-experienced. Only with the drug will my identity have a chance to make itself known. The belief in the existence of these memories is based solely on a voice in my head, a piece of Orange Silk, and the suspect recollections of an old man, but the belief is mine.

- 9 -

NATIVE LANGUAGE

Questions abound, they are reproducing exponentially, and their demand for answers has no end. It's exhausting being a slave to their relentless assault, as answering one inevitably leads to the creation of many more.

For some enquiries there are immediate solutions. Quick-fire queries with rapid responses; Where is that music coming from? The shop over there. How many times have I seen that person's face? Was it three or four, or more? What is the quickest way to The Park? Turn right here and then the second left.

Other questions need more consideration. Hours or days may pass before I am satisfied; Where can I find somewhere to wash? In the ocean, but where? There is a running tap I used not so long ago, where was it? The questions which occupy me on the deepest level are those suggesting an impossibility of finding any answers; How long have I been here? Weeks? Months? Where do I belong, and with whom?

The more you know the less you understand.

There are certain places in the metropolis I revisit many times over, feeling pulled towards them. In these places I can be myself, either resting or observing or more often both. I allow myself to stop, my motion being otherwise primary, and it is in these places I find solace.

There are open and sparsely peopled zones where I walk without any cares, away from the hustle of the more intense parts of town. I have hiding spots too - dark, tucked away recesses behind buildings or in shadowy corners, where I can stow myself away in small alleyways. These serve as a respite if pressure rises too high or mania becomes too strong.

Such locales form the nodes between which connections can be made. Time flows more slowly when I reach them, and I collect my thoughts whilst occupying them, before continuing with my explorations and searchings.

Being outside and feeling other, is now a familiar emotion. Not belonging to the human race and not really feeling fully integrated into my own I am neither one thing nor the other. I exist in a suspended limbo-land and whilst in this nameless pseudo country, mobile as I am within its undefined borders, I make my own rules.

The most pressing restrictions are the limitations of my languages.

Mandarin is all around, I hear it, I understand it, I can speak it. With four tones per sound it feels easy to me, natural, but I know it's something I have learned, and maybe not so long ago. But who was my teacher? My vocabulary grows, and I continue to learn.

Cantonese, I absorb with difficulty. It's harder for me to understand. With six, seven, eight or more tones it's as though my hearing isn't up for the task. Like trying to discern the differences between subtle shades of green leaves from different trees, my hearing just can't quite lock on. As a result all I hear is a garbled stream of tonal traffic, and one too fast for me to register. My inclination is that I will have to master this language, in spite of my difficulties with it, because it represents the strata of society with which I wish to communicate.

In addition there is a street slang, called Text, and this eludes me also. It has no obvious structure, or grammar which I can discern, no way to find a grip on its meanings and it seems to change form daily. I've given up with the mumblings and underlying curses of this lingo to accept that there's at least one method of communication I feel no need to associate with.

The English language I command has no such problems. It comes to me as naturally as the way I walk or the way I think. I don't have a set of rules I can access for its creation but nevertheless I seem perfectly able to utilise some code. I have instant access to speak it, however I see fit, and my thinking in this tongue is clear and fluid. When I hear it spoken by others, I feel at ease.

Ticker tells me that in this city English used to be more than just a second language. The place was once run by the English but, he told me, a time had come when they simply had to relinquish their control of what was then a colony and return it to those who ran it in the first place. Such a story of whole cities being owned by various different countries over time seemed incredible, but Ticker assured me that in trade and war, any such thing is possible.

My accent brings further complications. I'm aware, once more, of my differences, it's been pointed out to me that I sound American and this confounds me. If I've ever been there I have no recall of it, not even a vestigial curiosity of a memory, or suggestion of a clue. So how can this be?

The answer has come from a disparate categorisation of people whom I have learned to recognise and select for conversation and further analysis. They are travellers.

One of these people, a man who told me he came from Ireland, convinced me that I was Irish. He said that I had all the right qualities and that many Americans had their origins in Ireland. I believed him, as he was very persuasive. My lack of memories about my origin he put down to alcohol consumption, he said I'd most probably been drinking too much rice wine. It was a frightening thought but for many days I walked tall and proud as an Irishman.

The feeling wore off, particularly when I spoke with other travellers. Mostly younger people passing through on their way to other exotic locations such as Fiji, Australia and New Zealand. They were friendly as a rule and very informative. Fortunately for me, English was a common international language. Germans, French and a Brazilians talked to me in English so that I could easily make sense of them. But their accents were all different, strange and bizarre remnants from their native languages, mixed with the complexities of English, to produce startlingly humorous results. I don't know where or when I learned to laugh but with these people it was impossible not to.

They assumed that I was American and largely I would just go along with this. The problems came when they wanted to know where in America I was from. After some embarrassing moments I learned to lie, quite creatively and successfully, but the act of lying itself left a bad feeling in my gut. Why did I have to lie? Where were my memories of my home?

The truth revealed itself, as usual, by talking to other Synths. Perhaps I'd been speaking with the wrong ones. Ticker, was my go-to-guy about these things, and most of the Synths I knew were down and burned out in some way. By chance I locked eyes with a more advanced and fully functional model one day who seemed to be on top of everything, having full access to the information I needed.

Suited and carrying an attache case, he sat next to me on a bench and was drinking a coffee. We got to talking and I decide to broach the issue burning within me.

"Why is it, could you tell me, that I speak English with an American accent, yet I have no recall of ever having lived in America?"

He looked at me as a teacher to a pupil and spoke with English which had no trace of Americanisation, a fact in which I think he felt some pride.

"Ah. Well to be frank there are two reasons. One, from your appearance, and dare I say it your smell, I assume you are poorly connected and not currently on the correct course of REM. This would account for any memory impairment. Second, and not to put too fine a point on it, underneath any post-production modifications, we are all American."

I tried to take this on board but it went against my intuition. He could see from my speechless amazement that I needed clarification, and whilst in his teaching mode he was quite happy to give it.

"All Synths are designed in America, by CYBEX, which as most people over the age of five could tell you is a contraction of CYBERNETIC EXPLORATION. Its headquarters are in San Francisco, California, but we are all made here, in China. Fabrique en Chine as I believe the French say."

Not remembering how I first came to know of my Synth nature was disturbing, but   at least I now knew who my maker was. I was American, and perhaps America, San Francisco in particular, was somewhere I belonged, somewhere to be with people like me, somewhere to call my home.

- *10* -

Remember To Never Forget

With Ticker's directions, and his description of Viola, I found her quite easily. At this time I merely hoped that she would be my introduction to the MTR and my inroad to REM, nothing more.

Even at a distance I knew it was her. She was sitting on a low wall near the water, moving her legs back and forth as if in rhythm to some silent music. The choppy waves whipped the breeze up into small gusts of warm air, and as she sat drinking a coffee her shoulder length hair blew in a chaotic mess.

True perfection seems imperfect, yet it is perfectly itself. True fullness seems empty, yet it is fully present.

She turned her head towards me as I approached, our eyes locked and she registered my ID quickly. In that instant her face, with such harmonious subtleties, resounded deeply with me. Her whole person began to sink into my soul in ways that I knew were permanent. With the solidarity of Synths a given, it was like we were old friends immediately. That I found her incredibly beautiful wasn't something I could hide, a hitherto unfelt awkwardness, and embarrassment perhaps, giving away my feelings as our conversation unfolded. She spoke first as I came close.

"Hello."

I liked her husky voice from the start. "Hi, are you Viola?"

"That's me."

"Ticker sent me, they're calling me EZee."

"Well pleased to make your acquaintance."

"I suppose there's no need to make this complicated. I'm looking to get some REM."

"Join the queue my friend. What's your flavour?"

"I, er, I don't know. I've never, taken it."

"You never took it, what's going on with that? It's a surprise you can remember your own name."

"I'm not sure that's my real name anyway. It's my memory, it only goes back a couple of weeks, at best."

"You're lucky. There's folks round here can't remember where they slept last night. You're a new model, EZ1:613 right?"

"Right."

"So that makes you a Thirteen, lucky for some. Let me see your money."

"I don't have any."

"He wants REM and he hasn't got any cash! What's up with you, are you defective or something?"

"I might be, yeah, I think I am, it's not easy to tell, I mean how would you know, for sure that is? I'll work, for money."

Viola looked me up and down, she seemed to be sizing me up, as though she was trying to estimate my weight or calculate the dimensions of my body.

"What you gonna do? What's your function, my friend?"

"Again, I can't be accurate as to the nature of my programmed purpose. I would like to acquire the REM so that I can retrieve that information and come to form a better representation of my personal identity."

"Crazy. Well you sure know how to talk, in a certain way. Look the only way you're going to get the REM you want is work for the MTR, you ready to do that?"

"I'm ready to do whatever is required."

"Ok. I'm going to give you the details of a place, and you've got to be there tomorrow evening at 9pm. Hangar 8, Harbour Wall 316, can you remember that?"

I nodded.

"If you're not there, you don't get the gig. The guy's name is Robbie. He'll sort you out with a small amount, but only to sell, you understand?"

"Ok."

"You sell what he gives you and you go back the next morning, he'll pay you in REM, just for you. You might get a few days worth, that's if he's got some Thirteen in the first place."

"Can I get some for myself when I see him tomorrow?"

"Oh no, he won't be giving you any Thirteen tomorrow, not until he knows you can sell what he gives you in the first place. He needs to build up some trust. You know about trust, EZee?"

"No, not really."

"Yeah I thought as much, it's fairly rare these days, even among Synths. He'll give you a selection so you can feel out the city and help out the community. Do you have transport?"

"No. I think I used to have a bicycle, somewhere, at some time or other."

"It would certainly help, otherwise you're going to get mighty tired, walking around all day."

"You don't have any Thirteen on you right now?"

Viola stopped and looked me up and down again. This time I felt like she was scanning me for a fault diagnosis, but whatever it was she saw in me, it was my first lucky break.

"I've got one you can have."

She reached into a small courier bag and pulled out a pouch. Opening it revealed a row of fluorescent coloured capsules. She ran her fingers along the row and stopped at one which was vivid green. Removing it she held it up to the light.

"Pure REM. Well ninety-nine percent. You be careful with this stuff. Find somewhere safe to take it, with someone you know, Ticker would be perfect."

"Thank you."

I reached out to take it but she held it back an instant.

"Seeing as how this is your first time, the results may be a little… unpredictable. You might not like what you remember, you get me. Chances are, whatever's in that memory of yours isn't likely to be so happy and full of flowers and rainbows and unicorns and things. I'm just warning you."

She held out the capsule and I took it between my thumb and forefinger. It felt weird and so foreign but it held so much promise and was somehow like a little friend. I put it in my top shirt pocket. I thanked Viola and left, as I walked away she called out after me.

"Take it easy, EZee!"

"Yeah, that's what I do."

"Be seeing you."

"Hope so."

It wasn't the most romantic of encounters, but considering Viola's attitude towards me and the way she'd made something difficult feel ok, I felt it was something on which to build, but to build what I wasn't sure. I'd never really spoken to many young female Synths before, having kept mostly to the company of men. Viola didn't only represent a chance to climb up to a better place, she was a seemed to be a better example of our kind, someone to look up to and admire, even if only from a distance.

I smiled, and began walking back the way I had come, back towards Ticker. This was a new sensation, things were looking up. The capsule's energy in my pocket was pulsing with potential but it began to feel heavier as I came towards The Cathedral and the concrete underpass.

When I arrived there, Ticker was nowhere to be seen. I asked around but nobody knew where he'd gone. Finally I came across an old woman who was a friend of his. She looked at me and hung her head.

"He expired just a few hours ago now. Drinking more of that rice wine and singing. Kept calling out your name too, saying how life with EZee was easy. He went out on a high. We'll all miss him, that is until we forget."

She held her head down again. My heart was filled with sadness. It was a deep feeling which I would have remembered if I'd experience it before. A death, a life no more, and I felt alone again here. Some people had helped to take his body to the place they called The Exit, where it would be disposed of. The city continued with its great machine of a heart not missing a beat.

Life here was hard, there were precious few people to rely on and Ticker had been my only friend. A pain got a grip on me as I could still remember his face well, but I wondered how long this impression would last.

I re-doubled my determination to make good on my new direction. If I worked hard I would be able to remember everything. Viola was my only real contact now, and that being in the underworld of the MTR of which I would soon be a part.

Lying down on Ticker's mattress and I suddenly recognised the bicycle leaning up against a concrete pillar, just in the shadows. I knew in that moment, connection with real objects being a great memory trigger, that it, and my story had their beginnings some place a great distance from here. The black hole in my past seemed to get just a little smaller.

Taking the capsule of REM from my pocket, I placed it on my tongue and, swallowing it, lay back on the mattress. Some rays of sun filtered through the gaps in the concrete structure above me. I heard the hum of the electric traffic buzzing overhead. For some time I lay there, limp and lifeless myself, aware that I had replaced Ticker in a physical way, lying in his space. I wondered how long it would be before I might reach the same fate. There would be some poetry in youth taking over from the aged, only inevitably to follow it to The Exit in the course of time.

I focused on the rays of light flickering above and then without thinking about it too much shut them out by closing my eyes. As soon as the awareness of my surroundings had dropped to a point approaching sleep, a fierce recall of a most visceral nature burst into my being. In some recess of my mind a sharp fragment of memory had been found and now it played out, in razor-edged detail, in a fearful nightmare that could only be the very beginnings of my existence.

- *11* -

WITHIN THE VOID OF THE SYNTH FACTORY

Black. Deep. Warmth. Liquid. Floating. Peace. Dream.

Shock lightning pain, cuts in two. Electric spark reaches the mind. Severed.

Body within gelatinous bubble, falling, dropping through darkness. Impact. Distending, stretching, breaking point and burst. Life thrown down, struggling form dumped. Fluid spills across hard concrete surface.

Hard, bruising, aching pain travelling at speed through all neurones. Slipping, slippery sliding flesh on surface. Limbs flailing. Synapses firing in overdrive, pain receptors raw, maximum sensitivities. All sense data absorbing immense systems in play. Alive.

Initiation programming running, new energy source within activated, pulsing, beating. Electrons flowing through integrated rerouting circuits. Silicon wired tight into nervous system genetics. Pain seeking a response, demanding a reaction.

Lungs now spewing forth the last of the liquid, rib cage contracting tight to eject the remnants. Convulsing violently, gasping for first breath. Coughing and kicking, drawing air in, filling vacated spaces within body. Writhing slipping, naked abandonment, senses and nerves firing, seeking a purchase within psyche.

All is darkness. Moving in a spasm, a fit of fear and fury.

Sensory input assimilated, panic responses to emergency state. Continuous, instantaneous construction of inner and outer architecture. Fluctuating variables given necessary priority. Sentience achieved. Consciousness bursting in great waves throughout mind. Self-awareness emerging, making its presence felt.

All things are born of being. Being is born of non-being.

Dynamic, interactive spatial awareness coming to the fore, first reflex to stand. Sliding awkwardly, feedback loops engaging all muscular activity, fall, again, fall, again. Crashing headlong into steel structures, concrete pillars. Standing still, upright, head already wounded. Opening eyes fully, thick blood running into them, blinded in red zone of panic and fear.

Lights guiding first moves, few and dim in distant corners. Alarms sounding, lights flashing. Danger. Reaction required.

Malfunctions, basic directive wrong within frame of reference. Immediate perceptions, programming in conflict. Current condition not pre-programmed. Fall-back imperative response improvisation. Essential items missing. Aborted initiation.

First few risky steps, successful action. Sensation of self motivated movement in chosen direction. Parallax movement of lights ahead, orientation towards them. Move, faster.

Sounds coming through the darkness, bodies running.

No purpose, scramble, scared and alive, stay alive. Threat, avoid or confront? Searching chaotically, point sources of white and coloured light. Red beacon, flashing at eye level.

The body of another arriving at speed from one side, impact, hit, fall, and to the ground. Forces at work, strong and violent. Fight, increasing amounts of strength, combat assailant, origin of power unknown. Fierce, muscles struggling against each other.

Find moves and momentum. Standing up, lifted enemy, throwing it to the floor. Motionless. Recovering inner personal directive, moved towards flashing red light.

Cover the distance quickly. Standing still, facing wall. Red wavelengths intermittently illuminating. At peace, for precious seconds, more assailants approaching. Innovation of thought and action.

White light, image of a hand. Looking at my own hand, transfixing my attention. Placing my hand on the image, sliding door opens.

It springs into existence, unconscious, perfect, free, takes on a physical body, lets circumstances complete it.

Bright, white, broad daylight hits me with a wave of awakening. Step outside, naked, free of the void behind, sharp blades of grass beneath the soles of my feet. A free new life, running at fear-crazed speed, into the raw sensory data of a wide open world.

- *12* -

DEALING IN MEMORIES

It was the memory of a dark and gruesome ordeal. In spite of the blackness in which it took place I remembered being there and feeling those sensations. In a world of shadows, the force of the ejection from whatever foul machine I'd been an organic part of, had left a deep impression on my soul. A psychological scar, left over from what I could only imagine to have been a violent birth, ran across the fabric of my soul. This scar was a nightmarish memory, but it was a memory, and it was mine.

The time-frame involved felt like only minutes, but the duration of my recall of the event had been so much longer. In reality I had slept, for many hours I believe, sleep that I obviously needed. The energy required for the recovery of this memory was greater than I could have imagined but it had been well spent.

There now existed a sharp incision somewhere in my past which was a reference. It had not been what I'd expected, what I'd hoped for, but the REM had done the job and I intended to pursue this line of activity. I wanted all my memories and I was prepared to battle through any or all of them to find the moments which I felt certain would define me.

Further questions had now presented themselves. I had precious little hope of finding the answers but I asked them nonetheless. Where was the place in which this memory had been formed? What was my journey from there to here? How long ago was this memory made, how old was it? And assuming this was my birth, how old was I when I was born?

I had a story, or more accurately the beginning of a story, without it I was just a disjointed assemblage of meaningless events, but with it my soul had a unique place in this world. There was space for my story to grow, and to illuminate my understanding of why I feel so incomplete.

Seeing into darkness is clarity. Knowing how to yield is strength. Use your own light and return to the source of light. This is called practising eternity.

Without proper sustenance my hunger kept me awake in a sickly hallucination of sorts. I was experiencing the come down and side effects from this potent drug which were spiked and gnarly. More REM was the solution.

I spent the afternoon scavenging for food which was a difficult job, very unpleasant and usually quite unsuccessful. The city was meticulous with its litter collection, using a small army to keep the streets clean. Even so, to me there was a vile stench and a veneer of dirt, at all times, over the entire metropolis.

How much longer would I have to live like this? Without my very identity what was to stop me from descending into animalistic psychology. I had to regain my humanity, at least my Synth version of it, lest I become reduced to a mere collection of sense impressions. My soul deserved better than that.

Towards the evening I made my way to Hangar 8 down by the docks. It was a long way so I took the bicycle, feeling good to be moving at some speed. By the time I reached my destination I'd shaken off the after effects of the drug and felt stable, if a little high headed. For a few moments I felt something akin to being a better version of myself, caught in a brief daydream of possibilities.

With a little snooping around the hangar I saw a group of five people and made a judgement that Robbie might be among them. I walked over, pushing my bicycle and locked eyes with several of this sorry looking bunch. They were Synths alright, and they already had my number.

"I'm looking for Robbie."

"I'm Robbie, what do you want?"

"I was told you could help me. Maybe I can help you too."

"Well that's what we're all about my friend, helping each other out. Who sent you?"

"Viola."

"Ah, now she's a one. What are we talking about here?"

"Some REM, I want to shift some, get paid, you know."

"Mmm. Do you need REM, like for personal use?"

"That'd be a factor, yes?"

"EZ1:613, you're a Thirteen. New around here?"

"I've been kicking around a while, getting to know the city, just keeping to myself mainly."

"Mmm. You look fairly regular, I can see you could do with some food and a clean up though brother. Here's what I'll do, I'll offer you my start up package. You get a sample case, that's all sixteen, with the Thirteen removed of course. You sell what you can, and you come back tomorrow, with the Holo cash, and I'll let you have your Thirteen. And then we can talk some more. We got a deal?"

"That sounds fair."

Robbie produced a small sample bag, just like Viola had, opened it and removed the vivid green number Thirteen capsule, then shut the case and passed it towards me.

"One Holo for one capsule, think you can remember that?"

It meant little to me. I went to take it and he withdrew it at the last second.

"Now don't be thinking you can cheat on old Robbie here. No running off with the goods, I got your number remember? And I definitely don't recommend you think about trying any of these yourself."

"I got it." I took the case.

"Have you got a name brother?"

"EZee."

"EZee come, easy go, I like it. I'll see you tomorrow, around this time. By the way I suggest you try down-town first."

"Thanks."

I had a good last look at the others in the group, thinking I would most likely see some of them again, then turned, got on my bike and cycled away.

It was late but I didn't stop until I was right in the heart of the city. I stashed my transport in a bush by a park and walked towards the business district. I went to work.

Not having a clue as to my target market I scanned the streets looking for any Synth I could see. The first one I registered looked like a bum.

"Hey, do you need any REM?"

"Of course I do! But do I look like someone who can afford it? Get out of my face you joker."

He left me standing. I'd try higher up the ladder. It took half an hour to come across a very smart Synth sitting on a wall reading a real book. I clocked him and tried a casual approach.

"Would you be needing any REM today, sir?"

"You think I'd buy my REM from someone looking like you? Get a real job buddy, beat it."

Now I walked away feeling somehow less of myself, but I carried on.

A couple of hip looking girls were walking towards me, and saw me before I saw them. They were laughing and I took my chance as we got closer.

"Evening. Can I interest you in REM?"

They looked at each other, in a mischievous and knowing way, then one of them spoke.

"You got a Seven and a Nine?"

"Sure. One Holo a shot."

"Well, everyone knows that."

"Over here."

I moved just off the sidewalk into a space sheltered by the side of a building and we did the deal. They walked away happy and I had in my hand two Holo's. I felt I'd seen Holo's before, that I'd used them before, but I had no recollection of how I might have acquired them in the past.

I pushed on into the night. Getting faster, I asked more and more Synths, at random at first and then I began to specialise, approaching folks who looked more amenable. The younger, hipper generation were a good bet, as were professional types who looked a little ragged around the edges. It took hours but soon I was down to my last capsule. That one took an age to sell, it turned out no one needs a Sixteen, but eventually it went to an old gentleman in fact.

With fifteen Holo in my pocket I recovered my bike and cycled back to The Cathedral. Each night I slept there my thoughts were mixed with the changing complexion of the community which called it home.

Some of the time I felt deeply for them, at other times I was repelled by their degraded status. This was just a reaction to the knowledge that I could become one of them too, unless I hustled, unless I could remember, and break free of whatever had put me here.

I settled in for the night. Ticker's mattress a stark reminder of harsh change, and the unpredictable nature of a future which could become darker so quickly. I kept my Holo's safe and close, and although the hunger was bad, I rested well after my exertions for the MTR.

Tomorrow I'd be able to remember again, the first thing I'd had to look forward to. If I could pull memories into the present, my future might start to become more than a formless void, perhaps then life would be bearable. Was it possible to influence my destiny or must I accept an unknowable fate?

The memory I have of Viola is surrounded by a beautiful hazy cloud; soft, cool and bright.

- *13* -

Unwritten Rules

What I'm doing is illegal, but it doesn't concern me too much. That it should, or that a morality might stop me from pursing a particular course of action, has occurred to me, but sometimes the end justifies the means. My goals override my methods and morals must play out in the background.

Dealing in REM is tolerated, like kids skateboarding on the sidewalk. As long as there's no trouble, no violence or public disruption, or in the case of skateboarders, no collisions, then no one is too worried. Black market, street level REM, keeps the city turning over. Without it there would be no buffer. Occupation of the no-man's land which bridges acceptable REM consumption with the underworld, props up the city's less glamorous activities. It is in this zone that I now operate.

The structure and size of the MTR intrigues me. I'm aware now of these low level foundations but moving up through it's higher echelons is a challenge which seems to suit my sensibilities. It must have a leader, a head, someone who makes the decisions and controls the shots. Whoever is at the top of this organisation surely has great power and must be a figure of some interest to the authorities. I imagine such a person will also have enormous knowledge, answers to questions, and it is these I crave the most.

The MTR being an exclusively Synth organisation might be reason for a protected status of sorts. The authorities, indeed the overwhelming power of the government, may see it as simply an efficient enterprise servicing the community of Synths. But why then should it have to be so secretive? Toleration may be only an impression, giving the idea that Synths are taking care of themselves, doing jobs no one else wants to do. In this way they will feel that they are a benefit to society and will appear so to the wider human population. Perhaps the whole show is just a sanctioned business which rakes in a lot of dirty money for some corrupt people at the top.

I can only speculate. What I know for certain is that the police sometimes turn a blind eye, then at other times they want to be seen to be in control of the situation, making arrests here and there seemingly for the sake of appearance.

Folks here are afraid of the police, and for good reason. But it's not necessarily what you see of them which has impact. They actually have a very limited visual presence, a car or a motorbike here and there, sometimes a couple of uniformed officers walking the beat. One might think there aren't very many police in this city, that they aren't really required, as there is apparently very little actionable crime. I'm sure this is the image those in power wish to project.

However, as with many things in this city, the surfaces are misleading and conceal deeper, darker realities just a small distance beneath. It's not what you see of law enforcement, it's what you hear.

People, Synths and humans alike, often disappear. That's the reality, at least if you believe what you hear. You might be talking to someone one day, then enquire about them a couple of days later, and no one's seen or heard of them, their memories vanishing with them.

Within the groups of homeless Synths, for it's with them I mostly converse, this is a subject of much discussion. Individuals disappearing may not seem a great surprise in this type of transient community, as people often move on at sporadic intervals.

It's only when you look at the types who disappear, often outspoken troublemakers, anti-establishment agitators or militant demonstrators, that a pattern begins to emerge. And I've heard the same sentiment being expressed of humans who have disappeared, seemingly without a trace. No one sees anything but the rumours are rife. The realities of this situation creates an unease, a tension and a nausea on the street, but the disappearances are as accepted as more natural deaths, and just as regular.

It's not a taboo subject but, due to the inherent memory difficulties of Synths and our reliance on REM to compensate for this, the existence of those who are disappeared is often quickly forgotten.

With my initiation into MTR I'm feeling part of something bigger, something which I feel will give some degree of security and protection to my life. No longer a purely solo unit, I'm now one among many. It feels intrinsic to my nature to be a part of a whole.

I understand the world I see on another level. All these people are elements of a complex system, each of them playing some tiny part in a scheme of greater scope. Whether they are aware of this, and have eyes wide open to their panoramic reality, I can only guess. My instinct tells me their gaze has been trained to focus inwards, to fixate on the intricacies and details of their position, their role, their job. To have both perspectives may be a luxury afforded only to their superiors, and so on up. Perhaps there are but a few elite, privy to the truths of the full picture.

At ground level in every sense I'm thinking about the person at the top of the tree, and wondering what they are thinking. I can imagine him, or her, they can't be much different from me, just better connected, more experienced, broader thinking. I want to see a complete image of the world in which I live, and the apex of the MTR pyramid will be the best vantage point.

I will climb. To reach up is to reach out, to those who were once where I am now, but who have grown and evolved into a great wholeness. To be complete is to be free.

Even the other Synths have completion of sorts. Memory deficiency aside, those I register with cohere in ways I cannot. This solidarity is a mystery to me, one I cannot penetrate, or even find ways to express my feelings about. It's as though they share a secret, one which will remain so to me, or that they are members of a secret club into which I shall never be initiated.

The other morning there were four of them, four of us, I should say, as I stood nearby. They talked and I listened, their exchanges overlapping and interweaving between each other. Laughter and comprehension ensued as they shared what I can only describe as a communal spirit. I struggle with two way communication sometimes, one to one, but three or more presents a confusing babble where my attention flits from one to another, failing to grasp the direction and meaning. It's a source of great anguish for me and my inclination is to be alone with my thoughts.

My mind is perhaps trapped within a cage. It feels best suited to working within my own psychological boundaries, describing its own world. Is this the definition of a cage?

Whether I've always been like this is another unknown. Whether my condition is improving, or at least changing is impossible to predict. I continue as I am, my history a void and my hope of remembering it, a dream.

I have the voice to follow, the words of the monk which happily return, soaked into my soul as they are. Their rhythm is a clue, undulating patterns of the sound they make in my mind. Words laid down at some deeper level than the memories I think they point to. But who is the owner of this random verse? Who spoke it, and where and when?

Only REM can help me now, I have put all my faith in its transformative promise. There's nothing wrong with me, I tell myself, but I need food for my mind as well as my stomach. I've yet to find the nourishment which will fill my soul. Empty in so many ways, perhaps it's because I'm hollow that my thoughts echo inside. I am just a surface and underneath it, my character is only another surface. There are layers to describe who I am but the veneer is thin, and transparent too I fear.

I work with what I have, always with the impression I am missing what is essential, that I am in need of something which I cannot imagine. A musician needs an instrument, but if she doesn't know she is a musician, how will she exist? Who can tell her what she needs? Only someone who knows what she is, or was, or could be.

I am in this state. Sometimes I feel only an entity outside of my consciousness, will be able to change it. I've met people who believe such an entity does exist, but they are, in my experience in some kind of detrimental state themselves, with no material proof to show for this belief. It may be an illusion, it may be a delusion but with all honesty I too subscribe to it in my own way.

Knowing that I have a soul, that written within it is my life, and my destiny even, is of great comfort. But I have no evidence to show another person of its reality.

Practise not-doing and everything will fall into place.

All I have is a dirty piece of Orange material in my pocket, powerfully linked to my irrational faith. It is a nonsense to try to explain to anyone. So I keep quiet, only touching the Silk occasionally, to give my memories a fighting chance of returning in their full.

I listen to the voice and let it guide me. I trust it, indeed it is the only thing I do trust, because I can remember I trusted the person to whom it belongs. If I can bring back their face from the past I'll be able to see them talking to me, and I will know their name.

- *14* -

BLACK MARKET CUSTOMERS

Robbie was pleased with me and kept his end of the bargain. I got the impression he'd made this kind of deal many times before and it hadn't always worked out. My twenty-four hour turn around and complete sales impressed him. He gave me another sample case and once again I was in business.

With my patter perfected and my patch established I concentrated on repeat customers, working this time by the light of day. Sometimes I would walk about, stealthily scanning the seething sidewalk for Synths. Trying to keep out of sight of the police was tricky but quite possible.

At times I would sit and watch, taking in the fluxing behaviour of animated human traffic, learning about life from expressions and behaviour. Smiles and gestures, rhythms and pace, people trying to make manifest their ideas whilst attempting to manipulate the forces around them.

The theatre of lifestyles, both Synth and human, is rich in contrasting details. The ways of walking, attitudes and changing pace. Fashions and other expressions of creative life, the art of being and the self-generated forces that keep everyone in motion, all keeping the economy fluid.

Hierarchies within societies, levels of livelihood feeding off each other, or blocking one from the other. Everyone has their place, even me, we all have duties, all are required to live by some rules and some form of civilised decency.

Whether you go up the ladder or down it, your position is shaky. When you stand with your two feet on the ground you will always keep your balance.

The shady police were a subtle presence, but sinister somehow in the ways they moved. I had a few close calls as I tried to get a measure of their methods. Ultimately I just out ran them, something I was more than capable of, but with my observations I was more careful and operated in the shadows.

There were others I noticed, just like me, Synths most likely, competitors even, who were equally illusive. How many more were there, of us, invisible and silent? The total number of Synths in the city was an unknown to me. If the total on the streets was any indication, the figure could be huge.

The sounds of Mandarin hummed all around. From the Chinese rulers at the very top right down to street level. But Cantonese was favoured between Synths and most of my deals were done in this tongue, in the formerly prevalent language.

Smatterings of English fell on my ears every now and then. From the style of those using this code, gentleman in tailor-made suits, I became aware of another layer of society. I couldn't put my finger on it but perhaps these men were part of an organisation. If they were it was secretive, at least that's how it appeared to me. To those speaking Mandarin, Cantonese must have appeared a sub stratum, and to me as a Synth, the English I heard was a world in which I felt most comfortable.

I was enjoying myself with these thoughts. I appeared to be as adept at this type of activity as I was at dealing REM. Why it should be so, and what benefit this reflection was to me, I could only wonder. Maybe it was simply my mind's way of keeping itself busy, active and sharp.

Continuous thought was my only real companion at this time. The monk's voice came and went, its patterns and ideas with a mind of their own. My own inner voice grew with my activities, and I started to learn and feel a type of inner confidence too. It was as though my ego had been sleeping and only required the gentle encouragement of increasing contact with others to gently stir it from rest.

The day passed and so did others just like it. At given times I would report in with Robbie who would give me more REM in exchange for the Holo's I'd collected. After a few days he began paying me, not only in my necessary Thirteens, but in Holo's too. I began to build quite a collection of both.

The key was to create a database of customers. Specific individuals, yes, these were essential to keeping a regular base income, but character types too. I found myself logging everything from fashion sense and shoe styles to tattoos and piercings, all were clues to potential clients.

As my database grew so did the corresponding network. Expanding and cross referencing this meant that my business began to reach far and wide. I was like the centre of a wheel with all my connections being spokes to gather money from the spinning outer rim of underworld Synth society.

We join spokes together in a wheel, but it is the centre hub that makes the wagon move. We work with being, but non-being is what we use.

There were surprises too. Moving up from ground level there was easy money to be made from wealthier Synths. Once I had their details I often provided a delivery service to these folk.

The reasons Synths wanted REM were as diverse as the Synths themselves. Some were desperate, as I had been. Some had run out of their legitimate supply and needed a quick fix. Still more wanted them for one-off memory trips, perhaps to remember recent holidays or recently passed loved ones. I was just happy to be there for them and fulfil their needs.

All the while I was taking my own memory trip. The results weren't great, I was uncomfortably stuck with the one dark memory which I could only occasionally break free from. However, I took great pleasure analysing fragments of these images, laid down at a point which appeared to be at the start of my existence. The more I talked to other Synths they explained that this fixation on a single event was common in early stages of a course of REM. I was told to stick with it as there could well be an unfolding of imagery hidden deeper inside.

A higher aspect of my experience now was the creation of brand new memories as an ongoing and interactive narrative. I could recall many of my recent days in perfect detail. It was like my mind had its own Holo TV, like the ones I saw displaying their dreams in expensive shop windows.

Over the next few days and weeks the money began to accumulate to a point where I wasn't quite sure what to do with it. I sought the advice of Viola, with whom I wished to become friends. When I found her she was as fresh as I remembered her, upbeat and energised.

"So, Robbie tells me you're top of his leaderboard."

"Well, I didn't know that. I'm doing ok."

"He says you're a natural at sales. A machine I think he called you."

"Hah, that's funny. I'm focused, that's all, feel like I'm just getting started really."

"Must be banking a few Holo's then."

"About eight thousand."

"My god EZee! That's a lot of cash, have you been buying wholesale?"

"Well yes, actually, Robbie and I have an evolving relationship."

"Where are you living now?"

"At the Cathedral."

"For real?"

She gave me a long hard look up and down.

"It's not safe to be hanging around places like that with so much Holo in your coat pockets. If you like you can crash at mine for a while, get cleaned up. Don't be getting any ideas though."

I smiled and said yes.

It felt a natural development as there was trust and friendship between us. I'm not sure what she saw in me but in her I saw everything. Her femininity represented all that I was missing, her warmth, friendliness and her coolness of being suggested... the future, a concept I needed to hold close. The move meant the end of sleeping on poor old Ticker's mattress, underneath the concrete overpass.

Having the afternoon spare until Viola got off work, I decided to go back to The Cathedral for one last time to collect my bicycle. When I arrived the usual crowd were gathered in a ragged group, huddled together for safety and what comfort they could muster. I sat down on Ticker's spot, which I had made my own, and took out a Thirteen, to really look at it closely.

The neon green surface glistened in the sun as I touched the slightly raised edges of the binary number Ø11Ø1 printed along its side. I was fascinated by it and imagined it in use everywhere, throughout this city and in the world beyond. It really was something to behold. For my personal experience there was however a doubt.

It wasn't so much that I was disappointed with its performance, these past days and weeks were now so clear in my mind, but I was looking for something more. The dull ache at the core of my being was still there and I hankered for it to be soothed. Something profound was still missing. Although perfectly functional now, I felt broken inside as I had always done. It was just a bad feeling.

I took the pill, hoping for the breakthrough I sought. Slipping under into a sub-conscious zone, a sensory rush brought waves of intense recall, memories which could only be mine.

- *15* -

Origin of A Fugitive

Colours blind the eye. Sounds deafen the ear. Flavours numb the taste. Thoughts weaken the mind. Desires wither the heart. He observes the world but trusts his inner vision. He allows things to come and go. His heart is open as the sky.

These are my legs running. This is my heart beating. This is my my mind thinking. I am alone, I am one.

Here there is nothing, only… Nature. So familiar but all so new as well. Shapes and forms inside matching all I sense outside of me. Am I the first one here? I am inside myself and I am everywhere at once. And I am nobody, I am nothing. I walk for a while. Light is everywhere.

But I have everything within, it has been placed there just for me. How could it be otherwise? There is only one way and it is my way. I move forward, reality moves into the past. I look ahead I see the future approaching, the future is more of what has become the past. So this is the present.

I am zero. I am one, and two and three, and so on. Time, Space, Change.

Are these ideas? What are they for? I cannot hold onto them, they appear and disappear so fast. I just want to keep one and grow it for a while. But then here is another, and another, and more. Waves of thought passing through me, changing me.

Simple in actions and in thoughts, you return to the source of being.

Where am I? Where am I going? It's so hot.

- *16* -

MAINLAND CHINA

SOLITARY BROTHER

Zhang knew where he was and where he was going. He had walked this dusty old road many times before. In the middle of wide open country-side, it was still a few hours walk home to the monastery in the blistering heat. He was lucky his red robes were loose as they kept him relatively cool and free of sweat.

All Zhang's memories seemed to be dominated by the sun, framed by its path across the sky, lit from its constantly moving location, with the varying palette of colours it created.

His wooden cart, pulled by a darkly coloured ox, was old and frail. He'd never trusted it since a wheel had come off a few years ago. There was no end to the problems he'd endured with it since then. The nails were all rusty and often failed to hold it together adequately. The wood itself was split in many places, providing him with a steady supply of splinters in his hands.

The ox pulling it was even more temperamental. It snorted, it urinated and defecated at the most inconvenient of moments and far more often than seemed necessary. Most annoyingly it would simply stop, whenever it felt like it. There was no skill in getting it moving again. Hitting it with a stick just encouraged more snorting, and sometimes it would respond to this treatment by simply lying down. Once down it was even more difficult to restore any motion. Zhang had learned to treat it as a stubborn old lady, which is what she was. He had never given her a name preferring instead to exercise his scant vocabulary of swear words as a substitute. There was no sense in hurrying her. The best course of action being to stop and wait, and take the opportunity to rest.

It was on one such occasion that the monk found himself standing motionless, regarding his surroundings with a vaguely curious mind. It was quiet save for the sounds of nature. Some crickets in the nearby meadow were doing well to form a foundation to the soundscape. Layered on top in a fluxing wash of billowing waves was a wind pushing leaves against each other in the trees. Some delicate birdsong, barely audible at first began coming more strongly to the fore.

Looking up he located the tiny bird which was the source of the song, perching at the end of a long crooked branch. Then it stopped suddenly and flew away at speed for a reason only it could know. Zhang carried his gaze further upwards.

The blue was intense, the heavens free of cloud, clear and vast with no points of reference on which to focus. Zhang smiled for he knew the stars were just biding their time, and would soon puncture the purity of this blue, letting the black of night fill this vision with a far greater spectacle.

The ox stirred and began walking again of its own accord. Zhang was happy to be walking again, hoping to reach the monastery before night fell. With no moon he would otherwise be as good as blind.

He hadn't seen a soul for an hour or so but approaching him from not so far ahead in the distance, he could see a man, on his own, walking towards him on the path, wearing the clothes of a farmer perhaps. Perhaps they would talk with each other for a while, two men in the countryside exchanging news and a few simple truths about life.

However, as the man came closer, the distance between them now only twenty feet or so, Zhang became transfixed by the stranger's face. The defining feature of this otherwise unremarkable man was his wide, oversized jaw. It dominated his appearance and Zhang's interest. He'd only ever seen such a jaw on one other man, and that man was his father.

Zhang's stare was powerful in its strength as they passed each other. The stranger looked unnerved to see a monk so fiercely locked onto him and he looked away embarrassed without speaking.

Zhang was disturbed because he had only one memory of his father and now it had been brought back to him with perfect clarity. He continued walking, the ox leading the way, the path ahead empty once more.

His father had taken him to the monastery when at an undermined age. He must have been incredibly young for this memory was his very first memory of any kind. It was thus the first and the last memory of the man who had been his father, the man who had left him with the monks. He remembered beginning to cry in that moment, although he could not have been aware of what was happening to him.

The monks were his family, he'd grown up and become one of them. He was at one with them an he knew of no other way in life, in truth he knew very little of the way of the world outside the monastery. It was not until he was a much older boy that he'd become curious with a passion as to his origins; Where he had come from? Who and where was his father? Why were there no women in the monastery? And why did he have no mother?

There was a period during his teenage years of emoting the distress, sometimes angrily, at the lack of answers to these questions. An elderly brother took him aside one day, after he had been performing his duties chiming the bell at mediation.

In no more than a minute the old monk conveyed to him the only information he would ever know about his origins, his parentage and the source of his life. His mother had died giving birth to him. He had lived with his father for the first few years of his life in a small village an hour to the North. His father had then brought him to the monastery and had left him with the brotherhood. His father was a soldier who had been forced to go away to fight a war.

In spite of his burning curiosity to discover his true identity, Zhang had listened to these facts of his life with a cold, numb and detached acceptance. There was no other reaction needed, no appropriate emotion to express. However, he believed this revelation signalled the moment when his crying had ceased.

He set his mind to studying. It seemed he was above average intelligence, the desire to learn burning within him. The passions he'd not experienced and perhaps all the emotions he would have shared with his father, or his mother, he instead turned inwards.

The ancient texts he memorised and analysed. He spoke in great depth of these scriptures with his elders, aiming to unlock the secrets which they themselves had cultivated over their long lives.

Writing was taught to him as an exercise in art. Forming the characters with brushstrokes, he gave them the aesthetic their meaning deserved. But he chose to write for personal satisfaction too and kept diaries, wrote poems and even some songs.

He tried to learn from nature but the monks kept no text books on the natural sciences. Mathematics was another area where he was frustrated in his attempts to discover the necessary knowledge to make progress of any kind.

These days he mostly followed the drama of the monastery itself. He studied behaviour and recognised patterns. He saw his life only in the context of this place and he came to realise he lived in a microcosm.

There had never been a dream to leave as he'd evolved into a contented man who was at peace with the small world he knew. If he could wish for anything it would be only for a companion who understood his inner world on a deeper level than the monks. Unlike him, most of the brothers had come here of their own free will. Many had given up lives in the outer world, for a wide range of reasons.

Sometimes Zhang felt as if he had been born in the monastery.

The ox stopped dead in its tracks once more. Zhang accepted the event for what it was and stopped too. His thought process ended and was forgotten quickly as he took to looking at the word around him once again.

He stood and listened to nature humming to herself. There was no birdsong to be heard this time. Instead a quiet low roar was caught by the sensitive ear of the monk. He knew this sound and looked high up, scanning the blue for the source of the sound waves.

There it was, the long white needle leading to a shining silver dot, which proceeded at some unknown pace through the sky. The sound seemed to be coming from somewhere way back in the wake of its trajectory, near the tail of the cloudy white trail. He knew it was a passenger jet, at great height, and he watched it for a while as the evidence of its path slowly faded.

He didn't like them, these aeroplanes, scarring the sky as they did, even if it was only a temporary cut in the fabric of the world's roof. But then he didn't like advanced technology of any kind. For Zhang all man made machinery drew a path to technologies of war. War had taken his father away from him and it only led to death.

However, it wasn't death in itself which held any great dread for him, at least in theory. Death was just another part of life and he'd learned to believe that without death there is no life. When a being dies it is no more than a transformation of energy, and this energy becomes new life.

What really did concern Zhang, to the extent that it filled the core of his soul, was a question he couldn't answer. With the loss of life comes the loss of identity and without identity how can anything exist? It was a question he felt would always be with him and pursuing it kept him thinking only in circles. He welcomed any distraction from it, and on this occasion, in this very moment, it was something unusual in the scrub by the side of the road which caught his eye and broke his introspection.

Amidst a small collection of rough bushes he thought he saw something. It was definitely the figure of a person. Crouching and curled up amongst the greenery was a naked man hidden in the undergrowth. Surprised but curious at his find, Zhang moved forward to investigate.

- 17 -

THE ART OF THE WORLD

Entering Viola's loft apartment it was so vibrant and pulsing with her colour, music and energy, that it was impossible to absorb it all, even after several hours. It was larger than I'd imagined it would be, and full of so much stuff I didn't know where to start.

If you want to know me look inside your heart.

"Is this all yours?'

"Of course it's all mine, you think I stole it? You think I'm some low life hustler?"

She smiled at me and I felt awkward. Many of our interactions up to this point had been similar, with me showing my innocence, or maybe just my ignorance, and her taking a lead with a more experienced perspective.

"How do you afford all this?"

"Maybe I didn't let on, I'm a little higher up in MTR than I told you. As you've been finding out, employment brings with it increasing advantages."

In amongst all the furniture, which was mostly leather and wood, there were all types of lamps and rugs, sculptures and coffee tables.

Placed on the walls, with a balanced appreciation of the interior architecture, were several large paintings in bright powerful colours of abstract shapes and compositions.

I walked without talking as I scanned some more. It was hard for me, because I had so few reference points. I knew this was art, but of what kind and purpose?

The view from the fifth floor of this old block was outstanding. The sunset here was deep, dark purples and reds, coming over the harbour. Only a few minutes ago it had been light but now the wide open sky had moved in on itself, wrapping the city up tight in a swift, dark transition which shifted the mood.

I looked at the paintings again, "Where did you buy those?"

"Well I did't buy any of them, no one gave them to me, and I didn't steal them, so that really only leaves one option doesn't it... I painted them. I'm not exclusively an MTR girl. I've got my own things going on too you know."

"Is this a kind of play?"

"Well, I call it work."

I looked some more, it was difficult to look away from them, they had a hypnotic quality where colours placed next to each other moved together in blurry waves, merging then separating again.

"We'll eat later, I think you should clean up. The shower's through there."

I took my coat off and walked into the shower room. Something felt very familiar about this, but forgotten and old. I took all my clothes off and stepped into the shower, put the water on and cried out.

"Ahhh!" It was freezing!

Viola shouted out. "Don't worry, it will get hotter!"

The water warmed up and I cleaned away dirt ingrained in my body, during a time measured only by how difficult it was to remove. How far down I had gone before I could take this little step up. I washed with sweet smelling soap and was as deeply clean as I could be. This feeling was not new, but once more my memory of a previous experience, with which to compare it, failed me. I washed my beard and hair too, both were very long and matted. I enjoyed the rush of warm water over my head and body for so long, standing, but swaying and lost in an all over pleasure. Then I was finished. I stepped out of the shower to find that my clothes were missing.

I called out. "Where are my clothes?"

"I'm washing them. Use the towel!"

There was a red towel. The colour hit me hard. It was a dark red and I had a flashback to the robes I wore, the ones Ticker had said he'd first seen me wearing. I used it to dry, then wrapped it around myself, glanced my form in the mirror. I was animal, and human and Synth all at once, and despite close inspection my image could tell precious little of the character residing within.

Emerging into the room. I saw Viola. She looked at me with her judging scan again. "Mmm, better, but that… that hair has got to go."

Before I knew it, she had rearranged me to be sitting on a stool, and took a buzzing machine to both my head and face and then washed me down, head, neck and shoulders with water. I was clean and then with more rubbing I was dry.

"Let's have a look at you."

I stood there, wearing only the red towel, which unwrapped and fell to the ground. I looked at Viola my face reddening too and I remembered feeling something like this once before too.

"Mmm, they really build these new models right, don't they. Put these on." She handed me some clothes.

"Are these yours?"

"No, they're not mine silly. They belonged to… someone else. He was… nearly as big as you…"

I took the clothes and put them on. They were so clean and felt beautifully new to my skin. White underwear, grey trousers with a belt, and a white shirt. I stood there, not sure of what was expected of me next. This process had fazed me and left me without direction or purpose of any kind.

Viola walked me round a corner of the room and put me in front of a large, long mirror. Now I really did look at myself. It was me and superficially at least, I looked… complete.

"There you go, EZee Update."

"Thank you. I look, well, I look like, I look like someone."

"No worries. You look very handsome. I'm going to keep cooking, it'll be at least half an hour. Why don't you look around. Mi casa es su casa."

"Sorry?"

"My house is your house."

"Well it clearly isn't, it's your house."

"It means you are welcome here, this is your home too now."

I walked away. Home. Sounded nice. Walking past the paintings I noticed they were all made up from the sixteen different colours of REM. Although this was impressive and cool and everything, I thought the pervasive way it made itself present on these walls was difficult to accept. REM had never struck me as a miracle cure, more of a necessary evil.

The sculptures were very different however, obviously in format, but most strikingly in style. Made from metal and stone and plastics, they looked to be composed entirely from the flotsam and jetsam of urban life. Pieces of machinery, cogs and gears. Marine related items from boats and the like. Automobile parts, building materials and pieces of furniture. I imagined the constituent elements to have been collected with a great degree of love and care and had all been fused together into wonderful forms. It was only as I continued to stare that the sum of their parts coalesced to show the whole. Their fullness, their completeness and perhaps their meaning began to emerge for me in patterns which mapped onto parts of my soul which were previously hidden.

Without exception they were abstract pieces, and as I began to look at more of them I sensed a celebration of life. The themes I engaged with on a physical level were those of motion, a feeling of kinetic energy and movement of any kind in general. Once I had recognised this, their dynamic qualities really came alive, it was as if they were speeding through the room and had either been caught in freeze-frame or were in fact still moving, albeit imperceptibly slowly. In fact I found myself moving gently too, fine tuned muscles were slowly contracting and relaxing with a pulsing urge to sway.

The apartment revealed itself to be even bigger. Exploring quietly, I found the room where Viola worked on her paintings and sculptures, a great mess of creative chaos where the evidence of energy and work was staggering. There was a library with many real books, and then her bedroom.

The colours here were shades of mauve, and violet with pinks and reds as highlights. The room was a delightful, quiet and peaceful place, but I felt I was somewhat trespassing and left after a brief wander through it.

Catching myself in another mirror I was surprised again. I stopped and adjusted my shirt. I felt like one of those English gentleman I'd seen down in the business district. I went back to find Viola in the kitchen.

We sat down at a table to eat. Once more I could remember this as an experience I couldn't place. The soulful music which Viola played from a machine, and the beautiful tone of her sensual voice lulled any anxieties. I thought these moments were perhaps planned, but the way in which they played out, were blissfully spontaneous and natural.

The food was simple, but strong and in great abundance. I ate my fill. We drank a dark red liquid from glasses, which tasted smooth and rich. Viola told me it was wine from France, an advantageous acquisition via the MTR.

Be content with what you have; rejoice in the way things are. When you realise there is nothing lacking, the whole world belongs to you.

My head felt fuzzy, hazy and warm, as though my mind was bathing in slowly rotating, soft circles.

"Can I lie down please Viola?"

"Yeah, sure, do you have your REM with you?"

"Yes, why?"

"Let's go and lie down on my bed and take them together, it's much nicer after wine."

When male and female combine, all things achieve harmony.

She took my hand and led the way to her bedroom. The light was now a mixture of artificial lights from the streets and buildings outside. Tungsten and Neon and Fluorescent, the combined glow was one of warm Orange which spilled gently into the room through the large floor-to-ceiling window at one end of the room. Through it the city hummed below the velvet night sky, strewn with the perfect point sources of the stars.

We lay down on her large bed and she took out her capsule from a bedside table. I saw that she was a Ten which was Violet in colour. I found mine and we took them together, and lay together, holding each other. The music from the room next door played calm and moody, She was so warm and smelled so good. I was happy.

Whereas our minds and our memories may have been flawed, our bodies were a kind of perfection. Aware of our intimacy, perhaps a little shy of what must have been our innocence, we followed each other's moves, traced each other's feelings. With a touch we felt the fragility of our skin, goosebumps and giggles making way for the fullness of deeper sensations where hearts began beating more strongly and blood rushed through our souls. We became lost in ourselves.

More of a whole person than ever before, the transition into sleep was due to a feeling of oneness and physical exhaustion. In my dreams, aided by the drug, I was transported to memories of a place where light and life were one, and where time was a new concept.

- *18* -

Lost In A Strange Land

It's hot and the sun is blasting down, so that it blinds me every time I look up. I'm running again, fast and furious, fearful but focused. I'm heading West, I think, no mental map, no knowledge of this dry land, its layout or its time.

There are no people, only fields of open grassland and the sky is so wide as to make me feel meaningless. I cannot think, I can only run. I run until long after the sun has set and then I lie down in a ditch I've found by a road. I don't sleep for hours, kept awake by my dread and an animal instinct. The exhaustion finally gets the better of me and I slip under.

I am woken in the morning by a boy, who is standing in the dry dirt path looking at me. He is wearing a blue smock and baggy trousers, his mop of black hair sticks out in funny shapes. I realise that I have no hair of any kind. He beings laughing as he realises he has woken my and starts pointing at me as I stand. I cover myself realising for the first time my nakedness. Then he runs away and I am more lost than ever.

Walking along the path I find a pace that soothes me. I'm no longer running but I am striding out. The heat becomes almost unbearable once more and I sit and take shelter under a tree. There are berries on the floor all around, I try some but they are bitter and I spit them out. I feel safer here and I fall in and out of sleep, keeping one eye open.

I must have fallen fully asleep again because once more I am woken, this time by a young man, who appears to be the same type of person as me, in height and build. He also has no hair. He is wearing red material thrown over his whole body as a robe and stands next to a wooden cart which is attached to a huge beast. He has caught me unawares, as did the boy, but he seems to read my situation in a different way. Not laughing, instead he looks curious, mystified and puzzled.

He offers me a container but I do not understand what he wants me to do. He drinks from it then passes it to me, urging me to take it. I do as he did and drink in giant gulps and the fresh cool edge of the fluid fills a great hole inside of me. It's good, and the first of anything that I have put inside me.

The supreme good is like water which nourishes all things without trying to.

As I drink more of it he offers me something else, and he shows me how to eat. I eat it all. Although it is rough and dry in my throat, I swallow, and drink more and I know that it's also good. I finish drinking the water.

Finally he reaches back into the cart, the beast snorting occasionally as it jostles the great horns which come from its head. He pulls out a large piece of the red material and throws it towards me. It unfurls as it travels the distance between us and for a moment I'm completely underneath its lightness and redness. I stand and he motions me to wear it as he does. This takes quite a long time and he laughs a lot. But then I am standing next to him, clothed, looking as he does. He hits the great beast gently with a wooden stick and it begins to pull the wooden cart. We walk along the road together.

All the time he is speaking a language I cannot understand. Extremely quickly I begin to make out repeating patterns, hearing some of the sounds over and over. I store these patterns with little effort, knowing they are important if I'm to continue living. He doesn't stop talking and I don't stop listening as I know I am learning. We walk like this for many hours, my appreciation of time growing.

There is a building, and after following its wall for a while we enter through a large wooden door. Inside it's open and the plants have been ordered and put into beautifully symmetrical patterns. There are many other men just like my rescuer, all wearing the red material, all walking and talking or tending to the plants. A few of them look at me as we walk through this great wide space but I feel as one of them, nobody does anything to make me feel otherwise.

My friend leaves the beast and cart with another man and leads me through a narrow corridor and then into a cool, shaded room. From this room there is another, bare and empty. He turns a handle and water pours from a source above me. He motions me to take my clothes off and I step under the flowing liquid.

Nothing in the world is as soft and yielding as water. Yet for dissolving the hard and inflexible, nothing can surpass it.

This water, this pureness of the world is beauty in itself. It pours over my head and my body and I wash away the dirt and sweat and blood and the remains of some sticky substance which has clung to me with an acrid smell since the moment I remember starting to run. There is more, a sweet smelling, slippery block helps to clean off the mess I'm in, and I clean my bare head with it too.

When I have finished, the man, who has done nothing but help me since I first saw him, hands me a thicker piece of material and, as he has done from the start, acts out what I must do with it. I am clean and dry and soon I am wearing the red clothes again, this time they are new and clean also.

I sit with the man. He points to himself and says something. I don't know what he is doing. He does it again and again, until I repeat the sounds he makes. As this is the first time I have made a sound, it surprises me, in a way which causes me to smile, again a new sensation. He smiles too and points to me. I don't know what he wants me to say and I hang my head in shame. He has something that I know I do not have, but he is unconcerned.

Teaching without words, performing without actions.

I have retained many of the sounds he has made. I hold the red material I am wearing and point to it. He makes a sound and I repeat it. He smiles and I point to myself, to my face and repeat the sound. He laughs and points at me repeating the sound once more. I laugh, the most incredible of feelings, and I know why I am doing it, because I know that I now have a makeshift name. Even though it is only a sound, the sound of the word to describe a piece of red clothing, it is the only thing I have.

I lie down on a bed in the room. My friend leaves and I close my eyes. I am somewhere warm and safe, and I feel a peace and a strong solitude as I fall asleep.

As I sleep it is with a blackness that I welcome, I know this deep darkness is a place I've come from and that I'm at peace there. Then, from nowhere, I feel a jolt, a splinter cracks into me from a above and I begin to fall from way up high. Within myself, something terrible, something violent, runs through my head and down my spine, and I crash with all my weight onto a hard, cold unforgiving floor. I wake.

- 19 -

UPWARDLY MOBILE MEMORY

With my heart racing and in a cold sweat, I woke from suffering with those shadows, which felt as though they had lasted longer than the dream before them, sitting bolt upright in the bed. Viola was lying soundly asleep beside me and I wondered what memories and dreams were moving through her mind.

I wished for the serenity of this story of emotions in my history to continue. Who were the men in the robes and how long had I been with them?

Do you have the patience to wait till your mud settles and the water is clear? Can you remain unmoving till the right action arises by itself?

That is him. That is the voice of the man in the red robes. He found me and gave me food and water and shelter, and we spoke to each other and it is he who speaks to me still.

This sudden and overwhelming vision had now emerged from my memory. Resurfacing it brought with it an affirmation of myself, its clarity revealing to me what I hoped would be a great flood of further imagery.

How deep and how far back in time it went were questions which promised to have real answers. The facts of my existence had substance.

However, with some twisted irrational logic, I wanted to delve more completely into the nature of the earlier, dark event also, the moment before which there were no moments. If I could trace back, to find the cause I was certain I could find the truth of my condition. Mostly I wanted more of the present, more of Viola and more REM. I lay back down next to her and in the comfort and safety of this place was soon asleep once more.

The following days and weeks, I lost count, were a fantastic escalation of my dream-time and memory quality. I moved in with Viola permanently, at her invitation, her insistence even. She said she'd have a problem if she knew I was out there, alone among strangers, and that we'd be better off together. I felt wanted and needed.

I was taking great strides and improvements were continuously being made. The domino effect of my memories returning caused seismic shifts in my understanding of who I was, who I am. I had been someone, and I had grown into a new person because of it. I'm sure an external observer might have mistaken me for a completely different person, such was the wholesale change in my mental agility. I gained personality, so Viola told me and a character all of my own. For the first time there was also elation, a new sensation which came in glorious waves.

Viola, was a breath of fresh air. Her scheduling revolved around the MTR, she was a kind of accountant who kept various records and compiled statistical reports. She didn't really want to talk about it, calling it a chore, but it seemed to me it required some high level of skill and commitment. At times she would spend many hours at this, often working to a deadline, but when she wasn't deep into it, or when she had completed an assignment, she was nearly always working on her art. Bringing materials home and creating with a passion, sometimes well into the night, we still found plenty of time to ourselves.

Our friendship strengthened and grew, becoming deeper every day, a fact that came as a very pleasant addition to my life. We helped each other, grew closer to each other, shared everything with each other, loved each other. We began to socialise as a couple and we lived the lives we created together. We loved each other.

She soon introduced me to members higher up in the MTR network. I saw Robbie occasionally and it became clear that he was really only a minor player, and that there were many others like him. The people I began to meeting now however, people Viola was friendly with were wired in, closer to the top, closer to the source.

I started moving a lot more merchandise. Collecting larger amounts, turning it around and counting the Holo's as they came in. Very early on I figured out the bicycle was becoming a bottleneck in my system and so I bought a motorbike. It was an old petrol machine, but it was fast and I found a contact where I could get cheap fuel. I could make a lot more drop offs in a day because of it and I loved the adrenaline rush and the challenge of riding it around town, satisfaction was immediate.

As a machine it was an expression of me, and it fitted me like a glove. The way I took to its form and function was natural and I could handle it at speed with an easy attitude.

I gave the bicycle to a homeless Synth who looked like he needed it. Although I wasn't attached to it, and couldn't remember where I had acquired it, there was some symmetry I felt in giving it away like this. Perhaps one day, if he worked hard enough, he could become like me.

Taking my REM daily now because I could afford to, I decided I needed it for more than just reviewing my beautiful memories. Of great importance was to remember where I'd been, and what I was doing, because logistics were getting more and more complex. Viola told me I should slow down and cool it for a while, in case I began to attract attention from the wrong places. Control, in every aspect of my life, grew into a key concept for me, but was a natural evolution of my constitution.

There was no getting around it, I was on the up and up. With Viola's help and with my efforts focused I was mixing in higher circles. Some of these contacts came through the MTR, others via clients. One day I came to realise that there was just one person at the top of the organisation, The Minister as he was called. He had a mixed reputation among other Synths, ranging from admiration and respect to fear and suspicion. Few it seemed had actually met him.

I felt only a few steps away from him, and I wanted to meet him. The time had come to see eye to eye with the boss. I checked myself one night. I had been looking to this person for a long time, right from the moment I'd imagined that someone such as him simply must exist. Why did I feel the need to meet this person? It wasn't an easy question to answer.

As I looked back at my life, as much of it as I could remember, I came to the conclusion that I do not belong; not in this city, not in this country, not with humans but most worryingly of all, not with my own kind. I knew about belonging because I remember I used to feel it, I used to belong somewhere. Viola and I were one-to-one but other than this I felt no union with anything greater than myself. I was an outsider.

The Minister and the MTR were one, he represented the greater, bigger whole of which everyone was a part. But he was also at its apex, he was unitary, primary, singular, number one. He would know how I feel. He would know why I feel this way.

There was a quality I'd taken a long time to learn about Synths whilst among them. When we meet, we make a look, not a stare, just a short gaze. No one would notice it except for us. We not only exchange our ID numbers, there's a huge amount of data transfer in those seconds too. During this time there's an almost sub-conscious comparison; you instinctively know who's the fastest, the strongest, who has the biggest memory, the quickest mind with the most efficient internal architecture.

It's obvious really but it's a clever way of sharing crucial, beneficial protocols for how to proceed. You know about each other, at least some vital basics, and this means you know where you stand and what you can offer. It also means you rarely need to fight, because you always know which one of you would win. It's like a digital handshake, a sizing up and a trade deal all in one. Both parties benefit.

Always looking for people who could help me, as much as being able to help others, I'd found looking up to people was a bonus. Only someone in a position above you can help you up, especially if you don't want to be the kind of person who treads on others below you to advance in life.

I wanted to lock eyes with The Minister. I was fully aware that my psyche was still way out of balance, if not completely devastated. Whatever the event was that had seen me thrown headfirst into the darkness of this world it's effects felt permanent. If there was anyone who could give me what I needed to locate and rectify my flaws and errors, whatever they were, it was the boss of the MTR. The Minister was the highest positioned Synth I knew of. He had power, he had wealth, he had influence, he must have great knowledge too. If there were solutions for my problems, he would have them.

It was a question of trust. The Minister was at the centre of an inner circle and very few people were allowed in.

With Viola's help I got an appointment with a Synth called DJ who was in an outer circle of sorts. He'd heard of me and told me that I was on the The Minister's radar, due to my stellar efforts in obtaining such a large and reliable income. This was good news. He said he'd try and set up a meet, and sure enough, when he got back to me, the meeting was in place. It wouldn't be for some time yet but it was time I could spend contemplating, preparing. I knew I had to be ready for the encounter.

Stop trying to control. Let go of fixed plans and concepts, and the world will govern itself.

I took my REM and lay on the bed. I think Viola was painting. Lately the memories had taken on a dreamlike quality. As they came to me I relived them again in a full colour vision, with all the feelings, ideas, words and senses of the moment, woven into the textures of the fabric in which they were stored.

- 20 -

NATURAL TRANQUILITY

I'm gardening. It's a calm, warm day and the activity is both peaceful and productive. There are others around me who are also gardening.

The healthy flowers, bushes and plants all need to be watered daily and I must walk back and forth to large barrels, which have collected rain over the months during the winter and spring. The watering can I use is large, but still there are many journeys up and down the rows and bedding. I feel strong.

Most of the gardens are set to vegetables of all kinds. I don't know the names but the sizes, shapes and colours are so varied and extreme. The dank smell of the reddish soil itself is in the air always.

Gardening is my primary work and it takes up nearly my whole day. Pruning, weeding, planting and watering. Sometimes I have to dig great holes or move large amounts of soil from one place to another. We often work together to accomplish greater tasks, and this type of work is very rewarding.

When I sleep at night it is with aching muscles, but regular washing and a comfortable bed make for a good night's sleep. My dreams here are of nature and its nurture. There is a routine and a rhythm I have entered into which has brought about a great harmony. The synchronicity of my physical work and the workings of my mind blend into a unity which is with me throughout the day, rising and falling with the sun. It is my reality, the only one I know.

The vegetables supply almost enough food for the whole monastery, for that is what this place is. I've counted over sixty people here, all male with ages ranging from five to eighty-five. They all talk in Mandarin to me and I have picked up the language with some ease. Conversations are usually short and rarely deviate from the necessities of daily chores but I consider them all to be my friends and my brothers, for in our simple exchanges this is how they treat me.

I've worked in other parts of these buildings too, the variety being a welcome change. There are kitchens where much industrious collaboration is employed preparing and cooking the food we eat. There are large washing rooms where clothes and bed sheets and the like are cleaned and then dried outside. There are groups specialised in cleaning. They move about with a regular schedule washing floors, and latrines and in fact every part of the buildings.

There is a system for everything and a place for everyone. Every task is performed with care and pride. I have built up such pride myself in the work I do. The more I apply myself to the job, and study its particular requirements, the more I appreciate the skills and talents needed to perform it. An approach where one plays with possible alternative methods, leads to a heightened awareness and a strange feeling of perfection.

The monks, for that is what they are, what we are, occasionally leave the monastery with carts and the great beasts of burden. They're loaded with produce, mostly vegetables of which we apparently have a surplus, and return with other goods. I have learned that they trade the food for these products, things such as pots and pans, chairs, rope, anything in fact that they don't make within the monastery. I have yet to leave this place myself since I arrived but I begin to forget how long that might be. I cannot think of the events which occurred immediately prior to my arrival here with any clarity at all. It feels like an accident which happened a long time ago in an impossible past.

In the mornings and the evenings, the monk who saved me, whose name is Zhang, takes me for prayer and meditation. This regular experience is quite fascinating in many ways but mainly because I have not yet discovered its purpose. We are often in a group of ten to twenty others and assemble in a great room which I understand is solely for this activity. It has a high ceiling rising up to wooden rafters, the building I imagine to be very old, much older than me.

We sit down in rows, our legs crossed, and there are a series of sounds, chimes made with a bell by a young boy who sits up high at the front facing everyone. We wear our red robes, and sandals, and only these, at all times. And we just sit there, for long periods of time. Sometimes I close my eyes, sometimes I leave them open. We are there long enough for me to notice the light and shadows move across the floors and walls. Noticing the passing of time when in this state is certainly a powerful force to consider, especially when I realise for most of the day it is far from my mind. The bell is chimed and we stand and leave, and that's all it is.

I tried asking Zhang what these activities are for and what I am supposed to be doing all this time seated. He took a watering can and tapped his head and poured the water out. With only his actions to inform my understanding, I took him to mean that I must empty my mind.

I try to do this every time we meditate but it is very hard for me. Zhang tells me that it is not meant to be easy and sometimes it takes people a whole lifetime to master. There are moments, I don't know how long, in which I feel I am successful. In these periods it's as though the breeze is blowing both through me and around me. When we finish, an extreme sense of clarity and power moves within me in pulsing waves. I am both energised and relaxed and know that I am working as I should.

In the evenings it is harder to meditate because there is a whole day's worth of information to empty from your mind. It's easy for me to spend the time simply remembering what has happened during the day. The meditation is for me like the gardening, except that it is my mind I am exercising and tending to. When I remember my days, it is with great detail, as detailed as the structure of the leaves and petals of the flowers and plants. It's becoming obvious to me that in my case at least, and perhaps for all my brothers too, the ways of remembering and forgetting are woven together in the same fabric of the soul. There is a need to attend to both.

Empty your mind of all thoughts. Let you heart be at peace. Watch the turmoil of beings, but contemplate their return.

Zhang is also my tutor, and a very good one too. He is patient and methodical and has only my interests in his heart. We have become good friends. It is he who's taken to teaching me the language and it's from him I have learned as much as I have, both of this world and the world outside.

He tells me of great mountains of people living together on top of each other with the peaks of many of these mountains rising high into the sky. It seems hardly credible. He tells me that there are seas of salty water that stretch all the way to the horizon and that one can travel for many weeks on them, the land disappearing, with only waves in sight. I would like to see such a thing. And he tells me of many other things too; of wars between men where they kill each other, of little people living in small metal tubes up in the night sky with the stars, and of the countries of the world and their different languages.

Usually laughing and joking, Zhang became more serious once, sitting quietly together as he met my eyes. He said there are men in the world who are not men. Men who look like men but who are partly made with wheels inside them. These Future People, as he called them, are made by Man, but they have become separate from Man. I couldn't believe him as he talked, but he was just silent and stared into my eyes.

There was a bond between us in those seconds, it was strong, but it passed. He laughed again and gently pushed me and I pretended to fall over.

It was around this time that he began singing songs and poetry to me, I think to improve my grasp of the language. Some of the words rhymed, some repeated and it did help my vocabulary. However the meanings of these verses were clouded to me and gave difficulty for me to analyse. I persevered because they seemed to flow from some ancient source and over time I felt I gleaned great understanding from them.

I'm gardening again. It's hot and I sweat, my leg muscles are sometimes in pain from regularly squatting and standing, but I am content as this discomfort is always balanced by relief at the end of the day.

Approach it and there is no beginning; follow it and there is no end. You can't know it, but you can be it, at ease in your own life. Just realise where you come from: this is the essence of wisdom.

A stream flows by, and through, the monastery. It drives a water wheel, the energy being used to drive certain machines. I'm fascinated by the motion of the wheel and the sound the water makes as it turns the paddles, I feel a connection with this transformation of motion and energy as I feel it within me too. The sunlight plays with the surface of the stream as it flows smooth then breaks and cascades.

- *21* -

FREEZE FRAMING

With regularly repeated doses of REM I began to see beauty all around my enveloping environment. Not able, as yet anyway, to retrieve every distant memory, I was certainly beginning to make new ones of the here and now. The accumulation of these new memories was nothing less than a construction of my self. They became me. The sum of my senses and their arrangement into an order of my choosing created the palette from which I painted my ongoing life-story.

As I walked, both at day and night, through the realm which was my domain, I became adept at storing images for later retrieval. There was no method for this, nor indeed a pattern to the instant pictures I could record, but with effort I began to have some control over the storage of this mainly visual data.

I would be distracted by some motion or alluring arrangement of people and objects. I would focus, my mind as much as my eyes, on the elements of primary interest, then by means of an extended gaze, the scene would impress itself upon my memory, indelibly.

Initially there would be perhaps only ten or so of these events, each day, to which I could later have access and the opportunity to process and analyse. Later I would be able to build up a database of hundreds. In my down time, as I rested, their review was a source of immense happiness.

Can you cleanse you inner vision until you see nothing but the light?

The people of interest in these momentary memories were both human and Synth, not always being close enough for me to lock onto and discern the difference. Often oblivious to my attention, some were unknowing subjects, but others looked straight at me as the images were formed:

An old man stands upright with his eyes closed, holding a wooden spoon. In front of him is his livelihood, a steaming tray of several score of mottled eggs, boiled in their shells and ready for sale. A tea urn covered in Chinese symbols completes his offerings. A watch is loose on the wrist his other hand, hanging at rest by his side. A bus moves by in the background. His expression is one of serene meditation.

A round, happy man sits inside a big digging machine with caterpillar tracks. Road cones guard the site where the road is being dug up. Behind him a huge skyscraper rises. He looks straight at me, smiling and making the peace sign. He isn't doing any work, he's just looking at me, looking at him.

Seven people on bicycles are coming straight towards me, two women and five men. The bicycles all look very similar with handlebars that droop down. They look to be owning the road, they look about to run me down, but looking closer they are going so slowly and pass by on either side of me avoiding me completely.

At a busy street-crossing I follow behind a woman. The back of her denim jacket has its collar turned up, the back of her head has short black hair. I cannot see her face but she holds over her shoulder a child, a girl who stares straight back at me. A round face and wide eyes look into me, and her downturned mouth expresses indifference. A man in a suit and colourful tie walks the other way.

A middle aged man wearing a white tracksuit and white baseball cap sits aboard an archaic barge boat down by the docks. On the deck he operates a mechanical machine of gears and pulleys and chains, ropes criss-cross the area. With gloved hands he concentrates on this difficult task, pulling alternately on three levers, his feet working pedals.

A modern sports car juts out from the garage doors of a back street mechanic's garage. Two men are at work. One handles a piece of bodywork, wearing open sandals and squatting as he shapes the metal. The other sits by one of the car's wheels, manipulating some small machine which is partially hidden from view. Their faces are turned away.

A hotel employee, resplendent in his uniform stands outside his hotel by a railing. One hand in a white glove touches the railing. He looks out at some distant scene or object with calm and peaceful concentration. Gold braiding drops from his shoulder down the back of his jacket. His peaked hat completes his grandeur.

A group of four people with their backs to me pray at the entrance to a great hall. Inside, huge wired lanterns hang from high ceilings. Incense burns and fills the space with smoke and rays of light break through to illuminate the holy place, highlighting the smoke inside. Two of the people kneel, one stands with his hands behind his back, the other is beginning to leave. They wear casual modern clothes.

Two young men sit next to each other on folding chairs on the sidewalk. In front of them there is a hole in the ground surrounded by a safety cordon. One works on some cables which come from the hole, the other looks on intently, a large toolbox by his feet. An older suited man stands nearby with his hands in his pockets, leaning towards the other two, watching.

The central atrium of a shopping mall, seven stories high, and people line the balconies on every floor looking down at the scene below. Brightly lit and surrounded by advertising, a lone girl stands with a microphone singing a song. She looks tiny and frail but her shadow thrown by the lights is long and large.

A boy is having his hair cut. He sits with a cape around his neck, his head tilted forwards. Black hair is being formed into a neat shape. The old barber uses an electric cutter, the cable running around and away. He is focused on his work, a slightly furrowed brow and his own hair, grey and wispy is combed over a balding head.

The stern of a huge sea-going barge pulls away at a quay. Stacked up high in a haphazard way upon it, are twenty immense tyres, each ten feet across. Below these a line of washing hangs and below this two small men stand in a large opening.

An ancient woman sits laughing with a wide eyed toothless grin, in her doorway out onto the street. By her side, a tiny child wearing a cartoon top, holds a bottle in one hand, which she sucks from as she looks at me. They are holding hands.

A very young boy, wearing a small and poorly fitting, baggy check suit, and white trainers, is squatting. He has his hands together, tiny fingers interlinked in prayer.

- *22* -

Two Minds Better Than One

The closeness of our interactions meant that Viola and I began to share our most intimate thoughts. Our minds together were a perfect union and the experience generated was warm and fun. Her approach to life, was bright and refreshing as everything was seen by her as raw materials for the creation of something new. It didn't escape my attention that I was one such medium, ready to be shaped and formed into a better version of myself, but I was willing clay in her hands.

The engine of our relationship was total honesty, with no detail of our experiences left unexplored, transferred or transformed between us. Observations of our factual external environments, minutiae of our inner worlds, the quality of emerging feelings, thoughts and emotions, were all open for interpretation and subtle communication. Sharing without boundaries or conditions meant that effectively we became as one.

The spaces in my soul, she filled. All my zeros she turned into ones. I believe that for her I became the epitome of strength, upon which her confidence and character could grow. We laughed a lot, and when we clashed in our beliefs we sometimes argued, we lived. Without question my memory improved with her guidance, and sometimes her control. The recall of my former life was returning to me with a clarity and purity to match even that of immediate experience.

When he makes a mistake, he realises it. Having realised it, he admits it. Having admitted it, he corrects it.

One afternoon, we decided to head out of the city a little way on the bike. I'd bought another helmet for Viola and with a small bag packed with food we set off looking for a good spot. It was a long ride to find somewhere suitably remote, but when we found some fields by a river I parked up and we sat down in the shade of a willow tree. It was warm and close. Viola was excitable as she stepped of the bike.

"Where are we?"

"North, somewhere. It feels somehow familiar, like I may have passed through here once, but I've never been here before, I don't think."

The difficulties I had in remembering were sometimes mixed with uncertainties about the truth of what I actually could remember. In addition places like this seemed so familiar as to have been in a dream, or described to me by someone else. I was less and less troubled by my limitations and the unreliable perceptions they produced, as I'd learned to live in-between worlds, where the past merged with ideas of the future and both were often brought into a hazy now. Viola rarely thought like this, being carefree on the whole.

"I'm thinking of starting a new series of sculptures."

"What kind of thing are we talking about here?"

"Visions of the future, you know, how everything might be years from now."

"Well how would you even start doing such a thing? You could extrapolate from the present, project it into tomorrow but, years ahead? I don't see how. You wouldn't be able to… see that far ahead."

"Imagination."

"Oh, that."

"What do you mean, oh that! It's only like the biggest gift we have."

"Yeah, but it's not exactly… accurate, now is it."

"I'm not looking for accuracy dumb dumb, just an idea, an expression of what is yet to come."

"Ok, I got you now. Something similar to your cooking, when you have all the ingredients but you're not sure exactly what it is you're going to make yet."

"Shut up. You like my food don't you?"

"I do, I do. It's just, for me at least, I'd rather stick to some kind of plan in life, where you know what's going to happen."

"Well, that's just you saying you want a future that's all mapped out, and you just have to live it."

"There's nothing wrong with that."

"No, there's nothing wrong with it, in fact it's perfectly reasonably and desirable, it's just that it's only one of many alternate possible realities. I want to pick one that's… the most interesting."

"I know what you want, you want the dream. Some abstract beautiful idea of a future. Don't you think that's going to be forever just out of reach?"

"No, no I don't. I'm a dreamer and I'm a believer. Now eat your food and don't complain."

We ate and I told Viola all about my developing ability to make new memories with my freeze-frame mind pictures. I could see she was impressed. But as I described them to her, it felt like I wasn't doing them justice. Their visual quality didn't translate well into mere spoken words and I became a little perturbed at something else too.

"The thing is they're not really stories though are they?"

"I think they make lovely stories, there's something happening within them, they all have a story woven through their fabric. Keep with it, you might find they change over time, or that your way of capturing them improves with experience."

As always she made me feel better. I was less negative during these weeks but my preoccupations with completion and belonging, or rather the deep belief that I was fundamentally incomplete, and separate from my fellow Synth, kept returning. This concept of stories was yet another inroad into the investigation of my inner workings and their limitations.

It\s hard to enjoy yourself though, when you don't have a story, a story to tell yourself to make sense of who you are, and to communicate effectively to other people. The history of my earlier life in the monastery was coming back to me in ever increasing richness, I was at least beginning to recreate my life, perhaps soon I would have a complete story to tell.

Viola and I had the MTR, it was how we'd met and it was through it that we had come together. It was our story. This was a fact that had been weighing on my mind lately. As the umbrella organisation which protected us and provided the means for us to live, it was of great benefit, as it was for many other Synths. But that same umbrella threw a shadow over the two of us and I for one wanted to step out from under it, at some point in the future.

The Minister himself had dark auras surrounding him. He was, in the same breath, both the saviour of Synth culture and a stone around its neck. With one hand he gave, in the form of jobs and security, and with the other he kept a firm downward pressure upon all under his vigil. Viola was no different in her attitude towards him than most others within the city. She showed both respect and fear and this was a combination abhorrent to me. The opportunity to lock eyes with him, to see what he was made of was was just a day away. Aside from asking him the questions to which I felt only he would have the answers, more than anything now, I wanted to know if I had the measure of him.

It was simply impossible for all the stories about him to be true. It was said he had tortured both humans and Synths alike. There was talk of random killings. But also he had apparently organised the rescue and rehousing of many hundreds of displaced immigrants arriving near the city, dangerously overcrowded in overloaded boats. It was he who had built the MTR, from nothing, making the lives of hundreds, thousands of Synths, bearable. People thrived under his leadership.

Yet still, nothing was known of his personal history, and in this way we had a connection. The means by which he operated with so little interference from the authorities was a complete mystery. I could sense the darknesses which surrounded his dualities and tomorrow I was going to meet him, to know for myself their nature and depth.

Lately there was a real feeling that the split in my own character was healing. All Synths have a degree of tension between their human underpinnings, and all of that which is other within them. This duality is written in at a genetic level and cannot be escaped, we just have to live with it.

Further to the conflict, which this design inherently produces, my own personal crisis was still tangible. The clash between ancient and modern, between the peace of the monastery and the negative vibe of the city, was at the core of the my restlessness and disharmony. These opposing factions within couldn't be reconciled.

I knew that one dominant philosophy would surely win out over the other, for it is a noting less than a war which is taking place in the topography my soul. The manner of the victory, and the character of the victor, would be decided over time.

There must be a good reason why I've been lifted from such a holy place and put down in this gritty, corrupt city. Viola is my reason, my future here involves her as central to my being, of that I have no doubt. Together we talk of dreams, of exploring far away countries and living as though we were different people. We imagine a world where REM is no longer needed and we're free to live and remember as we wish.

The Minister holds all the keys, only he can unlock the doors through which I desire to pass. When I get close to him, I can assess him and I can make myself equal to him. I can use him to get what I want, as I'm sure he will do the same with me.

With my thoughts occupying my mind I was forgetting the beauty of the present and so I took one of my visual recordings:

Viola is lying down, propping herself up on one elbow. A large silver earring, which she made herself, hangs from a perfect ear, hair lifting in the breeze. A swooping branch of a willow tree drops low just behind her. Some sunlight reflects from the rippling surface of the river, points of light of varying intensities. She is turning to look at me.

The sky is clear and spacious, the earth is solid and full, all creatures flourish together, content with the way they are, endlessly repeating themselves, endlessly renewed.

The Minister, the city, the MTR, all seemed a thousand miles away again and we stayed in this state of bliss for several hours before returning to the dark city after nightfall. The harsh glare of artificial illumination wrapped around my visor as I cruised up to the apartment on the bike. The feelings of the afternoon seemed to be subsumed, and almost erased by an oppressive power of urban fear. I'd noticed it growing lately, obscuring my happiness, just as a misty smog which sometimes filled the streets, threatened to obscure my vision ahead.

- 23 -

Natural Beauty

In the large, bright, open space of her painting room, Viola moved with a natural grace, uncommon even in our kind. Gesturing to herself occasionally in some private language she listened to a gentle, mellow stream of music. Brush in hand, she was lost in the zone she needed to generate the work she desired.

The expansive canvas in front of her occupied almost the entire wall and was in an evolving state of progress, transitioning into a recognisable state.

She used a palette of two hundred and fifty six colours, each a distinct wavelength of visible light, each labelled with its wavelength value. She mixed them liberally but at this moment, a pure colour of 613 nanometers was neat on her kolinsky sable-hair paint brush. She preferred one with a fifty-fifty male/female hair, which was more of a yin and yang thing than any considerations of what might be the very finest quality.

The painting itself was a type of pointillism. She'd once seen this particular technique and had developed it into her own style. Currently the painting had the appearance of multicoloured chaos but she knew what she was doing, and knew the desired effect would eventually emerge.

It was a landscape, an abstraction of a New England scene in the Fall. Having only an old postcard to work with, Viola had channeled her imagination and then expanded it to begin expressing what it was she wanted.

Working this way was escapism, she knew this. The choice of an image from a far away land, the USA in particular being of great interest to her, wasn't a random one. The choice of a vision of wide open nature as opposed to the sprawling claustrophobia of her cityscape habitat was equally diametric to her reality. And then the choice of abstraction as opposed to some more realistic representation of the world was further evidence as to the location of her thinking. Viola accepted her lot in life but saw no reason why she shouldn't escape from it, if only in some virtual way on occasion, and this was how she did it.

She'd made studies of undersea scenes, African deserts, mountainous alpine regions, Arctic wastelands and now these forests. All were of natural vistas, all were places she was only able to imagine herself occupying.

When she looked through her window to the view of the city, it inspired only sadness. It was a civilisation for certain, but for her it was an ugly one.

Beauty kept her alive but it was so hard to find here, so she had learned to create it for herself. She found most people here ugly to look at too. Her experiences with humans hadn't been good and maybe because of this she saw only the distorted or corrupted sides of their characters. She felt despair when she watched their faces, as they tried with vanity to express themselves adequately.

She'd run away from a group of humans, whom she'd been placed with. A family they had called themselves, but as their maid, home-help and personal tutor she was not appreciated in the slightest. They had used her with no regard or respect for her femininity or indeed for her living soul, and she'd reached a limit, a breaking point. It was a realisation of their ugliness of spirit which had pushed her over the edge. Their superficial outward appearance mirrored their inner badness and once she perceived this she had fled and she'd never looked back.

Starting the creation of artwork, in a small way at first, shortly after this event, she had no illusions that it was a reaction due to the negative experience. It was her start in life. It had been a way to heal, to play and to re-invent herself anew. Now she felt that to be the artist of one's own life was no more a choice than it was a choice to be a Synth. It was an activity of life, on a par with breathing. In moments of hope she thought this might be the same for some enlightened humans.

Synths were just as mixed up and confused of course, and had all sorts of their own problems and shortcomings. However, by luck or by design, most were generally congenial and what's more she like they way they looked. Naturally she was biased. Each to their own.

Her own looks were a source of some fascination, she was quite obsessed with her own image. This was not narcissism, but rather the study of the subject which was most readily accessible to her. She modelled for herself and in some objective sense she liked what she saw.

Androgyny was an overused word. To be designed, to be synthesised and to some degree to be shaped in form and appearance by the human hand, meant that she was someone else's idea of beauty. But the idea that she was sexless, or that some other viewer might have difficulty determining her gender, was slightly cliched. She received compliments from time to time, from both men and women, human and Synth, but she believed in her own mind that her beauty lay within.

When she looked at EZee she liked what she saw, appreciating his external and internal aesthetic. The beauty of EZee was that he was now fully committed to her and although she couldn't let on to him, it was clear he had become her muse.

Thinking of him she allowed herself to slip into a little reverie as she continued painting quietly:

He's actually not so complicated. He had no past, but now he's started sharing what is is that he can remember we're closer. It would have made things difficult for us if his memory had not returned. There is simplicity when he shares with me. With his past so real, he's better able to be in the present, always aware and alert to my being.

I symbolise a new beginning for him, a start which needs no groundwork or foundations. It's often the beginning of a journey which contains the most hope and we exist in this eternal commencement,.

There's the matter of assimilation. It was so stark and brutal and obvious when we met that he wasn't connected to the Ultra Net. It was just something that wasn't there. From my conversations with the others it was perfectly clear to them too. He's just detached from Synth consciousness, who can tell what that might feel like? I've never seen it before, neither have the others.

How such a condition could come about seems impossible to fathom. I have theories but nothing concrete and not a clue as to how his situation could be changed. It would be an easier problem to solve if he were missing an eye.

How could you broach such a subject? It's not a case of being tactless or rude. The issue has gravity and an edge so as to make possible dialogue negate itself. It's a question of identity and to talk of it with him would cause irreparable doubt in his mind. It would lead to an existential crisis.

Without his memories he felt incomplete, but to be told he is missing something we all take for granted, that he is not as real as all other Synths, he would feel deficient in a fundamental way. It would cause him to question his sanity, being aware he is Synth but being aware in a factual way that he is outside of all Synths. He would neither know who he is or what he is. Without any material identity he would not be able to grasp the necessary orientation for continued life. He would malfunction, he would breakdown. I don't want to imagine what he would do by default in that state.

It was good we'd agreed unanimously to keep information regarding these considerations from him. It's much better for him this way.

Anyway, I like him just as he is. He doesn't have the advantages that we do, but his deficiency doesn't seem to have effected his will or drive. Being blissfully ignorant gives him a quality that's fresh and individual and strong. He is his own man, and quite literally more independent than any of us could ever be.

Besides, he does have an identity above and beyond the usual, he has me. He identifies with me, and I identify with him. Ours is an exclusive relationship, with a reality that nobody else could ever know.

In a strange sense he actually is connected to the Synth consciousness, only through my mind. My mind is the media through which he makes a rudimentary manual connection. Obviously he can't know he's trying to do this, but his own independent mind has a curiosity and a hunger for the knowledge, it's a harmony and oneness he senses with me. I don't know where he gets this from.

Eye to eye contact with him is like nothing I've felt before. The exchange of personal private data and values, the intensity and scope of the feeling, sometimes it's just too much for me. I know he feels this too, he's said as much and knowing that he's not assimilated makes these exchanges all the more intimate. Knowing that he's unaware of his lack of assimilation gives me a great feeling of responsibility for him. His being, detached and solo in his unitary state, makes me love him all the more.

I've never been loved by any man before. EZee's love for me feeds my mind, my body and my soul. The fact that we are connected by our love is all I need to know.

- 24 -

HIGHER POWER

Standing in front of the mirror I put my jacket on. Viola helped me with a tie, something I found impossible to master on my own.

The motorbike took me at speed to my destination and I parked in an alleyway to the side of the road. The building, known in the MTR as The Studio was guarded quite heavily by well-built Synths who looked like their primary objectives were protection, defence and security. They allowed me through with no fuss in this old warehouse space, which had a metal staircase leading to the upper floors. One step at a time I ascended with caution, looking for clues, looking for cracks. I heard music.

Then there were no more steps, I was at the top, and the only one up here was the boss. Through the few chairs and tables which were strewn about I scanned for The Minister. He was seated in the middle of a wide open space with a drink in his hand and in a nonchalant way he waved me over.

"Come, come, have a seat. Do you mind if we speak English?"

His English was perfect and clipped, already I looked forward to speaking this with him as I considered it my native tongue.

"Not at all." I realised now how my own accent was different, certainly from his, more drawn and elastic in some ways.

Walking over I could see the source of the music, huge panel speakers hung on the walls. The sounds were not loud but nevertheless filled the entire volume of the place, defined as it was by the bare stripped back ceiling and floor.

I walked slowly to where he was seated and placed myself opposite him, some three metres away, in a leather armchair similar to one in Viola's apartment.

The Minister wore a grey suit of the kind I had seen before, he looked… grand and rich. He was wearing eye protection of a type that made it impossible to register him and his ID. This unnerved me a little as it was a trick few played, it was underhand and a Synth would know it was counterproductive.

"Mister EZee, would you like a drink?"

"No, thank you, I'm not particularly thirsty."

He waved his hand in the direction of the speakers. "Do you like music Mister EZee?"

"I can't say that I've had much of a chance to listen to any. It's difficult to come by."

"It is, it is. One of the benefits of ample wealth. This is Beethoven, I have been able to get to know him rather well over the years. I think you could say we are quite good friends."

"That's nice for you. I wonder if we might get down to business."

"Ah yes, business, the small matter of REM distribution."

"I'm interested in, becoming more proactive within MTR, taking on a greater role."

"Well, you've certainly earned it. More than 25,000 Holo's in just a month, it's impressive."

"Thank you."

"But you will need more than a street dealer's instinct if you are to progress in this Synth organisation Mister EZee."

No one had called me Mister before and although I liked it on one level it was starting to grate on another. I thought I had yet to address him by his name, not knowing quite what was appropriate. The conversation was already growing one-sided and I didn't like it too much.

"I feel I'm versatile enough to take on most any challenge."

At this point in our interaction he removed his glasses and I was able to clock him in an instant, but with an amazement I was hardly able to conceal, there was nothing to register. The head of the MTR was not a Synth. So there was a human in control of the underworld too, it shouldn't have been a surprise, Synths were always under the thumb. He would know I was a Synth, before I had arrived, and so immediately had me at a disadvantage, I felt extremely uncomfortable and it was probably obvious. He put his glasses back on.

"Mmm. What do you know of shipping Mister EZee?"

"Precious little, but I can learn." I had gathered myself together remarkably well considering the scale of this recent revelation.

"You've built up some trust within this network and now I want to extend to you opportunities of a more lucrative nature. There's a cargo vessel coming into Hong Kong, down the coast, in a couple of days. We will be relieving it of one of its containers, within which there will be enough REM to keep us all swimming in memories for at least another year. Believers in reincarnation will probably be able to remember their previous lives. I'd like you to manage the operation."

I wanted this but in point of fact I couldn't say no, that is to say even if I'd wanted to I couldn't say that word. With a horrible involuntary acceptance I knew I was under the control of this person, this human. Some powerful programming at my core was commanding me to comply with his instruction and no matter how strong my will was I could only comply.

"I'm sure I can facilitate such activities."

"My usual man... became unwell, and has sadly retired. I can pay you well, in fact I will open up a line of credit for you, and the experience might prove useful, to us both, in the long term."

"I'm here to assist, Sir." I'd never called anyone Sir in my life, that I could remember, but I felt somehow obliged.

"Good. These are the details of your assignment. I won't expect to hear from you until the job is done." He stood, walked towards me and gave me a brown envelope.

"Are you sure you wouldn't like a drink, to toast the arrangement?"

"That won't be necessary, Sir."

"Fair enough. Good bye Mister EZee, and make sure it runs… perfectly… for me, won't you."

I turned and left the space, my heart rate had climbed, as so much had happened within such a short time. I took my time walking down the metal steps but only really breathed when I'd left the building and the air outside brought me back to a reality I recognised.

There being a human in control of the organisation came with a dawning dread that I couldn't tell anyone. It would sound like just another conspiracy theory and no one would believe me. But there must be others who knew, the guards surely. Were they psychologically shackled and under the same spell? I couldn't share this with anyone, I could feel it, the secret locked away inside of me, written in my code to silently obey, with a stress on the silence as much as the compliance. I was more along that ever.

We were all just slaves, and if everyone was the same as me, none of us could complain or refuse to take orders or rebel. All of us complicit in our ignorance and powerlessness, robbed of our free will under the perfect innate control or our ultimate creators.

What broke my heart was the now tainted image of the entire MTR, run and orchestrated by humans. I hated it, this was supposed to be our operation, our system, Synths working for Synths all together. Now I found the whole show was just being directed by some human dictator at the top, and my immediate question was, who was he working for?

Folding the envelope and putting it into my inside jacket pocket I got on the bike, started her up and blazed away. With Hong Kong lights streaming through my peripheral vision I didn't really care if the police caught me, I'd outrun them easily before. Racing through traffic I knew I'd entered the innermost circle of the city's Synth network and that I couldn't leave. I was just a wheel in a machine, over which I had no control. The Minister being a man left me stone cold, but it all fitted together when I zoomed out and looked at the picture with some objectivity.

Of course the MTR had to be made legitimate with a human controlling its direction. The law enforcement authorities would naturally be aware of this, otherwise it wouldn't be able to operate. They could turn a blind eye and the Synth population would get all the REM it needed in order to best serve its human masters. Everyone wins, except us.

What this did for the ongoing struggle for Synths rights, and moreover the Synth revolution which was sometimes talked about in hushed tones, was another matter. Humans stood on the shoulders of Synths and Synths were obliged to keep it that way. I wasn't happy about it, it was the way of the world, but on that journey back I knew I would fight it.

I arrived back at the apartment. Viola and I ate in silence before analysing the full contents of the envelope. We talked about it, as Viola would be involved in the operation. It was suddenly clear that I had leapfrogged her, jumped ahead of her in the MTR, but she wasn't worried.

I considered telling her about The Minister, but I knew she would think me crazy and even if I could convince of the truth I knew it would break her heart, her spirit and her resolve. Even so, on a couple of occasions I did to try to confide in her, but the horror of my condition meant I simply was not be able execute the necessary speech. I was logically, physically and mentally paralysed in this attempt. Even in moments of intimacy I was alone with my secret knowledge. Maybe it was a secret held by others, but one which defied sharing.

Viola had several roles within the organisation, some small, some larger and more important. Something of an accountant she prepared reports for The Minister, as well as having street level duties, directing sub-teams. Like most of the jobs within MTR, every cog was an essential piece of the machine. Viola was proud of being so essential. I on the other hand had been shown the truth behind the illusion, any pride I might have had was transformed into resentment and anger.

I lost a great deal of faith that day, even the voice of the monk, so often a comfort, failed to materialise and bring its usual peace to my mind. In a private moment alone in the bathroom I collapsed in on myself. Close to breakdown it took all I had to pull myself together, to reform my persona into something presentable to world and to Viola.

- 25 -

PERFECT PEOPLE

Late at night, and with only his security detail in the building, The Minister had been thinking. With his hands clasped behind his back, he paced at a steady rate around the perimeter of his huge room on the upper floor of The Studio. He muttered to himself, in a constant an almost inaudible string of words. Only he could hear what he was saying and even he was having difficulty clearly making out his voice. He began speaking slightly louder so that he could hear himself above the classical music filling the space.

Stumbling and stuttering at first, he grew in confidence with a more distinct enunciation of his phrases, making them clearer as he continued to pace. After a while he was in his stride, and as he spoke with greater force and conviction, his hands unclasped and they began to gesticulate in front of him, punctuating his delivery.

His thought process was, in itself, a monologue, more of a speech in reality. It was one he had rehearsed many times over. With each repetition, he would edit his thoughts, adding to them, censoring them and in his mind perfecting them.

Without knowing where or when, he felt sure that at sometime soon he would be called upon to deliver his speech. Perhaps when he received a promotion, or in the event of a restructuring, he would be offered an invitation to address an audience. He would be ready for the opportunity to inform an assembly of his peers as to the truths of society. He would tell them not just what they wanted to know, but what they needed to know. He would be able to teach them:

"A gradual and steady progress, is what we require, but vitally a perfectly planned one too. It is the way through, over and up into the future. Constant revolution of procedure is necessary and only through alignment with power can effective change be brought about.

The will of the human mind is to supersede, to overcome, and this can only be done by standing on the shoulders of those beneath. Organisation is supreme to bring this about. Without it nothing of lasting importance can be built, but with it anything and everything is possible.

Focus is the path to arrive at the goal. I focus, I plan, I prepare, I organise, I act and I meet my objective with unconditional success. One hundred percent. Perfection as an end-in-itself, self-fulfilling, self-perpetuating. Pure.

We are sacred, us humans. The human mind is perfect, that is true by definition and should be obvious to us all. Human thinking is pure mind. Pure thought is as perfect as mathematics and there is no way to dispute this.

It is only through interaction with the physical world that error and imperfection become apparent. It is because the physical world is imperfect that any association with it inevitably results in further imperfections. Even the flawless mind cannot make that which is inherently chaotic, orderly again.

So what are we to do, we possessors of conceptual purity, when faced with the horribly corrupted world in which we find ourselves?

Our perfect minds created synthetic life and this life should therefore be perfect too. As we know however, synthetic people a far from perfect; flawed genes, flawed memories and flawed characters. We must remember that we are not responsible for their misfortune, it is only the physical world which has intervened to spoil their design.

We have gone to extreme lengths to provide all conceivable corrections for their errors. The drug REM is of immaculate conception itself and we must be satisfied that we can do no more to remedy their condition. We must be content with ourselves and allow them to attempt their own rehabilitation of their faulty constitutions.

People say we should remove the cause of the imperfection, erase flaws at their origin. But the idea of a life of constantly removing flaws is tiresome to me. I prefer not to see them in the first place.

To be presented with only that which is already perfect is far more agreeable to me. I feel so much more comfortable that way. It is how life is meant to be. If only others could see that it is imperfection itself which creates imperfection!"

He stopped in his tracks, seemingly having forgotten the next part of his speech. Scanning his memory for the next sentence, and failing to find it, he became distracted by the positioning of one of the chairs in the room. He moved it a very small distance to be more aligned with the one next to it, and decided to leave the room.

- 26 -

TRADE IN GOODS

Zhang interrupted my gardening duties one day and asked if I'd like to go outside the monastery for a few hours with him. I paused and had to think as I'd become quite accustomed to being surrounded by the walls of this place. He told me it would be good for me to see the world and how it works.

We loaded up the cart with vegetables. There were; sacks of carrots, potatoes and beetroot, large piles of spinach and lettuce and beans, which meant the small cart was full to bursting. The final addition was a large tray of ginger. The great, black, four-legged beast was attached to the cart with a leather harness and we left the confines of the monastery, heading down the road.

It was a long walk. As usual Zhang couldn't stop talking. After a while he began to recite more verses, sometimes singing them, and sometimes insisting that I repeat them. It wasn't always easy to make the sounds but lately they were becoming somehow imprinted on my mind. Furthermore, my understanding of their meaning grew with every day.

Soon we came to a small collection of houses, a village of sorts. Here there were gathered many people, as many as thirty I counted. They all wore dull brown and blue clothes which were dry and ragged. Their shoes were old and worn and some wore hats of woven reeds. There was a hustle and bustle.

As we approached, individuals bowed to greet Zhang. This behaviour carried on the whole time we were here and I concluded that Zhang must be a very important man among this community, perhaps a prince or a king. I felt grand in my red and robes which were clean and smooth. The shoes Zhang and I wore were very rudimentary but a good design, strongly made and not as uncomfortable as bare feet.

We began to mix with the crowd, who were lively and talking in elevated moods. People here were busy, and happy, and all had a purpose. Zhang began unloading various items from the cart, and I helped with the larger sacks. He would give these to various people who in return would give him something back.

I watched these transactions carefully, trying to judge whether the one item was worth the other. For instance, a small bag of potatoes was swapped for five metal cups. A large handful of spinach and some ginger was traded for a small cooking knife. I don't know if these were fair exchanges but for the effort of work and time taken to make each item, I felt we received an equivalence of value for our produce.

Looking at other people, most were going about this activity in a very different way. These people were arguing about the value of items to be exchanged. Then they would swap small metal discs for the produce they wanted. Some would give, for example, just three small discs and receive large handfuls of the potatoes that we had just given away for several metal mugs. They seemed to be doing rather better than us and I was a little perturbed.

To my greater astonishment there were those who had rectangular pieces of paper, just paper, who would exchange just one piece and receive a whole chair in return! Furthermore the person who had given them a chair would then give them some of the metal discs also.

I almost stepped in to stop this nonsense but Zhang held me back.

Amongst the produce and goods I saw a man who was selling the flesh of dead animals. I knew that this was intended to be used as food, as I saw a young man eating a piece of it which had been cooked on a nearby open stove. I didn't know how to feel.

During the afternoon we accumulated; three steel cooking vessels, five metal cups, seven kitchen knives, lots of fruit and a bicycle wheel.

Walking home I asked Zhang about the meat I had seen. Why was it that people ate it and why did we not? He told me that many people all over the world killed and ate animals as they believed it gave them the power and spirit of those animals. He believed they were mistaken in this belief. The monks refrained from this practise as it was their belief that all animals have a soul, and that it was wrong to kill a being who possessed a soul. These ideas had great impact but I struggled with the idea of a soul, what it was and where it lived.

I also wanted to know more about the exchanges of discs and paper I had seen. He told me this was money and that it made the world go around. I wasn't sure what he meant so he stopped. With the help of an orange he explained to me that the world was a sphere which rotated upon an axis. Everyday it went around fully one whole turn. This he said is why the sun rises on the horizon, travels in an arc overhead during the day and sets again on the horizon the other side. He had used a large yellow melon as the sun to show me this, moving the orange around it in a circle and turning it at the same time. It was quite a demonstration and after a few moments to digest this new information I could see that it made a lot of sense.

Still I couldn't see how the metal discs and the paper were responsible for this. When I asked why Zhang didn't use the money he said that the monks didn't need it and didn't care for it, because although it was needed everywhere in the world, they believed that it also created much pain and suffering in peoples lives. I didn't quite follow the logic and was perplexed by this whole activity. Nevertheless I went away thinking that I would like some of the paper, should I have to walk through the world. I felt to carry some might be easier than using a wooden cart, and a huge black snorting beast, who kept leaving very smelly piles of waste matter behind it as we walked.

Zhang understood my difficulties with this subject but I believe this was the first disagreement we'd had. We were different, in appearance at least, and this was something that I knew intuitively on a deeper level too. It was a fact that Zhang had been trying to teach me and something I didn't want to accept.

With the money as a starting point he began to gently tell me that perhaps one day I would want to leave the monastery, to find my place in the world amongst the people. He felt I would want to seek out and find people of my own kind. I knew he was right but I fought him on this. I liked my life in the monastery. I wanted to stay. I wanted to be a gardener.

He said I would change my mind.

We returned home and unloaded our goods to the appropriate places. It was time to meditate and that evening I found the practise of this unusually hard. The bell sounded but within me there was a less sonorous noise, a grating and dissonant clash of all the wrong notes. I tried so much to quieten them, but they could not be silenced. With such a lack of harmony it was impossible to empty my mind in order to focus upon higher matters.

Zhang sensed my pain and decided that it would be advantageous to begin other paths of learning, in parallel to my meditations. We would begin in earnest the next day, and every day he would teach me in a more formal way.

I closed my eyes that night wishing that I hadn't gone to the market with Zhang. Had I stayed in the monastery I wouldn't be in the turmoil I felt now. I knew however, that this state of bliss, this state of unknowing as Zhang called it, could not last, and it would be best for me to embrace the realities of my condition.

That night I dreamt, and as I dreamed I travelled inside myself, a journey through the design of my interior. How we learn about ourselves? There are some things we have to be taught even about the very constitution of our own bodies. Then there are other forms of understanding that we simply know. I knew I could jump such a distance, before I attempted to jump it. I knew I had a heart because I could feel it beating. What else was there, specific to my nature that I would learn?

In my dream I thought I was one of the Future People, as Zhang had described them. There was no physical reason to believe this, but in my heart something such as this just might be true, and I entertained the idea in my dreams as I slept.

I saw cities that reached up into the stars and I saw the metal tubes amongst those stars which were the houses where the Future People lived. There were all kinds of machines in my dreams, with wheels spinning faster than the eyes could see, making sounds that I couldn't imagine. There were forces acting within these machines which were vast and also incomprehensible. And all these machines were black.

The blackness of my first memory also came back to me in that dream, even though its impression had been becoming more faint and faded of late. In the morning I wondered if the place I had been, the place I remembered coming from, had anything to do with the Future People of whom Zhang had spoken more and more often.

To those who have looked inside themselves, this nonsense makes perfect sense.

- *27* -

FLAWED PERFECTION

Viola had obligations with MTR business to attend to and was going to be out all night. After some time gazing with an empty mind at the Holo TV, I decided my own company was rather tedious and started thinking about going for a walk. It was still light, just, and warm too. Building up some momentum I left the apartment and soon I found myself wandering rather aimlessly around the city at dusk.

Drawn by old patterns I gravitated towards parts of town I couldn't remember having been to for a long time, places with which I was familiar but knew not why. The area I arrived in was called The Left Bank.

With the sun now setting these seedy zones of greater poverty and corruption were thrown into the shadows in which they thrived. I stalked my own shadow, feeling anonymous and discrete, observing myself as much as the people and scenes appearing before me.

The evening, and the subcultures who peopled it, was beginning to come alive. Fashion being the overriding element of communication on the streets, it was a visual conversation that was loud and argumentative. The clash of styles and colour, mirrored the moods expressed with every angle of subtlety and force. Throwbacks to decades gone by ran headlong into visions of the yet to come.

With the show of wealth blending into a spectrum with the flip-side realities of poverty, it was a playground where privilege existed on a dynamic plain, with the creativity of those forced to become somebody on the street. Overcome by the waterfall of inputs into my senses, and saturated by their qualities, I fell into a kind of waking dream, almost hypnotised by the present moment. Alive and alert I drifted for a while without thoughts of myself.

Tattoos and piercings, hair of any and every style, were all on display in a hyper modern competition for aesthetic attention and sexual advancement. This was the youth of the city, its future as unpredictable as the evolution of its styles.

Graffiti was everywhere here too. Old style spray paint on buildings and bridges. Manga mixed up in collaborative friezes stretching across the concrete canvas. The city as a gallery, the artists rising from the unknown to the legendary and beyond to be the next darlings of commercial success. A way forwards, upwards and out of the detritus of the wasted zones at the base of society.

Buskers hit their crazy cool instruments solo or in groups, micro amplifiers and splinter speakers taking their tunes through the cruising electric traffic, across streets to the next block. I sat and listened to one guy for a while who was hammering some kind of funky bass guitar, his thunder thumbs in a blur of a rhythm which seemed to evolve with no end in sight. His sidekick was rapping whilst tapping out a beat on some retro synth drums. I was caught in the sonic spell they cast over a crowd which waxed and then waned.

And then just a couple of streets down, the emptiness. Drinking fools and drug laden folk of all ages were gathering around a couple of alleyways where no one else dared to go. Bottles smashed, wounded old men pouring alcohol into their bearded mouths. The random, loose moves of people in a state of nothingness.

Vacant stares of people on rudely prepared drugs, the names of which I didn't want to know. Frightening effects of illegal highs transforming into hellish lows as vomit and coma lay next to each other. I hated this scene, there was nothing I could do here either, it was the arena of lost souls. Perhaps the medics would come later and try to clean them up, take them into rehab before releasing them back into the cracks of society. Their lives were short and ugly.

Those who'd got their act together were begging. They had set up shop and they were doing quite well. Enough to get a coffee and some food. Who knows how they got here, or where they could go. It was the saddest thing and I felt bad about myself just for looking. They're ignored, then tolerated, then taken away. Some probably don't return. Removed to secure locations they might be rehoused, but right now they know their future is in their own hands, and those hands are pushed out towards the public, asking for anything it can give.

A madman ran by in a frenzied panic. Crazed and screaming, moments ago he was probably in a deep paranoia. The dread of being disappeared by the people who're after him, no reason to believe he's done anything wrong, but the thought that he might have done. Blind fear had perhaps grown within him, whatever, he'd lost it and broken into a run for his life. He might make it, he may find a way, there might be a logic to his mayhem, but equally he could run straight off the cliff edge.

The prostitutes are both solo and organised. There's those who go it alone, driven to selling themselves as the only way to make it in the world. The MTR runs a kind of union for the more professional, career minded. There's hygiene and safety to be thought of, but viruses and disease are running in parallel with basic rights and income. Humans wanting Synths, Synths wanting humans, the combinations and boundaries blurred are difficult to imagine.

Right next door, are the clubs for the elite. Maybe they're here so that they can rub shoulders with the underclass, the underworld, say they've been slumming. Perhaps it gives them the edge they crave whilst working in the upper reaches of their glass towers. Easier for them to get their drugs too.

Stepping out of insanely expensive cars, the legs of a woman appear, one foot, clad in pearl shoes is placed on the sidewalk as she steps out of the luxurious interior. For a moment her body stands, wrapped in the fur of an almost extinct species of animal, then she's through rotating doors into the club. The beauty available to be seen by the likes of me for but a few precious seconds, a porthole into a world where money exists on a level that can't be grasped by any reasonable intellect.

The famous, the politically connected, children of the cosmos, and vitally, the business class which keeps the wheels of wealth well-oiled and in perpetual motion. All sitting, rubbing shoulders with each other around the swimming pools said to be floating at the top of the sky.

Architecture is king. Even now, in the black ceiling of the stars, it looms large. It peers down from one hundred stories high. The giants of the city are human, and made to lift other humans to what they surely perceive is their rightful place with the gods. I look up, and there they are, the shine and the sheen of these monsters in their reflective glass skin. At night they are an infinite darkness, by day the unlimited blueness of the heavens and the delicate whiteness of the clouds fill their surfaces. The structures are alive but their motionless presence reveals the guilt of those within.

Above, it isn't bright. Below it isn't dark. Seamless, unnamable, it returns to the realm of nothing. Form that includes all forms, image without an image, subtle, beyond all conception. Just realise where you come from: this is the essence of wisdom.

In their finest moments humans can achieve a type of perfection, but it's subjective to them, it's their perfection. The best of humanity can show itself to lift itself above itself, but only it seems at the extremes of art and mathematics. Genius at the zenith of physical achievement and in the design of things like these monetised monoliths.

I see the people on the streets and I feel myself making judgements as to their flaws and limitations and the lives these lead to. Looking inwards at myself and comparing my inner life to what I see outside, I realise something about my relationship to the world as a Synth.

He has no will of his own. He dwells in reality, and lets all illusions go.

The synthetic human is a design made with aspirations. Humans made us and we are meant to be an expression of their genius, we are meant to be perfect. But humans are born to make mistakes. They made Synths trying to create their ideal of perfection, but either they made a mistake or they succumbed to a kind of vanity and made us imperfect on purpose. Either way they created us with faulty memories and apparently, despite all the will in the world, and every technology at their disposal, this is a fault which is beyond repair.

As Synths we are, in essence, all mistakes, who by their programming are also trying to be perfect, but of course we are failing. We become as human as our creators but only by virtue of our flaws. In turn, whatever we try to create for ourselves is fated to be flawed too.

I see the world currently and I ask myself what is it to be human? The answer I have is that it is to be flawed, but also it is to have the belief that one is perfect in some, or many ways and that one can recreate this perfection. The truth that won't be accepted is that it's just not possible.

What is it to be Synth? It's to know that you are flawed and to learn how to live with this knowledge. In this respect I believe humans could learn a lot from Synths.

Is perfection itself even such a noble goal? Aren't there better, and more achievable virtues and goals to strive for?

I walked home, numb. There is a certain shame in the Synth condition. I hung my head just because of what I am. No one has the right to make someone feel like this.

- *28* -

Thieves In The Night

All day I was nervous, in fact I'd been feeling a little out of sorts for a few days. The side effects of REM were well documented and not negligible. The worries associated with the darker aspects of memory retrieval were in a negative feedback loop. You scored big on the perfection within the dream-like stories you could access in your past, but it came at a cost. The nitty gritty, dark and dirty facts of my origins were still a recurring nightmare of sorts. I was certainly a match for these feelings, knowing that it was necessary to accept the good and the bad as part of a whole.

The night which had been selected for the theft of the REM container arrived. Our intended prize was somewhere onboard a freight ship which had arrived in the port earlier that day. It had started raining hard. It was a black rain that came down from a moonless, starless charcoal sky. The only light was from the eternally brilliant street glare, and the sometimes random, sometimes patterned office lighting, shining out from the windows of the midnight buildings. I wore my old clothes and prepared for a long hard slog which would go all the way through until the morning. Tonight I was just doing a job.

The mark of a moderate man is freedom from his own ideas. Tolerant like the sky, all-pervading like sunlight, firm like a mountain, supple like a tree in the wind, he has no destination in view and makes use of anything life happens to bring his way.

The operation would be by the numbers. The cargo ship had already docked in the harbour and was in the system, its checks and documents in order. The company it represented was perfectly legal and had been in legitimate business for many years. Tonight it would be hit by a smooth Synth operation and it wouldn't know what had happened until a long time after the fact.

I took the motorcycle out and after driving through the rain, parked some distance away from the container port. I was wet and miserable and working against my will in many ways. Still I had no intention of screwing this up, or getting caught or doing anything less than achieving perfection. The Minister's words were ringing in my ears, and although I hated the fact that I was working with an edge of fear, I didn't want to bring any hurt down on myself. It was best just to keep my head down and get the job done.

Synths and humans alike had been paid upfront, either in Holo's or REMs, and a certain level of insurance, and assurance had been so attained. They all had a part to play at specific times, and would do their efficient best.

Most of the Synth men and women were fully paid up MTR members and were familiar with this kind of play. Some humans were paid to look the other way, some were more active and more vital to the running of things. I was the director of the show and I'd done my homework. That brown envelope The Minister had handed me contained all I needed to know.

Truth be told I'm sure the thing would have rolled along nicely without me, such was the clockwork nature of planned events. But sometimes you need someone to facilitate, to oversee, to manage any little unforeseen upsets.

The rain came down in sheets. Even with my coat, I was drenched. At the first level of port security I locked eyes with the security guard, number 637, and I was inside the cargo containment area.

Making my way through the complex, the map of this place securely memorised, I confirmed for myself the ship in dock. It was a monumental creation of metal that grew up and out of the sea like a monolithic rock outcrop. Somewhere on that ship was our container.

There was a lot of hanging around and nodding at various Synths on the job. I tried to keep undercover, out of sight and out of the rain. There was nothing to give away the running of our operation. Anyone watching might have seen a few unfamiliar faces loitering around, but the security here was a low key affair.

With everything slotting into place like an automatic puzzle, our immense steel box, full of REM capsules, had been moved in a number of pre-planned steps from one specific location, to another one, all as defined by the crew I'd assembled.

After only a few hours a truck pulled up, I tagged the registration plate and jumped on. The driver nodded and didn't say a thing. He was all hooked up and pulling the container behind, and I was onboard just to tell him where we needed to go. We left the port with all the clearances needed and when we were on the other side, I jumped out again and hopped on the bike. The truck following me closely behind.

Hangar 8, manned as usual by Robbie, was our destination. The rain still hammered down and I drove slowly through it for half an hour, checking the lorry behind was still following me all the while.

I pulled up. With the help of a couple of other guys, Robbie opened the immense sliding doors with a grating, rasping clang, and suddenly we were in the dry. Parking up the bike, it was not only dry but quiet too. Robbie was smiling.

"Any problems?"

"None. Just the rain."

"Nice little box of sweets we've got here."

"Several million, I reckon."

The truck driver used his automated rig to remove the contents of the container and deposit them in the hangar, a system I watched with great interest. Its concertina, hydraulic mechanism folded and squeezed, manoeuvring to extract our goods and deposit them within our warehouse. Then he disappeared, with the container now empty, saying nothing. Robbie and I looked at our consignment with great smiles.

Twelve crates of REM, wrapped in cellophane, straight from the source. Millions of little capsules of memory inducing chemicals that were enough to keep a whole city of Synths in memories. The memory banks of Synth culture were now guaranteed and with this amount of product the price might even come down.

I felt proud of our night's achievement, it had gone very smoothly indeed. No one was hurt, no one was arrested, it was a clinical procedure and a complete success. But for the first time in my memory there was a feeling of shame about this crime. Ok it was sanctioned from way up high but that was a problem too.

I was now working for a human and it didn't sit too well with me. He had me as one of his operatives, a servant, perhaps even a slave of sorts. He had my number and it would be easy for him to exploit my less than legal status with contacts he no doubt enjoyed in the police. How rich was he really? How powerful, and how greedy? I'd begun hearing very bad things about him lately. Partly I didn't want to know the answer to these questions, but another influential part, perhaps wholly a human part needed to know.

Now I was really no better than one of his grunts, the ones who stood and guarded his domain. I was taking orders from him and handing them down to other folks, Synths among them. What had I become? Was I mostly Synth or was more human?

Having been free in so many ways, after tonight I was forever tied to him and his network. I would have to keep my head down, bide my time, wait for moments where my skills could create greater advantages both for me and for Viola. I got on the bike, and I made sure Robbie locked up our booty. As I was leaving Robbie said, "Nice job, Sir."

I nodded. It didn't feel right him calling me Sir. How had things evolved so quickly? Is this what I wanted? I drove back through the rain to the apartment.

It had been a thrill, mainly because it was big time. What would be my next assignment? I'd been keeping an eye on my own prize too as the line of credit The Minister had arranged for me was more than generous. It's easy to be swayed by money, but its potential for changing one's circumstances is beyond comparison.

Viola, from whom I held an unsharable secret, wasn't the least bit impressed. She said I'd become a gangster and that this would be business as usual from now on. She was more concerned with getting me out of my wet clothes.

Before going to bed I stood on the small balcony and stared out and up into the night, the background buzz of electric traffic in my subconscious. After the excitement of the night had worn off, I felt smaller and insignificant in a way. The rain had stopped, and the wind had blown gaping holes in the clouds so that I was able to see the stars intermittently.

I was sure that there were many worlds in the vast expanse of Space, and in the far reaches of all corners of The Earth, and clearly within this one city upon it. I existed in this apartment, in a world which included Viola, but I also lived in my own private world. I had access to my deepest memories, and I although I was king of this inner domain, I couldn't escape it. Even whilst fully awake, the sublime blend of dream life in my mind was just an enhancement brought about solely through the chemistry of REM.

My eyes hunted through the sketchy sky, projecting my life into the night and scanning for signs of life above. I remembered Zhang, my Chinese brother, telling me of the Future People who lived up there, going around and around the Earth in their metal homes. Were they also prisoners of their realities? Were they even real or were they simply some fantastical story he'd spun for me, to make me wonder, to make me dream?

- *29* -

THE HOME OF THE FUTURE PEOPLE

James Jones, JJ to his friends, floated peacefully in a state of permanent free-fall. Seemingly weightless in this microgravity environment he let his synthetic mind drift, as he found himself doing more often lately. Thoughts flowed like a fast flowing stream running through lush meadows, a reflection of the North Carolina countryside he called home.

In Space he felt closed in, an irony not lost on his soul which was liberated in so many other ways. There was little room for any real motion, or dynamic expression inside THE CYBEX ORBITAL SPACE HUB, which everyone simply referred to as The C.O.S.H.

This was a commercial facility, ultimately it was simply another asset of CYBEX, a company interested largely in making money. They made Synthetic Lifeforms and they had a presence in Space greater than any individual nation on Earth. JJ was another employee and his work, although interesting, had no lofty idealistic goals which was something he would have liked. In addition the actual quality of life here was frustrating to say the least. He spent a lot of his time thinking about his North Carolina home in the Spring, and looked forward to his mission end date.

Daydreaming was a way to zone out the saturation of technology which filled his work life. Currently, with intense focus, he was occupied at a computer terminal attached to the bulkhead of Module Three. For over an hour he'd been reformulating some algorithms, his Eureka watch, floating loosely around his wrist, marking the time.

Engineering the future with him, were his two female co-workers, one Japanese and one Russian. Both looked his way as he spoke.

"Dammit, why can't they just send me the data from fifteen minutes ago?"

Kristina, the Russian, was concerned and moved towards him in one graceful motion, bridging the space between them in a few seconds. The serene beauty of Earth, the blue marble planet, filled a nearby viewing port. It was perfect, and an everyday sight for the crew.

Now by his side she put her hand on his arm.

"What's up JJ?"

"Oh, it's just that solar data, I've been… Oh it's ok, there it is, they must have realised what they did, they've sorted it."

"If you're done, maybe you can help me with that thing I told you about earlier."

The Japanese astronaut, Totua Ishimoto, was the captain of this CYBEX satellite, and was known simply as Toto by everyone in the program. JJ looked to see that she had left the module, before speaking quietly in his hushed, low American tones.

"Kristina, is this what I think it is?"

"It's whatever you want it to be, isn't it?"

"But it's not what we agreed on two months ago now, is it?"

"It isn't, but that was two months ago. This is now."

"It's not good to have unresolved emotions flying around when we're up here."

"Well resolve them then."

With one hand still on his arm, she put the other on his shoulder. Their faces just a few inches away from each other, a kiss seemed inevitable, but JJ moved away, and spoke in a slightly irritated way.

"Boy, you really know how to get inside my head, don't you."

"Just being friendly."

"Right now, I belong to CYBEX, Kristina."

"What, every little bit of you?"

"You're terrible."

"I'm just a poor little Russian girl. Call me!"

Kristina released him, and pushing herself away, waved as they both began floating apart.

JJ smiled, with the realisation of just how much he liked her, "I don't have your number…"

Kristina laughed, and blew a kiss as she left through a port to another module, "Well, maybe we'll bump into each other again sometime…"

He continued working whilst simultaneously internalising his thought process:

If she only knew. If I told her, what then? Not even sure that's allowed in my contract. Maybe it would make no difference to her, no more than the fact that I'm black. That doesn't faze her, but then why would it? Rules are different up here, nowhere to hide, accept maybe outside. Could do with that escape, the isolation, the freedom, untethered, and alone.

A little later, Toto had just finished calling up her son on the video link and arrived not so far away from JJ, busying herself at another computer terminal. She spoke to him in her perfect English.

"Ah, JJ, there's a note for you here. About… that EZ1 Synth unit you've been tracking."

"Thanks. I'll get to it in a bit."

JJ returned to his drifting dream-state. The truth was he'd been having a lot of second thoughts about his situation. It wasn't just the job, or Kristina, it was his whole direction. Going around and around the world in circles might seem glamorous to many hopefuls down on the planet, but his entire existence had become a series of repeating circular journeys back to the beginning.

Yes, he'd signed up for all this, he was dedicated and qualified and skilled enough to perform at the highest level, but everyone can have doubts, can't they?

The answer to the question of what type of work he could do, if he should quit CYBEX, wasn't obvious to him. There would be opportunities, he'd banked huge credit which could be invested in all sorts of different kinds of projects. He made a mental note to inspect his contract closely, to get a real idea of what his options might be with regards to the small print.

The stupid thing was, if it hadn't been for Kristina he probably wouldn't be here at all. Their relationship starting as it did, and the complex psychologies and politics which had unfolded leading up to this mission, meant that they were tied at the hip. Their interdependence professionally was one of the primary reasons why they now found themselves in this impossible romantic situation. The clandestine nature of their relationship, at first a thrill, was fast becoming a real worry as JJ was having great difficulties assimilating his occupational requirements with his new emotional states.

If all this wasn't enough Toto was always on his case. He was pretty sure she didn't suspect anything but was, by her nature, a rather controlling character. He didn't mind taking orders, and those orders coming from a woman didn't bother him at all either. She had no more idea that he was a Synth than Kristina did, so he couldn't feel hard done by as a result of some human superiority complex either. No, it was just her attitude. She wasn't cool, Toto only worked theory and a rigorous, testable, academic approach. But being cool wasn't an exam question, and even if it was she would have flunked that part of the test.

The EZ1 unit malfunction was about the most interesting thing that had happened up here in a long while, most everything else being somewhat routine. It was a challenge and a knotty problem, just the type he savoured.

JJ had been tracking the unit in order to figure out the logic behind its movements since leaving the process and the facility. He'd been having a hard time piecing together what appeared to be largely random moves and changes. In the bigger picture one errant Synth wasn't a huge deal for CYBEX, in fact he thought Command had forgotten about it for the most part. He felt they'd already written it off as a lost asset. Maybe the latest note was some new intel.

He felt he needed some new raw data, something he could get his teeth into, something that would take his mind off the very obvious charms of Kristina for a while. It wasn't that he didn't like her, far from it, perhaps he liked her too much, but he was finding it hard to concentrate with her appetite for the very obvious physical side of their clandestine relationship. Maybe Toto would stop hassling him too, if she knew he was engaged in some serious work.

He had to admit to himself he'd also taken rather a brotherly shine to the EZ1 unit. There was a connection there which he hadn't yet fully explored.

- *30* -

STAYING FOCUSED

A mixture of emotions, concerns and reflections on his personal life, left JJ in a limbo state. This mental wandering was not unusual for him and had in fact been identified as an issue on Earth during training. The aimless behaviour had been all but eliminated, the cause had not, and so the behaviour had re-emerged.

There were three other company Space Hubs and together the facilities controlled many of the CYBEX installations on Earth. All operations were interlinked and the C.O.S.H. space craft provided vital infrastructure to the organisation. All company assets were registered in Space for tax purposes.

JJ had orders from several key sites below to execute, but currently he was just drifting at one extremity of the ship, vaguely following a drama on the Holo TV. Toto, who'd noticed his dream-state before, caught him off guard.

"JJ! What's happening?"

"Oh, I was just, checking out the lightning storms over Africa. Take a look."

She closed the distance between them and was soon by JJ's side. The storm over Central Africa was vast, a natural phenomenon to be marvelled at. But there was work to be done and this was company time being spent fruitlessly observing the natural world.

"Have you finished the analysis on the solar data yet?"

"Ah, Kristina and I are working on it together. It's been through the first wave of algorithms, we just need to, er.. collate the conclusions. Quite honestly I'm not sure there is so much to worry about."

"Just get it done and sent. And JJ, are you ok?"

"Me, yep, I'm just fine."

"I only ask because you seem a little... distant lately."

"Really? Maybe I'm just missing home, been up here a while now."

"I'd appreciate it if you'd focus." Toto moved away.

"No problems Toto, will do."

JJ turned off the Holo TV returning to a train of thought which often recurred:

Do your job, get paid. I work as hard as the others. Went through the same training, company could have given me some privileges. I'd rather everyone knew. Guess they're waiting 'til I get home, make sure nothing goes wrong. Maybe I'll get some kind of hero's welcome, or a promotion, maybe they'll just analyse the results. You think they'd be proud. Not so cool being just another secret experiment.

Kristina intercepted him on the way to a terminal, disturbing his introspection.

"JJ, I wondered if we might talk."

"Not now, I've got to get on with some stuff, Toto's on my case, again."

"Ok, ok, I'll catch you later."

"Yep."

JJ spent the next hour working on the new solar data, debating why Command couldn't do this back on Earth. It was work of a kind he didn't enjoy too much. Sometimes he felt his mind was being wasted on this kind of thing, but then he knew he had an uncanny knack for it.

He preferred tracking Synths on the planet below, currently monitoring over three hundred units in various positions all over the globe.

As a kind of spy in the night sky, he sometimes felt conflicted though. Was it right keeping tabs on his own kind? Didn't they have their privacy? The fact that most of them would know they were being followed can't have been nice, but they were company property, they had duties and obligations, having free will was surely enough recompense.

To influence for the better the lives of his compatriots was an honour for JJ, one in which he took much personal pride. He felt that if they knew him personally and knew that it was he who was in charge of this sometimes delicate work up here, they would feel mightily reassured.

EZ1:613 was a special case for several reasons, foremost amongst these being that JJ himself was an EZ1 model. He'd been one of the first in the series, which had so far been a great success. He knew the strengths and limitations of this version personally, he knew how it was meant to work and what kind of problems a compromised system might cause. JJ felt that the problem was perhaps not with a flaw in the design of the model itself, but of course he was bound to think this way. Even so he believed that the problem may have been an anomaly, a freak occurrence, something outside of the control of all systems involved.

The new note that had come through wasn't of great help. It was the Artificial Intelligence report from Alpha 8 and simply stated that the reason for the rejection of the EZ1 unit from production was 'ERROR CODE 1138.' All this translated to was the presence of a singular syntax error within the transmitted microcode. This extra information wasn't of great help, seeing as he'd checked the code as it was transmitted and it was perfect.

Looking down on Earth he wondered how such a flawed unit would fare. The contrast between life up here and what might pass for life at ground level was immense. He felt an affinity for the model and an empathy too. He'd wracked his brain for ways that he might help but kept coming up with a blank. It was very frustrating for him.

- *31* -

Timing Is Everything

He was re-reading the file on EZ1:613. There were only two messages. One was the original directive from Command, and then the other was the subsequent communication after the event. This was not much to work with as he continued to investigate the cause of the unfortunate situation.

> 04:27:2049
>23:43:21 UTC
>FINAL MODIFICATIONS TO EZ1:613 UNIT
>LOCATION SZECHWAN DISTRICT FACTORY ALPHA : EIGHT
>HI JJ. WE NEED TO RECONFIGURE SOME OF THE MICROCODE ON THIS EZ1 UNIT'S WETWARE ARCHITECTURE. WE'VE GIVEN YOU THE NEW CODE, IT'S REALLY ONLY A THOUSAND LINES OR SO. CAN YOU ZIP IT DOWN TO THE FACTORY DIRECT FOR ME? WE'RE DOING IT THIS WAY NOW BECAUSE OF THAT FOUL UP SIX MONTHS AGO. THERE'S NO POINT GOING THROUGH ALL THAT AGAIN. CAN YOU EXECUTE BEFORE 00:15:00 AND LET ME KNOW WHEN IT'S DONE.

AND I NEED YOU TO KEEP AN EYE ON THE UNIT'S DEVELOPMENT
TOO, WHEN IT COMES ONLINE. IT'S A PROTOTYPE AND WE WANT
TO MAKE SURE IT WORKS OUT NICE FOR ONE AND ALL. THANKS JJ.
CODE PACKAGE ATTACHED BELOW.
>COLONEL HARRY RAINES

> 04:28:2049
>00:47:22 UTC
>JJ WE HAVE A BIG PROBLEM WITH THAT LAST ALPHA EIGHT
TRANSMISSION FOR EZ1:613. THERE WAS A SERIOUS ERROR WITH
THE MODIFICATION. AND THAT'S ONLY THE HALF OF IT I'M AFRAID.
WE HAD SOME KIND OF DEFAULT REJECTION OF THE UNIT AND TO
CUT IT SHORT THE THING HAS LEFT THE PREMISES OF THE FACTORY
INCOMPLETE. IT'S A REAL MESS DOWN THERE. TO BE FRANK WE'VE
NEVER EXPERIENCED THIS TYPE OF MALFUNCTION BEFORE AND
WE'RE INITIALISING A THOROUGH ANALYSIS TO IDENTIFY THE
CAUSE. IT HAD ALREADY DEVELOPED PAST PHASE #87 SO ITS
WETWARE AND IMPLANTS ARE ALL FULLY INSTALLED BUT ITS NOT
CONNECTED TO THE SYSTEM. THAT'S NO ULTRA-NET INTEGRATION.
YOU MIGHT HAVE GATHERED FROM THE UPDATE THAT THIS IS A
PROTOTYPE UNIT AND WE'RE STILL VERY INTERESTED IN FINDING
OUT QUITE WHAT IT MIGHT BE ABLE TO DO. WE HAD A CRISIS
MEETING HERE TO TRY TO FIGURE OUT OUR OPTIONS AND FOR

NOW WE JUST WANT YOU TO TRACK IT, THAT'S ALL. IF WE'RE LUCKY WE MIGHT BE ABLE TO GET SOME RAW DATA BEFORE IT EXPIRES. WE'LL GET TO THE ROOT OF THE PROBLEM AND YOU'LL BE THE FIRST TO KNOW ABOUT IT WHEN WE DO.
>COLONEL HARRY RAINES

He had another peek at the microcode attachment that he'd personally transmitted direct to the facility at the time. He was curious, and scanning the code his suspicions about this particular little assignment grew. It was a clever little subroutine, jumping over and even bypassing certain programming protocol. There was something slightly sinister about it though, the coding was written in some novel language with which he wasn't fully familiar. This was military software, he was sure.

Kristina appeared, silently as always. "What's up tiger?"

"Some code I had to send down to a Synth Farm."

"Those Synths, greedy for code, can't get enough of it."

"Kristina, do you know what these lines are, these just here?"

"Let me see. Yeah, that's in PICO, the new language. Let me see… Oh right, that's a kill code."

"Kill code, like as in self-termination?"

"No, no, it overrides all safeties, they're calling it the Will to Kill, they're going to be installing them to create soldier units. Looks like that's exactly what this is."

fried en route. Who knew what kind of a package was eventually delivered to the recipient.

At least he knew now. He had knowledge of the sudden abort procedure that had rejected the imperfect EZ1:613 unit from the production process. The Artificial Intelligence at Alpha 8 must have found the flaw in the unit incompatible to the essence of its own design. This flaw, and it's subsequent rejection, went a long way to begin explaining the unit's errant behaviour following the incident.

There was simply no way of knowing whether the modification, this Will to Kill, would have been successful. JJ's guess was that compromised code would necessarily lead to a non-functional operation, but he might be wrong. There were all sorts of ways the unit's personal AI might have filled in the blanks or found alternative routes around the glitchy syntax error. This EZ1 unit could be a killer. That would certainly be of interest to CYBEX, but for now JJ decided to keep his theories to himself.

Having only the basic Synth tracker to work with and no operational Ultra-Net link with the unit, there had been no way to perform what would have been far more revealing diagnostics.

- 32 -

WORKING RELATIONSHIP

"Kristina, come and take a look at this."

JJ was in front to the ship's main screen on which was displayed a map. Kristina finished stowing a small box containing some micro-tools and drifted over to the console.

"What are we looking at?"

"You remember that EZ1 unit that aborted a while back?"

"Elvis has left the building…"

"Yep that's the one. It turned out to be during an intense period of solar activity, I think that's what sparked the whole thing."

"Did they ever find him?"

"No, no, not yet but look, he's still alive, look, I've been tracking him."

"This is China?"

"Yeah. Now see, here's the Alpha 8 factory. Day One, he ran about 48km at an average speed of 20km per hour."

"That's amazing, marathon pace."

"Well, I know, the EZ1 is an athletic model. Then he stops here overnight and goes here in the morning and he stays there for three months! Now I don't know what he could have been doing for three months."

"What's at that location?"

"I have no idea, there are still places of rural China completely unmapped, but from up here it looks to be a complex of old buildings five or so kilometres squared. There's nothing there as far as I can see, except a small river of some kind running through the place."

"Where'd our guy go to next?"

"Get this. After those few months he moves, at around 15km per hour this time, he must be in some sort of transport, and he just keeps going. Including stops overnight he covers nearly three hundred kilometres in four days. He gets to downtown Hong Kong and he stops."

"Hong Kong, bit of a change of scenery for him."

"He's been there ever since, for nearly two months now."

"What's he doing all that time?"

"Well for the first month, he seemed to do very little, but then suddenly he started moving around a lot more, until one day he must have found some transport or other and he's all over the place, at quite high speeds."

"I wonder how he's surviving. Poor thing's probably scared."

"I've got my suspicions. Check this out. Two nights ago there was a theft of an REM pharmaceuticals consignment from Hong Kong's shipping port. It made the CYBEX news feed and I caught it this morning. A whole container of the drug went missing."

"That's terrible."

"Well yes, but not really, there were about fifty more identical containers on board, CYBEX will register the loss, but I can't see them doing much else except leaving it to the authorities."

"Aren't they able to track those containers?"

"Well, yes of course, and apparently they did, but by the time they knew it was missing, the first location they had for the container, it was at a building site on the outskirts of the city. They found it dumped there, empty."

"Professional job, probably organised crime, there's a lot of that in Hong Kong isn't there?"

"Apparently so. But here's the killer. Where was our boy on the night in question? At the shipping port… all night."

"Mmm, that's a little fishy but hardly conclusive."

"If he's into some illegal activities, I don't know, should we inform the authorities?"

"No! Look, he probably needs help if he's in that kind of trouble. Can't you do something, throw him a line?"

"No, no I can't. Unless he registers in some legal way with the infrastructure they have there, and pops up on a database somewhere, I can't do a thing."

"Well, at least he has the Ultra-Net."

"Er, no he doesn't. All units are connected at inception but, he didn't reach inception."

"You mean to say he's done all that under his own steam, working with only his own system?"

"That's the long and short of it, and it's most likely a very faulty system too."

"How is that even possible for a Synth?"

"My guess is he's been operating solely by using visual recognition, eye contact and ID intercepts. It's really basic but he could have built up some kind of do-it-yourself rudimentary network over that time. You're right though, without the universal sharing of consciousness with all other Synths he's really just a one man band. He won't get much further."

"Don't count on it. Look how far he's come. If he was part of that, what do you call it... heist, he's maybe wired tight into the underground, the underworld scene they have there. He'll be getting help from someone, in some shape or other."

"I'm going to keep tabs on him. If he comes to the surface we'll see him."

"CYBEX knows who you are, where you are, and what you are."

"Absolutely."

Toto breezed in holding a large leafed plant. "What are you guys doing?"

"Oh nothing much." Toto noticed JJ was being a little secretive as he shut off the display on the screen before she came closer with her plant.

"I thought this might cheer the place up a little, it's from the eco-lab."

"It's beautiful." Kristina found anything natural, especially things with bright colours, to be a soothing antidote to the hard technology of space engineering. The three of them floated around for a bit without saying anything until Toto spoke up.

"Sorry, I wasn't interrupting anything was I?"

"No."

"No."

- *33* -

Two Of A Kind

The Orbital Space Station moved at 7.7 km per second over the USA at night. Bright lights speckled the cities and somewhere down there on the outskirts of San Francisco, CYBEX Headquarters stood as a beacon to modernity. It's sprawling slipstream architecture, with curves carved from glass and steel, contained the combined scientific industries of all the world, at the height of its powers.

JJ was concerned. His allegiances to various parties were becoming torn and even conflicted. His loyalties were in question and he worried about Kristina. Then there was this EZ1 unit.

He had yet to give a report concerning his part in the malfunction and it seemed command had forgotten about it, either that or it was of such low priority as to warrant no further action. He didn't want to tell them what he'd found with his simple tracking of the Synth. And it was this professional question about his obligations to his employer that was creating a tear within him.

Further to this he felt something of a bond with EZ1:613, it was after all his fault that the circumstances of the unit's conception had been so compromised, his failure to transmit before a given time being the first cause. There was uncertainty within him as to whether Command was aware of his failings as to the timing of the modification transmit and subsequent catastrophe. The loss of one unit represented quite a considerable financial hit, he hoped there wouldn't be any repercussions. Maybe his concerns about career direction would be taken care of for him.

He felt responsible for EZ1, and he felt guilty. It couldn't be easy down on Earth for anyone to adapt to the environment in a place like Hong Kong, most especially if you've been abandoned by your maker in an unprepared state.

Then there was the problem of Kristina, he cared for her deeply, that went without question. It was obvious she had a terrible crush on him and he knew it wasn't just because he was there to comfort her when she needed someone. She liked him for who he was, and he knew it wasn't just going to go away, she had told him as much. The issue was that she didn't really appreciate what he was.

Relationships between couples of extremely contrasting origins had always been a source of tension in the wider community. It was human history to inter-breed between different races, colours, creeds and even other species and always this had come with its conflicts and criticisms for those who didn't want to see difference and diversity. The fact that such unions had helped, and even been fundamental to great leaps forward in the biological, psychological and cultural advancement of mankind was lost on some people, people who only wanted uniformity and the continuity of the status quo.

So the interaction of humans and Synths had been no exception. There was great resistance, much suffering and little acceptance. These relationships took place in the shadows and on the edges of society. They weren't forbidden but when they were exposed they were attacked verbally, sometimes physically, sometimes with loss of life, both and human and synthetic.

Now JJ found himself in the middle of such issues. He wanted Kristina and she wanted him, and that might be enough for anyone in normal circumstances. But they weren't in normal circumstances and the difficulties he'd been having lately in processing his feelings could really only be explained as the effects of Love. Therefore he was in trouble.

Of course, this was all rather hypothetical as Kristina didn't know he was a Synth, if she did, she might think very differently of her attraction towards him. She had none of the bigoted, narrow minded views towards Synths he'd experienced all his life, but then he just didn't know how she'd react. He felt cowardly in that he didn't want to risk what they had together at the moment. He needed courage, excellence in timing and a degree of good luck and, given recent events, he wasn't confident he could find any of these, especially whilst floating around in the confined quarters of C.O.S.H.

If he was at home, he'd go for a run, maybe have a beer with a Synth friend and talk it all through. Up here he was the only man and the only Synth, and he didn't think Toto would make for a good confidant, women talk to each other, and astronauts are no different. It was driving him mad and his default position was only to leave it until things became worse, until he broke into another mode which would rectify his dilemmas.

They were over Russia now, still under the veil of night, but the seamless transition between countries which had in recent times been enemies of sorts, gave JJ grounds for hope. Space exploration had become an international affair for many years now. The combined and complimentary qualities of Synth and human natures had been put to great use on Earth, and now in Space. Perhaps the cross fertilisation of ideas it had produced could also be the scene for bold progress in the realm of Synth and human personal relationships.

Of course the irony of this is that Synths don't look different. Hybrid couples can walk down the street anywhere in the world and no one is any the wiser. In this kind of mixed relationship, and one in which the Synth has been open about their status, there is the fantastic possibility of walking down that street with a shared secret, knowing something that no one else knows. The idea of doing that seemed very attractive right now.

Synth eyes can tell so much, but if beauty is within, humans might see the beauty within Synths too. With all this modernity the issues and feelings around the subject were taboo, JJ knew it and he would be keenly aware that, should he tell her, Kristina would feel it too. Putting her in this awkward position, in orbit around Earth of all places, might be too much, for her, for him and indeed for Toto, who would have to take on board the aftershock. He'd put it off for a while longer.

- *34* -

Constructive Interference

In between exchanges of small kisses over the exposed parts of their bodies which weren't covered by regulation CYBEX clothing, JJ and Kristina made use of the privacy of Pod Six and conversed quietly. JJ was fully immersed in the concentration required for both these romantic gestures and the more complex problems which currently occupied his mind.

"You know, there might just be a way we can help that EZ1 unit after all."

"Oh, how do you figure that?"

"We'll be passing directly over Hong Kong…er … about this time tomorrow. There's a chance we could catch him."

"I thought you said…"

"Yeah I know, that's via the Ultra-Net. However, but thanks to CYBEX involvement with the government, we have military options open to us on board this commercial baby."

"JJ, what are you thinking of?"

"We fly directly overhead. If we can catch him outside, unobstructed straight down, and if he stands still for more than a couple of seconds, I can fire a firmware update straight down to him. It'll be practically instantaneous."

"I don't know… aren't those firmware updates a bit buggy?"

"Well they used to be but… look our boy has been surviving on nothing for months. He can't be much better off than, a homeless person or something. I think he needs all the help he can get."

"I'm with you all the way on that but is this even safe?"

"It's perfectly safe."

"Have you done it before?"

"Twice."

"Expand."

"First time was for the bodyguard of the CEO of CYBEX himself. You remember last year there was that attack on the headquarters and The Chief nearly bought the farm."

"Of course I remember."

"Well his security detail took a blow to the head and went down like a sack of spuds. I was passing overhead and they sent me a swift instruction to reboot the guy."

"Was it a success?"

"Of course, apparently he was up and running, a little bit worse for wear, in less than a minute. The military love stuff like that."

"And?"

"And what?"

"The second time."

"Oh we don't need to talk about that.. that was just something that.. it's not so important."

"JJ, spill."

"Alright, alright, it was this Synth guy I got to know in New York. He helped me out with some investments and asked if I could sort him out."

"How do you mean?"

"I'd stupidly told him about some algorithms, some business modelling tools that I'd seen... they were giving them out to top business advisors. He wanted me to hook him up."

"On company time from up here?!"

"It couldn't be done through regular channels, security clearance and all that. Up here's there's just me and the, the er... Laser."

"And you did this for a Synth?"

"Well I owed him one. So, I arranged it with him, and when we were over New York one morning. I, you know... zapped him."

"What happened, when you... zapped him?"

"He told me later it was just a weird tingling sensation for a few seconds, and his vision went all fuzzy for an hour or so, then he was just fine."

"Just fine, poor guy."

"Look Kristina, this is all tried and tested hardware, and anyway it doesn't hurt to gather more data in the way of feedback, quality control and all that."

"So how did he turn out, I mean afterwards, with his new algorithms and everything?"

"Oh he became a billionaire. Still runs my portfolio too. It's good to have friends in high places."

Kristina was staring in disbelief, "You remember what happened last time we tried to improve the life of this EZ1 character. Maybe we should just leave him be, let him go."

"This is different, this is direct, the Laser doesn't lie."

Kristina started nodding. "Ok, ok. So tomorrow, lets say we give this EZ1 guy a quick brain lift, how will we know if it's worked?"

"We won't, not straight away. First he'll have to legally register with the authorities in some way, for Citizen Status for example."

"That's if he does, why would he?"

"It's the smart thing to do, that's what I'd do if I wanted to get some kind of legitimacy. He could move on up, and out if he wanted. Other wise, you know he's stuck there, for good."

"Well, we don't want that. What happens if he makes himself known?"

"If he registers, the update that we'll give him will register too. Then, after that, the first time he makes any formal interaction with the global system will automatically trigger connection with the Ultra-Net. He'll have all Synth user privileges, including access to all the usual AI sharing between other units. We'll be able to run full diagnostics too."

"You go this all worked out, but it sounds like a long shot to me cowboy."

"Look, I'm not saying it won't take a long time, but if he's as intelligent as I think he is, he'll go down this route at some point in the future. If and when he does, we can make sure he gets what is rightfully his."

"It would be a major advantage for a solo Synth trying to make it in the world. Mmm, it's his birthright as you say. We should do it, we should."

JJ smiled, "I knew you'd see it from my point of view."

The next day, at approximately 16:35 Hong Kong local time, JJ prepared the firmware update on the computer and aligned the Laser. With Kristina floating free next to him they waited to lock onto his signal. EZee was outside but he was moving, quite fast. They waited some more and after a few minutes he stopped. The Laser then locked onto its target and after waiting another ten seconds for confirmation, JJ hit the button and a massive machine code data stream travelled at the speed of light via an electromagnetic pulse straight into EZee's central nervous system.

The two astronauts were quiet as the inevitable silence which followed filled the space in the air between them. JJ realised there was nothing more to do.

"Well, that's it. I guess now we wait."

Kristina was one step ahead of him.

"Do you want to go and fool around in Pod Six?"

"Where's Toto?"

"Sleeping."

"Well absolutely then."

- 35 -

LIGHTNING STRIKES

EZee took a couple of turns at high speed, making light work of the traffic. The sensation of riding the motorbike was the best feeling he knew of, leaning into the curves, opening the throttle, the warm humid air pummelling against his chest.

He dismounted in a street where many people parked their bikes, took off his helmet and was just locking it to the bike when lightning struck. He stood bolt upright and dropped the helmet.

The jolt grew in strength and power, reaching a peak of some magnitude, then receded and disappeared. The complete transfer of data was over in less than a second. He bent down to pick the helmet up and had been alert enough to hear it hit the sidewalk. Anyone watching would have noticed nothing and EZee was not the slightest bit aware that foundational elements of his being had been significantly altered.

He locked the helmet to the bike and walked the remaining few hundred metres to the Holo Cinema. Viola had told him about it. She didn't like it herself, too much violence she said, but thought that he might find it a welcome distraction from REM distribution.

He'd been so wrapped up in the business, with a continuity and focus and he realised he needed a break. It was a first, to give this time to himself, and he knew he'd earned it. The idea of breaks, and vacations and holidays was one to be entertained by others. He, and Viola too, were mostly satisfied with a lifestyle which enjoyed little relief from working, and surviving. That's how they'd arrived where they were and that's the way they saw it continuing. Once she'd mentioned it though, The Holo Cinema had taken on an aura of a vacation from life itself.

There were plenty of Synth actors who'd made a name for themselves playing all manner of characters on the Cine-stage, apparently being strangely gifted in this area. EZee wanted to take in this experience for himself. He'd decided to try it once at any rate and report back to Viola with his impressions. The only thing he feared was that he'd be bored, or perhaps find the whole show ridiculous. With this experience there was only one way to discover his opinion.

There were all types of Flicks, as they were called; Space operas, historical dramas, musicals, eco-epics, secret agent action stories, road trips, westerns and gangster stories. EZee was most interested in the last of these, he'd been told there would be intrigue, street wars, good guys and bad guys.

He'd chosen a story called Solitaire. Having read the introduction it was going to be all about this guy who was a retired hit man, played by the Synth actor Joe Tanner. The plot outline was that the ex-hit man, decides to plan a heist to get some money to help a group of down and out immigrants. Viola said it was a stupid storyline, that there would be extreme deadly violence and a predictable moralising ending, she thought he should pick something else. EZee felt his selection sounded rather good.

He went into the theatre and paid. This excursion wasn't cheap, the Holo Cinema being a relatively new phenomenon, and one requiring some expensive laser technology. But now EZee had a sizeable line of credit and rarely had to worry about costs, of anything.

He took his seat amidst a congregation of no more than forty others and the lights went down. He was already transported to some other zone.

There on the stage were life-size people in a perfect environment, walking and talking as though there was no one watching them. They were of course holographic, even EZee knew that, but it was slightly uncanny and one might have trouble telling these players from real live people should there be one walking onto the stage.

The sound was all around and music accompanied the story. There was a clever way they went from this space to that, a sort of transition which pulled your eye naturally into the scenes. EZee let himself relax and was wide open to the ideas within the tale. Thoroughly suspended in the moment he could follow every twist and turn, every now and then remembering something from earlier in the story and occasionally thinking ahead to what might come next.

The time, two hours or so, went quickly, but when it was over EZee stayed in his seat, dumbstruck. The play he'd witnessed was some alternate reality, he knew it was fiction but it blended so easily with what he knew to be fact. The fusion of illusion and fantasy, with reality and everyday perception, was a heady mixture leading him to decide there and then that he'd be coming back for more.

He walked slowly back to the bike, carefree and not thinking of anything in particular except what he would say to Viola. With his helmet on, he was away, once more moving through the Hong Kong streets which were now under cover of the night, but rich in neon lights.

As he drove, his command of the bike's movements now feeling largely automatic, his memories of living within the monastery began passing through his conscious mind once more. The Holo Cinema, with its panoramic scope had tapped into his psyche at a multitude of levels, and had triggered this new memory sequence in a subtle new way. There was a strange combination of the movement of the bike and the graceful play of these gentle memories that was fresh and cool.

The quality was incredible. Whilst his eyes received all the information he needed to drive safely, in the theatre of his mind's eye another experience played out.

He could see the waving of the coloured robes as they dried on the washing lines in a slow motion furl, he could feel the light touch of his own robes on his skin. The smell of the warm earth as he worked it, and the texture of it on his fingers and hands, and then the feel of the raised ink letters on the dry parchments as he ran those same fingers across the paper during tutoring with Zhang. The undulating pitch of Zhang's voice whilst giving those lesson and the echoes of the chimes of the bell when beginning meditation. The taste of an orange from one of the trees and the clean rain water washing it down his throat as he swallowed.

The stream of sense data was almost overwhelming, not simply remembering it now, but living and reliving it. It was all that EZee could do to drive the bike and he was glad to be off it. Arriving at the apartment, with this waterfall of sensations still running through his soul in an hallucinatory bathing of his mind, he made his way to Viola.

Knowing he didn't have the words, and was not in any way equipped to describe this type of internal experience to Viola, his choice was to talk about the Holo Cinema. Which he did until he ran out of words for that too. Viola laughed at him. "You're like a little boy."

After dinner he stood on the balcony with a beer, looking out towards the harbour. Still in an affected state he was thinking how it might be nice now to get a bigger, better apartment, Viola would like that, she could have more space for her art. Looking down he suddenly felt dizzy, light headed and slightly sick. He dropped his beer and watched it get smaller and smaller, in a silent free fall, until it smashed on the concrete below with a vicious crack of glass and explosion of carbonated liquid. He felt weak at the knees, grabbed the door and managed to bring himself inside before he collapsed on the floor.

The dark void was upon him once more, the earliest memory, the source of his being but also the darkness which haunted him. Now he wasn't just remembering it, he was reliving it too. He was back there, on the floor, kicking and screaming in the dark, helpless, and in a full body agony.

Viola was quick to his side and held him. "Oh my god, Oh my god what's happening?! Talk to me, tell me what's happening. EZee!"

Fortunately this acute suffering lasted less than a minute and he was soon sitting up.

"I'm ok… I'm ok."

"What happened?"

"I don't know… It was like a nightmare, except I wasn't asleep."

"You were screaming."

"I know… I was back there, at the beginning again. I.. I don't want to go back anymore. I just want… to stay here, be here now."

"I've got you. I've got you now, you're here with me, you're safe."

But something had changed that day. The fierce bolt of energy which had passed through him, the dissolving of boundaries between subject and object he'd felt in the cinema and then this sudden collapse into a primal state. Somewhere on this day his ego had been altered, destroyed even, and with the disintegration of the 'I' of his mind he felt lost.

If it hadn't been for the close embrace of Viola he felt he would have ceased to be. And as he took comfort in her arms he became aware of the possibility of a new feeling. Much of his solitary aloneness began slipping away making room for a greater and more encompassing feeling of 'Us.'

- 36 -

Visionary Imagery

He couldn't sleep. Hours had drifted by already, with the sound of the city creating a low rumbling soundtrack to his awareness. Lying in bed on his back, Viola asleep by his side, he gazed, mind wide open at one of her paintings on the wall. Its slippery forms and intricate patterns appeared to shimmer in the artificial street light which came in through the window.

As he let Viola's artwork dissolve into his consciousness it was with a melancholy thinking his self had dissolved somewhere that day too. As consolation, missing elements of his existence had been supplied, and these he could sense as one might have the feeling of recovering one's strength after a long illness. Although he was not complete in any real way, he felt he would know wholeness should it present itself, suddenly he had potential. Like a hungry man given a good meal, there was now at least the opportunity for real work to be done. He was more prepared than he had been in the past, but it was a fiendish mystery as to what he might be prepared for.

Now was that there was a chance, not just for him, but for the two of them. However, today's very real loss of a personal identity, which he had carefully been building all his life, was all too apparent. His gaze became a vacant trance and the REM wasn't working properly. Instead of being whisked away to idyllic memories within a dream sleep, another, more visionary hallucination came over him.

This wasn't the past though, or even some assimilation of the recent present. This was an idea of a future beyond his known reality. His imagination was running free, constructing bizarre links between what was hoped for, what was dreamt and what was meant to be. He resisted for a while but then gave in and freed his mind, which flowed until he was in a trance:

Swimming underwater in a pool, surfacing to find himself at a party in full swing. Sweltering heat, climbing out of the water, surrounded by people drinking, laughing and talking through the day. Humans, but they're all behaving artificially, as though they want to be other people.

One woman is talking up close to him, she's beautiful and seductive, but it's not Viola. She whispers in his ear but he can't hear what she's saying. Why is he here? There are no other Synths, he is alone among these people who all want to talk with him, be with him. But he finds them to be cheap and malleable, like plastic, and walks away.

Now swimming in the sea. Fish, and every kind of colourful animal swimming with him. A nature of fluidity and never ending change.

In a huge ship sailing across the seas, the motion lulling him into a sleepy daze. Flat sea, sharp horizon with windless, cloudless vista stretching forever out of reach. Wind whipping up, waves in anger, black storm rising throwing the ship through vicious swells and tilting, leaning, unstable forces, threatening life. Storm passing, insane stillness once more, waves disappearing.

On a motorcycle on a dead straight infinity road, solo, travelling through the night. Vanishing point of black ribbon running headlong into disappearing horizons where his way, his journey, meets the sky. Incredible speed, shooting through the days and nights, stars scrolling by, half moon arcing overhead. Sunrise, sunset, through the night again and again.

To arrive at his maker… To confront him and to challenge him. Asking for an identity, a unity to be at one with. But his maker cannot help him, and he realises he is not even a god, he is only a man. He is not even a man, he is just a hologram, an image of a man, and the person he represents is already dead.

Within a small locked room, sitting opposite him is a human man and both of them are wearing the same clothes. This man is his father, but his father cannot help him, cannot tell him who he is. It's alright, because he can help his father, and that's enough, to be a son.

Walking with his father through trees in a forest, the light shining through the canopy, a stream nearby. They talk and rest and recover, and then his father is no longer there.

He is trapped inside a machine, trying to locate a memory.

He walks alone until the monk in the red robes is beside him, walking and talking. All is well and then the monk is gone too, and he is left walking, but he is no longer naked, he is wrapped in The Orange Silk. The material is cool, and he is calm and at peace. There is no one to share this with, but he is at one.

Hours had passed and EZee had been staring at the painting all the time. Having travelled this path through his mind he was only stirred by the quality of the light falling on the picture changing. The colour temperatures shifted as the artificial lights were replaced by the morning sunlight, the change alerting EZee to the passing of time and to the end of his vision, and the beginning of a new day.

Sleepless, but not tired, his fate was to continue with his life, without knowing where it would lead.

- *37* -

CREDIT RATING

EZee went about his business. There was no repetition of his collapse or indeed further descent into the darkness which he now knew intimately. The feeling was still there though, he still felt the grip of the void in his mind, and the angst it created, the twisting strands of elastic metal tightening his soul. Also there was a warp in his perception, a blind spot in his peripheral vision, and the subliminal feeling that a jackhammer was constantly at work, always half a block away.

He hadn't seen The Minister again since the single meeting he'd had with him, and that was just fine by him. He had a bad feeling about the man, hearing he'd tortured a Synth once, and resented the degree of freedom he'd lost when signing up to the bigger picture the boss represented. Still, he was the biggest fish in the pond and EZee knew full well it was only intelligent to be nothing other than a firm and trusted ally.

Receiving tasks and commands from the top was commonplace. The Minister had him running all around town on various diverse errands. He had become in one way somewhat of a courier, albeit one entrusted with deliveries of a very sensitive or valuable type. An envelope or a box would be waiting for him at one location and EZee would simply have to take it somewhere else, generally confirming that it was safely in the hands of a specific recipient.

Occasionally his shuttle runs were accompanied by a verbal message, once again to be delivered in person to one individual only. These jobs weren't so easy. He had to find the associate in question, who was not always the kind of person who wanted to be found. Then he had to ensure that the information imparted was not overheard by others. The discreet nature of this means of communication was essential to the runnings of the MTR, but it involved many meetings in shady places, back alleys, underpasses and the like.

Often there would be a response, which EZee had then to return to the appropriate person. Packages and pieces of paper, code data, and sometimes just a 'yes' or a 'no'. In this world of hackable high security connections and breakable encrypted intelligence, EZee's personal service was of the utmost value. Plus of course it had that personal touch, and this was something EZee learned was of great importance to The Minister.

His credit balance was increasing all the time, so much so that EZee wasn't sure what to do with it. He liked his bike, he loved his bike, but it was getting a lot of use and it really was quite an old model. Finding a replacement was a sound move.

He took a trip out to a dealership. It wasn't so far and when he arrived it was some kind of heaven he thought. With all the specs of all the bikes on offer memorised it was a question of aesthetics. The shapes and styles were a riot of design philosophies combined with full-on aerodynamics. The colours were metallic and glossy, shouting out money and speed even when stationary.

One manufacturer built only a single model, The Plasma. Sixteen identical examples of this model were lined up inside the expansive, well-lit show room, but each was painted in the sixteen different colours of REM. He knew these colours well, even having the value of the wavelengths of light they represented imprinted in his mind. EZee walked up to the neon green, number Thirteen and reached out his hand, gently letting it rest on the machine. This one was his.

He didn't need to take the thing for a test drive, this model was notorious for its slick handling and breathtaking performance. He paid for it with his credit, getting a relatively poor deal on the trade in of his old bike, which now looked sad and horribly dated. He told himself that he had no sentimental attachment to it.

Pulling away carefully on The Plasma he took it nice and easy through to the outskirts of the city. As soon as he reached some wider roads he opened up the throttle and took off towards the hills. This monster was twitchy and highly strung, but soon getting a feel for its energy release system and dynamics, he was racing without fear.

EZee knew everything about the boundaries and limitations of his body, and the calculations which were constantly being made to stabilise his motion. However, safety was only one consideration to be taken into account whilst pushing those limits, pure enjoyment and the maximisation of speed being vital factors too.

It was for these reasons that Synths had been banned from many sports, they had the edge and were just too good. It had been suggested that they form their own sporting competitions, to compete against each other, and in some sports this is exactly what they had done.

It was perhaps two hours later that he came back to the apartment. Viola wasn't in, she had her work with the MTR to take care of, and she took pride in doing it. She knew her role within the organisation wasn't as important and certainly not as lucrative as EZee's, but helping out her fellow Synths, particularly those in need was a priority to her. It fed into her work as an artist, the two in a symbiotic relationship and it was this relationship and the environment in which it lived which was the life-blood of her existence in Hong Kong.

He made some food. It was quiet. Viola usually played her music, and he was a big fan of her tastes. It was another facet to her character, when she was around there was music in all meanings of the word. But he knew nothing of the history of music and had little idea of which styles were the ones he liked. He just liked Viola's collection but without her the apartment remained silent, as did he.

Looking around him, at the apartment, at Viola's art, at this home she had made for them both, he was continuously impressed by her. She'd run away from an abusive owner in her early twenties and come from nothing to make her life just so. In a way their stories were similar, trying to make something from nothing.

Viola had a different problem though. Whilst he was fascinated, obsessed even, with his past and his origins, Viola was always running away from hers, in a bid to escape events about which she simply wouldn't talk. More and more EZee wanted the details of his history in order to illuminate his identity, whilst Viola looked to the future to evolve her character, always reinventing herself, always growing, or trying to grow away from the shadows of her beginnings.

Her residual fear showed itself one day whilst walking along the street in the centre of the city. They had just been for a really relaxing walk through the park when Viola darted and hid herself to one side of the street. He thought she was playing some kind of game and he'd laughed.

"What are you doing?"

Then he'd noticed she was genuinely really scared. She thought she'd seen the son of her previous employer walking towards them on the sidewalk, only to realise it actually wasn't him. EZee wanted to protect her, he put his arm around her, and they walked back to the apartment quietly. He wasn't afraid of anyone, and he would do anything to defend her against any person who might cause her harm, whether they be Synth or human, it didn't matter.

As for REM, it was no longer just a mission, a habit, an addiction or a job, it had become a way of life. He popped a Thirteen and lay down, letting his stories wash over him. The saturation of the drug in his being ensured an increasingly vivid and detailed memory stream. In his mind he was now living his past as an alternative virtual present.

Nevertheless, in his daily life, he'd noticed lately that the monk's voice had faded from his consciousness. The words that seemed to be whispered in his ear had faded away. Without the monk's wisdom as a companion, EZee was looking to other places within him for inspiration. He was looking for another voice, perhaps a version of his own voice, to be his guide. He needed some presence to show him more than his memories, someone or something to show him a way to his future.

- *38* -

THE STORY OF SILK

One cool, bright morning Zhang asked if I would like to go for a long walk with him, there was a place he wanted to show me. Of course I said yes.

We left the monastery before the sun had warmed the earth and we walked in silence for a while. Zhang, usually spoke to me all the time, encouraging me to talk and exercise my language but on this occasion we just walked without talking. I had the chance to look up above me once when I heard a low rumble in the sky, to see a long white scar, a track left by a white object which glinted with reflected light. I was quite overcome with excitement.

"Look!" I said, pointing upwards. "It's one of the ships you spoke of where the Future People live."

"Ah… no, the ship I told you of is a star ship, and the people who travel in her live even higher up in the sky. They can only be seen on a clear night as a star which moves slowly through the other stars from one horizon to the other. The object you can see there, is an aeroplane. It too contains people but these people, rather than travelling between the stars, travel from one country to another country, very quickly. I have seen one of these aeroplanes on the ground, it looks like a giant bird."

I was still looking up, marvelling at the white line that seemed to disappear as I looked at it. "What is a bird?"

Zhang stopped walking, "Stop, and listen."

I stopped in my tracks, we were near a tree, and I used my ears. There were no people around and there was silence all about.

"I can hear nothing."

"Focus, close your eyes, imagine that you are meditating."

I did as he said and then suddenly I could hear it. High pitched notes in random orders, no, in all kinds of patterns. "I can hear it!"

"You can hear birds. Open your eyes. Now watch the tree."

I opened my eyes and Zhang clapped his hands together loudly several times. Suddenly, as many as twenty of these birds flew high up into the sky in all different directions. They didn't fly in straight lines, like the aircraft but in swooping, curving arcs and twisting tumbling drops and climbs. It was fascinating. Some kept flying, I watched them as they flew so far away they became small dots and then disappeared. Others flew around overhead and many returned to the tree.

"Why couldn't I see or hear them before?"

"Your mind was closed. I knew it to be so. I think it was already closed when I found you. It is good now that you have opened your mind. Things will become much easier for you now."

I was a little sad because I knew he was speaking the truth, and I wondered about all the sounds I had not heard beforehand, but his encouragement boosted me. I was very happy this moment had happened and I restored myself.

"Do they always live in trees?"

"They rest in them and make houses in them. However, their spirit is to fly, to fly and to be free. All animals have a spirit, that which they are born to do and born to be. I think that you may also have the spirit of a bird."

"But I cannot fly."

"Oh, but you can. You must explore the world around you, then fly through the world inside your mind. Then you will be able to fly through the world itself. You must find out for yourself how to do this. One day you will find a way to fly and you will do it in your own way."

We walked much further in silence. Now I was listening to everything all around me. It was as though listening to the songs of the birds had made my hearing clear to me. It was nothing less than a revealing of this sense to me.

There was of course the rough crunch of our steps on the stony road beneath our shoes, but now also the wind moving through the long blades of grasses in the fields so close nearby, rustling in waves as they rubbed against each other. I was lost in my contentment over this heightening of my soundscape.

We arrived at a set of old buildings and Zhang led us towards the side of one. Climbing high on one side of the open structure were great wide sheets, ribbons of colourful material stretching up high into the roof space and over wooden rollers. Perhaps forty lengths of this material rose up from great vats of colourful liquid, up and over the rollers, and then down again where they then blew freely in the wind. As they flapped back and forth I could hear them, as they occasionally made a snapping sound in a stronger gust.

We stayed there for some time. Zhang could see that I was transfixed by these rich colours which appeared to me as having the concentrated qualities of the flowers in the monastery garden. There were deep Blues, subtle Mauves, intense Yellows, vibrating Purples and Pinks, dark Greens and a blistering Sun Orange.

Zhang introduced me to a man who arrived by our side after a while. He was a short man with funny teeth and a large straw hat, and he and Zhang seemed to know each other very well. From my grasp of the language I was able to learn that Zhang was ordering some more of the red material which made their robes. They talked for a while over the trade that would be fair and then the man gave Zhang a folded piece of Orange material. The man nodded and bowed to me, I bowed back, and then Zhang and I left, returning the way we'd come.

On the way home, Zhang told me a story about a very important animal, a Silk worm. Its spirit was to make clothes for kings and queens, so he told me. Kings and queens, Zhang explained to me, were people who ruled over countries and decided what would happen to all the people who lived in those countries. That there should be such people was incredible but I believed Zhang as I always did.

What was more puzzling was that their clothes were made by worms! I had seen many worms in the earth whilst gardening, and it was extremely unclear to me how they might make clothes for kings and queens. Still I had an open mind now and listened carefully as Zhang explained that these were different kinds of worms.

People fed the worms with mulberry leaves. These worms then created a capsule, around themselves, called a cocoon, by spinning a fine line of thread with their bodies and wrapping it around themselves completely. Usually the worms would then begin to change into moths, a type of flying insect. But before they changed completely, the cocoons were boiled, and then dried, and the fine threads were unravelled by a clever machine. The threads were then woven into a fine material, called Silk, which could then be dyed with colour as we had seen. After this the fabric was made into clothes worn by kings and queens.

I was speechless. Zhang stopped walking, I did the same, and he offered me the Orange material he'd been carrying, holding it out to me with both hands.

"You need a new name. You are no longer just the name of a red robe. You are a king and your new name is... The Silk King."

The name that can be named is not the eternal name. The unnamable is the eternal real. Naming is the origin of all particular things.

I breathed, registering this name, and I took the material into my hands. It was the smoothest most delicate thing that I knew of and the Orange colour shimmered in the light. I didn't know what I should say, so I bowed and Zhang bowed, and we carried on walking until we reached the monastery.

When I was alone in my room I unfolded the Silk and felt myself to be the most wealthy man in the world, like a king.

The gentlest thing in the world overcomes the hardest thing in the world.

- 39 -

COMPONENT PARTS

There was a list which Viola had been compiling, a shopping list in effect, and EZee had a day free. He decided to drive himself around the city on his bike, and try to get everything on the list, or as many of the items as he could.

Consisting entirely of elements for a new sculpture she had been planning, the design was a throwback to the cyber-punk craze of some sixty years past, but she had placed her own fluid dynamic style into its regeneration.

It was a commission, her first, and therefore a cause of much excitement for her, followed by development and focus. She would be welding the whole piece together herself and it would be partly painted and partly polished metal in construction.

The work was to be done in the yard outside on the ground floor apartment block. Then it would be lifted by crane onto a truck and delivered to the client, who was a wealthy start up business with new premises in an up and coming part of the city. The company founders had seen some of her pieces on display and had approached Viola through the gallery. This was real success as the finished work would sit in their foyer, where thousands of people would see it every year, it represented a step into a bigger world.

This was only the first, most exploratory list, a short one, and was planned to allow Viola to make a start mapping out her design in a physical way. Very specific in detail however, the description of the items included all relevant dimensions.

So EZee set out on his mission, on the bike with a big empty bag on his back, thinking it would be a simple process.

There was a sprawling industrial park quite some drive away, but it contained an automotive spare parts centre, mainly open to the trade. He intended to get most, if not all the items on the list at this place, and when inside at the front desk the scale of the operation gave him the impression he'd be successful.

List in hand he went through the components one by one.

At the top, four suspension springs between 0.4m and 0.5m and at least 0.12m in diameter. The clerk handling orders needed to know which exact model of car they were for, and which year of manufacture. Of course he didn't have this information, it wasn't necessary to the project, and he didn't need to know, except of course now he did.

They spoke at length until the employee was able to use an older data base in which to input the dimensions. There was a perfect match with the search criteria. It transpired that the suspension springs of a particular Italian sports car, a Zorista, built between 2030 and 2032 had such springs. However they were 1900 credits, for each spring, and there were only two of them in stock.

Dejected, he went through the other items on the list, one by one, with a similar outcome following each. He left disappointed and carrying only a one metre piece of rubber sealing tube in a plastic bag. At less than one credit, it was a cheap product, clearly essential to the design of Viola's sculpture but nevertheless only a small reward for having come so far.

EZee was a product too. Synths were made for all reasons, for all purposes and sold to a large variety of customers. Some were pre-ordered years in advance, with detailed, personalised specifications and preferences. All had an intended final destination, even EZee, but of course he had never reached his.

All he had were dark garbled recollections of a violent birth into a cold unforgiving world, but he did know that he was a product, and a pretty sophisticated one at that. This self knowledge was a comfort of sorts, but it wasn't an identity, it was still only a code. Looking at the label on the plastic bag in his hand he felt some affinity with it.

The unpleasant feeling accompanying the purchase was that even this simple product was new, clean and sterile within its hermetically sealed delivery device. It had probably never even been touched by human hands. Crucially it was perfect and complete.

EZee was unfinished, never packaged and delivered to a new owner in order to fulfil his purpose. It was this intense feeling of not having been completed which cut to his core. He had tried to share this with Viola, many times, but how does one describe something which is not there? He found himself spiralling into an abyss, it was as though he had been born without his very hands, and was attempting to tell her, an artist of all people, how this felt! It had always been this hole in his soul which was the source of his negativity, his despair, but it was also the feeling which drove him onward, he had hope.

Purchasers of Synths signed a maintenance contract. They were buying not only the product but the servicing of that product for many years to come. EZee was not part of such a contract. He came without a warranty. There was no lifetime guarantee of zero defects. He had not been through the mandatory quality control. He didn't come as advertised and there were no terms and conditions in any small print to suggest that any owner, if he had one, might be able to get his money back. Maybe he should trade himself in for spares or repairs.

He chose to try another approach in his mission to find the necessary parts for Viola. On the other side of the city, again quite a way, there was an automotive breakers. This was a series of giant warehouses where cars, and bikes, of all ages and makes, were brought in every kind of state of disrepair to be disassembled, and broken into their constituent parts. These parts were then catalogued and were for sale.

From the outset he was more hopeful. There was a huge sculpture here too, in the parking area, a robot in a classical design, made entirely from spare parts stood some six metres tall. He thought it looked like a giant toy, and this in turn gave him a fresh perspective on the possible relationship between humans and Synths. He went in.

This place was more like it. Rough and ready but carefully thought out and organised. Starting at the bottom of the list and slowly working his way up, he ticked off every single item. He had; ball joints, gearbox gears, differential gears, brake discs and tappets, all of the correct sizes and he was very pleased.

It came to the last objects, the suspension springs, and he wasn't so optimistic, neither was the guy who was helping him. Then EZee explained from what type of car they could be found and the man's eyes lit up. They'd had a Zorista come in only last week. Some banker type had thrown it round a corner and straight into the side of a concrete bridge. The driver was fine but his rather expensive piece of Italian automotive history was not. It was a tangled mess and a write off, but the suspension springs should be fine.

He took EZee to have a look at it. Clearly it had once been a thing of beauty and no doubt extremely expensive. It had already been broken into its saleable, deconstructed pieces and all that was left was the twisted body. EZee felt some affinity with this product too, how it had started its life, the life it had enjoyed and what it had become. But it was still of use, some benefit could still be gained from it even after its demise.

They went back inside and the man located the springs for EZee. They were found on shelf A17 of row 387, a location where they'd only been sitting a couple of days, and which took a mechanical robot less than five minutes to find and retrieve. EZee paid up and lifting his huge bag full of heavy metal booty onto his back with some difficulty, set off back to the apartment.

The bag was so big and heavy that he had to make great adjustments to his driving style to remain safe. Slowly around corners and just as importantly, careful when stopping at lights, a few times he nearly went over.

Upon returning, Viola was home. Proud of his efforts he removed the objects, one at a time for her inspection. It was all good. Saving the best to last, he told the story of the suspension springs and the Zorista, Viola listening intently. And the springs themselves, they were perfect. But he needn't have worried unduly about the dimensions, they were really only there as a guide.

This was they way they loved each other.

- 40 -

Rapid Expansion of Horizons

Word got about that The Minister wanted to see him, as soon as possible. EZee had mixed feelings about this. The rumours he'd been hearing about various Synths being removed from their positions within MTR had been confirmed to him by several people. More troubling, accounts of Synths being tortured in various ways as recompense for certain failings were as yet unsubstantiated, but EZee's sources were usually reliable. What was he going to do? This was the boss.

He hit the road, repeating in his mind a kind of mantra, as he drove, some of the words the Monk used to recite to him.

He remains as calm at the end as at the beginning. He has nothing, thus has nothing to lose. What he desires is non-desire; what he learns is to unlearn. He simply reminds people of who they have always been.

He wasn't fearful of The Minister, although perhaps he should have been, but he no longer looked up to him either. There was some respect for how he must have achieved his position and built the MTR but how he'd maintained this status was a mystery.

The Minister was, after all, a human being, but as a criminal it didn't seem as though he was particularly rough or from a heavy background. In fact, his refined nature was probably a result of a good education, a privileged background even. It didn't add up and, asking around, no one seemed to be able to provide him with any details of his history.

It occurred to him that The Minister, as his name suggested, was nothing more than a bureaucrat, an administrator of the businesses of his domain, and this was more troubling. An executive style of leadership may well be more efficient but its cold methods and calculations were more likely to be unaffected by personal considerations.

In this way, The Minister was more closely aligned with the inaccurate stereotyping of a purely logical, synthetic approach, than the supposedly higher and more emotional sensibilities of a human.

In contrast, EZee now saw himself as something of a model Synth, with all the strengths and limitations which that brought. He had the necessary blend of human and machine infrastructure to achieve a successful character, someone who could think and feel as well as anyone else, Synth or human.

Ironically it was the dark, mysterious and unknown quality of his origins, and the memories they subsequently produced which he believed gave him a further edge. He had to suffer and grapple inside in order to create his life and this fight made him stronger, keener, more ready to adapt and to survive.

The Studio had presence and stood as testimony to the size and longevity of MTR. EZee parked up and went in. The security guards were naturally expecting him, some even called him by his name. His reputation as a key player had grown along with his credit balance. He was known.

For the second time he climbed the steel staircase to arrive at the uppermost floor and the offices of The Minister. The man was pacing, classical music was playing. EZee walked into the room, now familiar with its layout, and feel.

"Mister EZee, good day to you. Enter."

EZee approached slowly, and gracefully. "I heard you wanted to see me."

"That's right, that's right. This won't take long."

They stood some three metres apart, The Minister keeping his distance.

"I have another job for you, rather an important one in fact."

The Minister seemed to fall into some kind of reverie whilst he spoke.

"As many as two thousand years ago there was a network of trade routes which connected the East and West, it was vast and proved very lucrative to all parties for many of hundreds of years. It was called The Silk Road and in my own fashion I would like to resurrect it."

"I'm sorry Sir, I'm not sure I understand."

"Miami is a city on the East Coast of the United States of America. It is the perfect place to... start out on a new enterprise."

"And how does such a far away place relate to us?"

"Our core business is here. Hong Kong is a natural point of departure to many parts of the world and as you know our merchandise has its origins not so far away. I'm intending to expand the reach of the MTR and break into the American market, and I want you to take charge of this operation."

"Why me?"

"You have a proven track record here and, perhaps it has escaped your attention, your English is rather, how shall I say, rather American itself. You'll fit right in."

EZee processed this new information slowly and carefully, examining all of its ramifications. Whilst remaining in a state of flux, variables changing and conclusions unresolved, he kept his mind alive.

"How exactly would this proposed situation be realised?"

"You would be taking the most part of the shipment we confiscated, with much thanks to yourself, and travel by sea, through the Panama Canal to a rendezvous in St. Lucia, an island in the Caribbean. From there it would be on to Miami where you would disembark with our cargo and initiate the business. I already have a particular cruise ship in mind for the journey, you would be travelling in the lap of luxury. This relocation, and... er... promotion, would of course be accompanied by considerable credit, and it would be permanent."

The Minister was pacing whilst he spoke, this was clearly no small matter. EZee remained motionless, it was an opportunity of some considerable scale, and a way to leave this city, but his immediate thoughts were with Viola. This was a decision he could not make on his own.

"I'd like to think about your offer Sir, and get back to you, if that's agreeable to you."

"Certainly Mister EZee, Certainly."

"When would we be leaving?"

"Ah, that's the thing. Due to the scheduling of the cruise operator, something over which I have no control, you will have to leave in nine days. And there is another small detail. Do you have a passport?"

"No, no I'm afraid I don't"

"I thought that might be the case. This mission is contingent upon such an item and, should you agree to accept, you will have to obtain one. I have many contacts, but the system being exclusively automated and very secure, I will have no influence over your application. The system is extremely swift in its processing, a matter of days, but it is, you might say, in the lap of the gods."

EZee had been integrating and extrapolating this data too. He hesitated, then delivered his summary.

"My agreement will depend on several factors. First I would like to consult with my partner, she is a very hard working member of MTR. I can say that I would only depart this city with her, and that she would be a valuable asset in such a start up operation, as well as a trusted companion. If she is also accepting of your offer we would both need to apply for the required documentation. Then of course the actualisation of the process would develop with the success of those applications."

EZee was pleased, yet unsurprised at his abilities to summarise the realities of this possible future event. He was already imagining the conversation with Viola. The Minister continued to pace.

"I think we have a plan Mister EZee. Send me word when you have decided, and make those applications immediately. You are my primary, preferred agent, but I must say, if there is some friction at any point, I do have other secondary candidates in mind, so please be as quick as you can."

"Thank you for this opportunity Sir, I will be in touch."

"Goodbye Mister EZee. Good bye."

The Minister turned away and EZee left the room. Everything looked slightly different now. The security guards appeared to be completely stationary and solid, as though they were statues. When he came out into the light on the streets the city no longer seemed to surround him, to oppress him so greatly. He had a vision outside of it, beyond it. The idea of Viola and he moving across the seas, far away from the dark and gritty texture of Hong Kong, meant that for the only time in his life EZee had an idea of a future.

Riding towards the apartment he began thinking many steps ahead. On The Plasma and in this elevated state of mind, the traffic was moving through his mind. From his REM saturated cortex emerged the richly illuminated story of his past. It streamed through his consciousness with colour and beauty.

- 41 -

WRITING IN THE FABRIC OF THE SOUL

This lesson was to be our last. Sitting in the small room where he'd been tutoring me these months, with only a window, a table and two chairs for distraction, Zhang's patience and wisdom were as great as his heart. After some rather technical instruction in points of grammar, and then some historical notes concerning the symbols used for writing, I asked a question.

"Zhang, the Silk material you gave to me, is it for me to wear?"

"For now you must be satisfied with the robes of a monk. However, in the future, if you become a king you might choose to wear it. It is your soul."

Sometimes I felt that Zhang used these words to confuse me, however, if I asked for clarification he would give it, and usually then I would understand. Mostly I think he simply forgot that there were some things to which I had yet to be properly introduced.

"What is the soul, I have heard you mention it before?"

"Aha!" He laughed. "Many people have asked that same question without finding an answer, but it is in fact quite simple."

He breathed in deeply and out again, as he sometimes did before speaking.

"Your soul is the fabric upon which your life is written. Your soul is your Silk and you must write your ideas, your memories, your knowledge, your dreams and your visions upon it and within it. When you have done this you will be able to read from your soul and others will be able to read from it also."

I was quiet distraught, "But Zhang, I cannot write."

Zhang took another deep breath in and out, he seemed heavier in his mood now as though he was about to communicate to me a lesson of serious importance.

"It is of no consequence. You see my soul is made of paper, the paper that you see here."

He picked up one of the pieces of parchment he had been reading from.

"I must write my life upon it in these symbols. It is something I have done all my life. I was taught to write when I was very young, indeed by a great teacher. He showed me how to make these marks so that some permanence might be attained to otherwise fleeting moments. But in truth my life is already written."

He seemed sad, so I tried to keep him talking.

"I must learn to write the symbols, so that I can write my life."

"No. It is not for you this life of symbols, they often carry double meanings, and one often needs keys to decipher them. No, you must write your life in pictures, and choices and decisions and actions!"

As he said this last word he hit the table with his fist, it made me jump and he looked at me long and hard.

"This is the way of the modern world. To live your life you will have to weave it the way the Silk is woven, with the threads of stories. To record your life you must make patterns in the material and fold it, many hundred times over. Only in these folds will you find your identity, your character and your soul. Only then will you see a pattern in the fabric of time, only then will you understand who you are."

I liked hearing Zhang talk this way with strength and emotion, but it was as clear to me, as it obviously was to him, that I had yet to understand very much. He read some more from the parchments, the words making a deep impression on my soul of Silk.

I have just three things to teach; simplicity, patience, compassion. These three are your greatest treasures. Simple in actions and in thoughts, you return to the source of being.

Zhang looked up from the writings, and looked at me in my entirety.

"Stand up, I want to try something," he said. So I stood up.

"Move this table over here."

We moved the table and chairs to one side of the room, so there was a larger space, then Zhang picked up one of the chairs and walked as far away from me as he could in the small room.

"I want to see if you can defend yourself, it is a very important lesson. I am going to attack you with this chair as my weapon and I want you to protect yourself, your body, from my attack. Do you understand?"

"Yes, I think so."

"No, do not think, just act. This is the essence of the lesson. Are you ready?"

"Yes."

Next, Zhang, baring his teeth, let out a huge, wailing scream of a cry and ran at me with the chair held above his head. He accelerated and was very close to me at speed, his robes billowing in the air. I computed the necessary vectors, using some matrices, and was able to swiftly move my weight to one side slightly. Taking the chair from him, and spinning as he passed, I arrested his movement with an arm around his neck. I held him so, and the chair aloft, for several long seconds before I realised I was causing Zhang to have breathing difficulties. I loosened my grip.

He took a deep in breath of air and called out, "I yield!"

He spoke with difficulty as I released him but quickly regained his composure and then with something of a laugh, tried to convince me of something I didn't quite understand.

"You see... by yielding, it is I who have effectively won."

He rubbed his neck and I worried that I may have hurt him slightly, although this had not been my intent. He straightened up and spoke to me seriously.

"Good… It's good to know, that you are able to handle yourself, it must be all the gardening you have been doing."

"Shall we try the other way around?" I suggested.

"No, I don't think we need to do that, you have learned your lesson."

I was satisfied to know that I could behave and move in the way that had been prompted, but in point of fact, prior to this test of sorts, it hadn't occurred to me that I couldn't.

I learned so deeply from Zhang in such diverse ways. The knowledge he taught of the world outside these walls, and the way of life that occurred within them, blended together into a unity.

That was the first and only time I saw Zhang behave in this way, indeed all the monks, although highly active, moved with a slow and peaceful grace that was counter to such aggression. I admired this way of living greatly and it was the first impression I attempted to write into the fabric of my soul.

- 42 -

LEAP OF FAITH

I didn't know what Viola would say. The depth of the proposition presented a choice that would be hard for anyone to make. We hadn't had to make many decisions together, and never one this weighty. I knew what I hoped she'd say but I had no intention of forcing my point of view. It was a burning question and it couldn't wait.

In the apartment I could hear her listening to music in her art room and walked there trying to ascertain the appropriate attitude. Standing by the door she had her back to me, leaning over a canvas on the floor, she was singing to the music, something about meeting someone by a bridge in the rain. She had a great singing voice and I just stood and listened.

Then she sensed my presence with a bit of a start.

"Hey! I didn't see you, how long have you been standing there?"

"Oh, I was just watching you paint, I didn't mean to make you jump."

"Hold on, I'll just turn this music down, getting a bit crazy with it, what do you think?"

"It's huge!"

"Yeah, you noticed... I made up some king size canvases, thought I'd broaden my horizons..."

"You've certainly gone to town with the colours, they're all over the show."

"Mmm... I'm thinking you can't have too much colour for this job."

"What's your concept?"

"It's supposed to give a feeling of extreme chaos, insanity even, on the cusp of a tipping point, or breaking through into order and a state of grace." Viola, had her head tilted to one side as she tried to get the measure of her own work.

"Well, I'm sold, but then I'm fairly in touch with the elements of your brief. It's a crazy mixed up world alright, but maybe there's some peace around the corner. I feel like I'm bringing my own rather unique perspective but I love what you're doing, I really do."

"It's supposed to connect with existence and perception on a barely conscious level."

"Are you saying you have to be half asleep to appreciate it?"

"No, dummy! It's just a piece designed to reach its potential at the interface between the artist and the viewer."

"So that's you and me right here then."

"It asks a question; is what we see a mental representation of reality or partly our imagined reality. Does our constructed space represent who we are?"

"It works for me, and I can see the transition you're after, chaos into order, I can… identify with it."

"Do you actually like it though?"

"I like it, I do, its cool."

"That's all you had to say. What kind of day did you have?" Viola began walking around her studio, looking at her work from different angles.

"I saw The Minister."

She stopped walking. "Oh. What did he want with you?"

"I think maybe we should sit down somewhere."

"Sounds a bit serious. Don't muck about. Just tell me, what was it?"

"He's asked me to do something, to go somewhere, but I told him I've got to talk it over with you."

"So talk, where's he want you to go?"

"Miami, The U.S.A. I want you to come."

"I… The U.S.A. What for, I mean when?"

"Very soon actually, it has to be that way, it's an all or nothing thing."

Viola, moved her head around trying to find a reference of some kind, coming back to look at EZee.

"We just pack our bags and go?"

"That's the long and the short of it. It's a big decision in a very small window of opportunity. If you want to think about for a while, I think we have to decide by tomorrow, even then we're really going to have to move it."

"I'd have to leave the apartment, all of this?" She waved around the studio, incredulous but trying to keep it together. EZee kept his focus on her.

"If you don't want to go I won't go either and someone else will go instead. It's a one way ticket. We would have plenty of money."

"You're really putting me on the spot here, you know. I don't feel I have enough to go on. I mean… Why leave? Why go? I mean if you're saying we can go, I'd just like to know why we're going. Do you want to go? Or are you just doing this because he wants you to?"

"I want it. I want out of this city. I've climbed out of the sewers and now I get this chance, and I want to take it, for me, for us. I was thinking you might like the idea of turning your back on the city too, waving goodbye from a cruise liner."

"A cruise liner, sounds nice, you didn't mention that. Miami though, why Miami?" She was talking quickly, process this new data as fast as she could.

"It's the place where The Minister wants to set up, and then expand the REM distribution business in The States."

"Ah, so that's the deal. How do you, how would we, fit into this little business venture?"

"It's a matter of babysitting a consignment of REM on the cruise ship, taking it through the Panama Canal and then on up to Miami, via some Caribbean Island."

"An island. Well now you're talking my language. Which island?"

"St. Lucia."

"Mmm… We don't have passports."

"We apply for them, if we get them in time we go, if we don't get them, we don't."

"It has a horrible logic. I've heard you can register and get a passport pretty quick."

"We have enough time, we just have to commit, or say no. So, what's it going to be?"

"It's a future isn't it?"

"It is, and it's a dream too."

"We could see The Miami Dolphins."

"We could make it an integral part of the arrangement."

"Well then we better buy some luggage."

Viola ran across the room, the tension in the air having dissipated completely. She jumped up on EZee and threw her arms and legs around him. There was paint all over the two of them and as they hugged each other tight they were more together now than ever before. They were unified.

EZee sent word to The Minister of their decision via the usual channels, the message being relayed by a rapid chain of Synths. Word came back swiftly giving the ok. The ball was in play, the mission had begun and they knew this was going to be a sprint. The idea of their race in tandem reaching a finishing line onboard a ship, and leaving the city behind them was the common goal they now shared.

The next day they made a trip to the appropriate government offices, having to apply for the passports in person. Retina scans, thumb prints and voice patterns were all taken and documented. Of course there was privacy but their Synth status was also registered, a fact that would be embedded in their passports but only accessible at certain levels of security. As previously undocumented citizens, official names would be randomly generated for them and they would each be able to choose from one of five forenames and five surnames.

The day was in fact a lot of fun, becoming legitimate people was an activity and a condition they had never needed to consider before. Although their applications were separate it felt to them as though they were getting married in a civil ceremony of sorts. Either that or signing up to join the Army together. They had great purpose but the time frame was such that they couldn't afford to relax.

They would have to wait only three days for the applications to be processed, days of anticipation requiring patience. There was a huge amount to be done but during this time Viola found some distraction in cleaning, washing and tidying everything in the apartment.

"EZee, I found this material stuffed in the long pocket of your old coat. It's Silk isn't it?"

"Yes, that's… that's very important to me."

"I washed it in cold water with some gentle soap, as you're supposed to do. It was filthy dirty but it's come up really clean. It's a beautiful colour, and it feels so… smooth."

She handed the folded material to him and he took it, remembering the moment it was given to him.

"A brother gave this to me, on a hot afternoon. He explained to me that it represented my soul, at least I think that's what he meant. He told me I must write my future in its weave and folds."

"How cool is that. You didn't tell me you had a brother…"

"I had a whole life it seems, before I arrived in Hong Kong."

"You've mentioned it, I know but… I never ask because… because I think you say what you need to say, when you need to say it. That's your thing."

"We're going to have a lot of time to talk and I think there's a huge amount for us to talk about. Thank you for washing it, that means the world, it feels brand new."

He wrapped the Orange Silk around her head and underneath it he kissed her, and they embraced for a beautiful moment. EZee looked at her up close under the cover of the Silk and spoke quietly.

"We'll be away from here soon, and our pasts will seem like dark dusty paths we walked down a lifetime ago. Ahead will be only wide open roads and we'll be able to draw our own maps."

"I love it when you talk like that, baby."

"Well, you know I was just saying…"

"Keep going, haven't you got any more?"

"I'm not sure, I was just you know, speaking my mind."

"I love your mind."

"Come on now, give me a break here."

"You can't stop now, go on, it was something about maps and dusty paths."

- *43* -

HARMONISATION

He'd always been leaving, perhaps because he couldn't remember arriving; for him every movement was always a movement away. His every gesture signalled departure but now he had a future his totality was synchronised with his reality.

Viola on the other hand had found a way of staying, of being at one with herself in a place. It was because she'd made that place all by herself, for herself. It was because she'd had no choice, no means of escape, no hope of daring to dream of another way. Now there was such a hope, and a dream it came wrapped up in. There existed the possibility of a life outside of the one she knew.

She had EZee, and together they were a whole, he completed the picture she was unable to paint alone. They reflected each other, they were the contrast needed to see themselves in each other's eyes. In every way they were made for each other and she was committed to staying with him, wherever that took them.

There was the question of the commissioned piece. She needed to tell the company she would no longer be able to complete the work, and she'd have to give back the credit she'd received upfront. She'd clicked with the client on a creative level and this was perhaps the greatest sacrifice.

EZee would have to sell his bike, he hadn't owned it for very long, and he loved the thing. But they were going on adventure, there would be endless unimaginable surprises in store, and every day would be one of wonder and enchantment. Viola had never allowed herself to believe in magic but now she immersed herself in its flow and charm.

Viola's mind was a subtle creation, a fragile one that mirrored the beauty of the soul in which it lived. At this moment Viola's slightly anxious situation was alleviated by her imagination, which was one of marvellous escapism and fantasy. It roamed through fields and skies of every colour, imagining exotic lands, where the threads of stories swerved freely between all things. She was in a blissed-out haze, her feelings, thoughts and emotions mixed so as to be indiscernible and undecipherable. Only she knew the languages she spoke to herself in these moments.

EZee's attitude during these hours and days was more pragmatic. There was so much to be done, and there would be a time to let his mind run free later. Only when they were clear and away would he celebrate and allow his anticipated joy a free reign. There were details to be taken care of, and this was important.

Essentials such as an adequate supply of REM for them both, for the whole trip, made EZee smile considering the cargo they would be custodians of across the oceans. It was business too, and he hadn't forgotten the reputation of The Minister. Until all parties had been satisfied, and he and Viola were safely sailing away onboard the cruise liner, he would continue to maintain a business-like approach.

It was memory once again which fascinated him as he made these arrangements. With daily REM both his and Viola's memories were merging in wonderful ways. All that they did together formed flawless memories, seen from slightly differing view points, which when fused formed a third, even more vivid recollection. Everything that they did apart they related to each other with their unique descriptions, and so the story of their lives together grew into patterns they could both understand.

The more distant recollections EZee enjoyed regularly were shaped within him so superbly that he thought some other kind of mechanism was at work. After all, to his knowledge, he hadn't been taking REM at the time these memories were made, even if he had no real idea when that was.

Was it possible that there was something about him which made memory formation possible without the drug? Was there some unique quality of his constitution which made him significantly different in some way? Perhaps it was the very same thing which had made him feel so alone and incomplete.

There was currently no way of answering these questions, but he had his theory and now believed it was possible for him to exist, to remember and to make new memories, without the REM. He believed this, but as with his belief in his soul, he had no proof, no concrete evidence on which to base these beliefs. To many they would seem as delusional ideas, mistaken foolish dreams.

This was a way of thinking that was a negation to how he truly felt. He knew he was alone in this beliefs but this isolation was of no concern to him. The idea that REM could be removed completely from the equation gave him the greatest hope and drive for the entirety of the Synth species. If he could crack this code with the unusual insight he'd been given, he might help many of his kind.

With this increased intensity of action he noticed parallel thinking in Viola, where one problem was being worked on concurrently with others. Sometimes she would conclude several of these strands during a short space of time and solutions to several intractable confusions would appear all at once. It gave the appearance of a type of genius, which is what it really was, but for a Synth it was just a means of keeping the totality of one's mind busy.

Viola had switched states and was furiously multitasking right now, calculating and scheduling in such ways as to prioritise and be as efficient as possible. This was necessary as the moment of their planned departure was close, and getting closer. Creating objectives in time and space, logistics with criteria for success, came naturally to her and EZee loved his little genius. Sometimes he would just watch her, imagining the millions of operations her brain was making every second.

Theirs was a love few Synths knew, and even fewer humans. With their psychologies complementary and their physicality coming from the same source, they laughed often with each other. In so doing, they proved to themselves that they were real.

When they were apart they were thinking of one another, when they were together it was as two parts of a whole, they were yin and yang. They unified and they harmonised.

Even so, the completeness EZee had always yearned for, whilst so beautifully close, seemed to him to be forever out of reach. There was something of a hatred for this state of affairs, as the angst felt at once both permanent and pointless.

At this time, he concentrated his entire being on the necessary path through the difficult present towards his future. He had a tight grip on reality but refused to give up his irrational belief in the future containing the belonging he desired. He wouldn't let it go of it, holding onto it as he had done with the Orange Silk for so long. The continued and forever unfolding recollections of his brother, his tutor, played out in a peaceful place in his soul where he found an endless supply of hope to fuel this belief.

- *44* -

Revolutionary

The bicycle in front of us was broken and in many pieces. Zhang told me it could be repaired easily but that it would require time and patience. So we set to work together with the goal of making it functional.

I had seen these machines on occasion passing by on the road to the side of the monastery. I thought they were somewhat magical machines which could propel the driver, sometimes at great speeds, and sometimes carrying substantial loads. All the seated driver had to do was move his or her legs up and down so that the feet moved in circles, and the machine would then move forwards at a rate dependent on the number of revolutions per second which the legs and feet could create. It was simplicity itself and an integration of man and machine to be marvelled at.

It would be a whole day before I could try to animate myself on this device. We had a huge number of mechanical parts to assemble first, Zhang telling me these individual items were collected from a number of other, similar bicycles. I had my doubts as to whether we could build a whole machine from these boxes of constituent objects, but we set to it nevertheless.

Act without doing; work without effort. Think of the small as large and the few as many. Confront the difficult while it is still easy; accomplish the great task by a series of small acts.

As we worked, Zhang, who seemed to be somewhat of an expert in this field, talked as he usually did.

"I've been thinking long and hard about your situation and the environment in which you currently live with us."

"It's very agreeable to me, you have made me welcome in your home and I am most grateful for your company and teachings."

"It is kind of you to say this and I hope we have given you a sense of belonging."

"We are one here together."

"This is true but I have the strongest of feelings that you have another home, elsewhere, a place which you must find for yourself."

"It is hard for me to imagine the kind of place you talk of."

"Nonetheless, I believe it is in your best interests, for your life journey, to seek this new home."

"What is it that I must do?"

"You must leave the monastery, and you must leave soon."

I had begun to feel an ache in my stomach at this talk. I never doubted anything which Zhang said for he had always been kind and put my interests at the front of his thinking, but with this talk grew a sad energy.

"When and for how long?"

"Tomorrow and forever."

In a burst of confusion I raised my voice.

"I do not wish to do this and there is nowhere for me to go."

"Your purpose is outside the monastery, hand me that tool please."

"I only have purpose here, there is nothing for me to do in the village, unless you think I should join the market permanently and have my own stall."

"No, that is not what I wish. Please be calm. You may have noticed that you are different from all your other brothers in this place."

"It is only a difference in form and size of facial features and body type. Our hairs are a different colour and my skin is a slightly different shade, but we are all people here and these differences are only on the surface."

"Everyone here likes you, but you know within you that you are special and apart from us. I believe it is these differences which indicate you have a unique calling, one that cannot be attained whilst you remain within these walls. You have qualities and ways about you which make you unique."

I wasn't sure whether to be happy or sad about this. Zhang knew I was having difficulties adjusting to this new condition and as always he found a way to aid my understanding.

"It is like the birds in the sky. They all fly, but some look different from each other and fly so differently too."

I found energy to protest.

"But they are all in the sky and they all make their homes in the trees."

Zhang's demeanour was one of reluctance, he sighed, but continued with his explanation.

"Whatever kind of bird you are, you need to learn to fly too."

"But you are here, and you feel no need to leave here, to fly away."

"But I am not a bird, or if I am, I am like… a chicken in that I cannot fly very far."

He laughed to himself. "You need to be free. You can travel great distances in your mind but your body needs to be free also. You must leave this tree and make your home in another tree, far from here."

"Where would I go to find a tree as beautiful and plentiful as the one I have here?"

"You will go to the big city, a place called Hong Kong. There you will find people who are like you, people who look like you and speak like you, people with whom you can be friends and make a home with. You do not want to be a simple brother, a brother who knows only other brothers, not for all your life."

"That is what you are."

My insistence to be contrary and my lack of ability to accept was making Zhang's efforts difficult for him.

"Yes, but I have chosen this way of life, chosen it over all other ways. You have yet to see and experience other ways, in order to be able to make any choice at all."

"Perhaps, if I see this city, I will decide that I do not like it, and I will decide to come back here."

"This you cannot do. Time moves only in one direction and you must do the same. You must keep moving and you must never stop. If you stop you may forget everything you have learned whilst you are here, you may even forget who you are, and that you were here at all."

"I can hardly see how that is possible."

"Nevertheless, I'm afraid that it is."

"How far away is this city?"

"It is less than a week's travelling."

"A week! That is much farther than I have ever walked before."

"You will not be walking, you will ride on this bicycle. You can sleep by the side of the road at nights, as it is so warm during these months, and I will give you plenty of food for your journey."

"This you have already decided for me."

"I have talked with the others and it is our belief this is the road you must travel along."

I was quiet for a long time as we continued mending the bicycle, the work taking on a new meaning for me. After several hours we were almost complete and then Zhang produced the front wheel, which we had received in trade at the market. He connected it to the bicycle and span it around with great glee.

"There, we are finished!"

There was something about his happiness which I admired so greatly. He often whistled to himself and enjoyed breaking into song when reciting the verses. I wanted to be like him in this respect but as I prepared myself to leave this place, I was aware of the possibility that I might be happier somewhere else. It was only a feeling, but it was growing inside. Maybe this was only a small part of the world, maybe the other worlds outside of it would be more fascinating. I thought of the Future People living in the night sky and how different their lives might be.

Zhang stood before me, resplendent in his robes, with the bicycle in front of him.

"Now you must learn to ride like the wind. I will show you how."

Zhang sat on the bicycle and then with a rather shaky start, set off around the courtyard wobbling and often just missing stationary objects. He returned, got off the bicycle and handed it over to me. I sat on it and cycled the same route he had taken, before coming back to him at speed. Using the brakes and stopping quickly, the rear wheel locked up leaving a long trail in the gravel.

"Mmm… You've done this before?"

"No, but it is very enjoyable."

"Mmm… It's just like riding a bike."

I didn't understand this as it didn't seem to make any sense but it didn't really matter.

"This is your bicycle now, you must take care of it, and it will take you where you want to go."

I felt a sense of pride in having worked together to animate this machine and had faith that it would now do as Zhang said.

Something of wonder occurred to me that night. My acceptance of this change in my life direction was in fact an acceptance of change itself. There was an eternal changing of the world happening all at once, all the time, and to fight it was to be fighting oneself. To know that we are beings of change, in a world of change, was a wonderful realisation and an acceptance of this state was confirmation of my place within the world.

I slept trying to imagine the character of the city I would be travelling to. As a much larger tree than I was used to, I would have to share it with many more people. To be one among so many made we wonder if I would feel larger or smaller.

- *45* -

LOST IN A MOMENT

The two synthetic lovers had never before experienced so much fun in so few hours. They went shopping together and allowed themselves to be open and free and alive in their behaviour, as if they were already in Miami. Viola gave up any vestiges of fear over her past, as she skipped and danced down the sidewalk. EZee succumbed to Viola's infectious expression of freedom and found himself breathing in the fresh aura she created around them both.

They chose luggage first; expensive, durable and sizeable enough to carry all the clothes they were to buy. Everything was on credit and everything would be delivered to the apartment later that evening. The shopping spree allowed them to throw off all cautiousness, which had been bottled up so long. It was an acceptance of a decadence which they could afford, in which they became transformed by the power of purchasing.

Their brand new identities would be accompanied by a remodelled look, their styles and tastes reinvented for their changing lives. Finally they could both become updated versions of themselves, a metamorphosis of their souls was taking place and an exploration lay ahead.

There was no opportunity for legal marriage between Synths, not anywhere in the world. Such advances often take time and the precedents only set by brave and forward thinking countries. They had their basic rights, but not the right to be publicly recognised as husband and wife. Still, Synths often had coupling or connecting ceremonies privately, but it simply wasn't the same thing.

Sometimes couples would wear rings and EZee and Viola chose to do this as tangible reminders of the completeness they created within each other, for each other. The circle was perfect, and for them this was the perfection of the love they had discovered. Choosing wedding bands in a jewellery store was with a mischievous and playful act. They knew they were pretending to be human, but also that the employee serving them wouldn't have a clue. They chose platinum and diamonds, simple, classical matching designs and putting it on credit meant nothing to worry about.

Down by the sea, not far from where they had first met each other, they said their impromptu vows and placed the rings on each other's ring finger. Walking along the shorefront, hand in hand, anybody who saw them might think that they were married, a real married human couple. None of these people would know that they were going on the honeymoon holiday of lifetime to shores so far away, and indeed that they would be away forever. But Viola and EZee did know, and this made for the most beautiful feelings within them.

In the afternoon Viola had a trick up her sleeve. She'd made an appointment with a downtown tailor. Outside the shop EZee was none the wiser.

Viola was excited. "This is it!"

"I don't get it."

"Turn around and look."

"It's a tailor."

"Yep, come on, we're going in."

They entered the shop, which occupied only a small area, but reached up some five metres to the ceiling. Lining the walls, all the way up to the top, were row upon row of fabrics, rolled onto great three meter rolls. A tall, thin Englishman appeared with a tape measure around his neck.

"Mister EZee?"

"I guess that's me yes."

"Hello, and you I assume are Mrs. EZee, with whom I spoke earlier?"

"Yes, that is I."

"Sir is requiring a suit for a long voyage abroad?"

"Apparently so, Sir is ready to go."

"Good, now then, we'll be moving swiftly along, the measurements if you will allow me…"

The man measured up EZee, a series of well-rehearsed and practised actions which took in every inch of his frame. After this the discussion moved to the type and style of the garment. Viola had a few ideas on this.

"I was thinking black, black linen."

The two men looked at each other.

"Linen is a quality fabric, certainly, but for a substantial journey one might consider other options. Black is obviously a classic choice, but I have to say there is the possibility of growing tired of it or of finding fewer and fewer opportunities when one can wear it."

EZee had his own thoughts.

"I've seen quite a large number of English gentlemen around the city wearing three piece suits which I believe may be made from wool. Do you ever have cause to provide suits for such men?"

"Indeed, the greater part of my clientele is of English origin, in name at least."

Viola liked this, the Tailor looked at her and she nodded.

"Let's go with that." She said.

"Fantastic."

They chose a particular fabric, a hard wearing, dark grey, wool mix with an extremely light, almost invisible check woven throughout. They were almost finished when Viola played her trump card. She spoke to the Tailor with a slight hesitation.

"What did you have in mind for a lining?"

"A simple grey Satin is standard but of course there are always options which one might entertain."

"What about this?" She removed EZee's Orange Silk from her bag and handed it to the tailor. EZee smiled at his wife and the ingenuity of her thinking. The tailor ran the material through his hands and was for a while lost in a quiet contemplation of its quality. When he spoke it was with an elevated interest in the special nature of this new job.

"Yes, Silk, very hard to come by these days and very expensive. This would make an excellent lining. In spite of what one might imagine, I'm not averse to bright colours and the use of this as a lining, hidden as it is, would give the wearer, a knowing secret, if you catch my drift. Do you think that would be agreeable to Sir?"

"It's very agreeable."

"Good."

They made a time in a couple of days for EZee to return for a fitting, and then the finished suit would be available to collect just a few days later. It would be cutting it a bit close as they were due to depart on the cruise liner that day. However, the tailor insisted that this was the fastest service available.

They left the shop in high spirits, the experience having been a novel and slightly peculiar one, but one of the utmost fun.

Later that afternoon, fate played the cruellest of blows. There was no rhyme or reason to the nature of the event, just a dull and ordinary fact. They were trying on shoes in a fabulously decorated shop where footwear of the highest quality was on offer to a certain customer. Viola had been running low on her supply of REM and had her last few doses in her bag. Putting it down on the floor for a moment, in a slightly hurried rush to help EZee with his choice, the bag slowly leaned over onto one side, and the wallet containing her REM slipped out onto the ground. It came to rest, concealed from view behind a standing mirror.

When the couple left the shop, it was with a pair of very expensive new shoes for each of them but without Viola's capsules of REM. The wallet containing them lay unseen and untouched for several hours until a cleaner found it and surreptitiously slipped the item into her pocket.

Viola didn't miss her REM until the next day when, in a panic, she couldn't locate them in her bag. She had rather a large number of duties to perform for the MTR and would be unable to get some more from her regular supplier.

"EZee?"

"When you get a chance, can you pop out and get some more REM for me, I've run out."

"What do you mean, you've run out?"

"I've misplaced the last of mine, no idea where they've gone, I'd do it myself only I'm really busy today."

"I'll sort it out straight away. I'm going to the Citizen's Centre in a minute anyway to check on our applications. I'll get some while I'm out."

"Thank you."

EZee didn't blink, he was after all a well-connected REM dealer, and soon to be international distributor, finding a good amount of Ten for Viola wouldn't be difficult. It was something he had to do anyway for the both of them to prepare for the trip.

- 46 -

MATERIALISM

The tailor had enjoyed serving his most recent customers. Alone in his shop now, he had only an inner conversation with himself for company. It was often this way, he rarely if ever said a word aloud, but such was the solitude of his existence and the longevity of his career, that he had developed a strong narrative in his mind. Over the years it was only natural that ideas, which had begun as idle musings, had grown into a fully formed system of beliefs which informed his way of life. He was single, he was human and perhaps he was a little sad, but in his shop he was a philosopher and a master of his craft. He whispered to himself as he went about his chores to close up the shop for the evening.

"Measurements are, one would think, all one needs in order to cut the cloth, in order to create a new garment for a customer. This is a common misconception, for one must also have the measure of the character of the customer.

One does not create a suit to cover an object of certain dimensions, it is fact a micro-habitat within which a living, breathing person lives their life. Moreover, this person is a dynamic entity, and he or she moves by virtue of their anima and inner power. Their muscles flex and they exist at a certain pace, displaying varying rhythms as they move, as they develop, as they grow. These factors must be taken into account when cutting the cloth.

The 'look', one might think to be mere frivolous appearance, superficial and purely in the service of vanity. Nothing could be farther from the truth. This appearance, and not just the form, but the colour and pattern too, are a reflection of the customer's tastes and style, and as such constitute an integral part of their identity. And it is this identity with which we are concerned.

The garment must say who you are, what you are, and give an idea of your purpose. It must show intent. It must show to the customer what they are capable of themselves, and to those with whom they interact it must suggest such intentions too. Some customers might choose to hide this information from other parties, and the design of the garment must be capable of doing this too. It is a great deal for a tailor to consider, let alone to achieve.

As if all this weren't enough, there is yet another consideration which must be taken into account, namely the 'feel.'

How one feels when wearing the garment, in all manner of wide and diverse situations and conditions, will dictate the confidence inspired within the wearer. It is this confidence which creates the possibility of action, and we are fundamentally creatures of action are we not? To feel able to realise our dreams we must first feel empowered, liberated and simply able to act.

That's not all one must know about the feeling of being ensconced in a made-to-measure suit. To the touch it must be more than simply to the customer's liking. This touch, the texture of the fabric, of the fibres themselves, must create a sensation which evokes in the wearer something of their own personality. It must both remind them of who they are and conjure up in them a feeling of who they can become.

Perhaps if a person is able to utilise their attire to grow into a more evolved version of themselves they will eventually require a new suit, for a developed purpose. The standard of work is aimed at attracting such repeat custom. A business can only survive if people who partake of its services return regularly, over long periods of time. And this is brought about by a consistency of standard.

It is for all of these reasons that the tailor must be the measure of a man in so many more ways than the measuring tape can provide.

This last customer for example, with his beautiful partner. They are obviously a young couple in love. It is not so difficult to tell such things when you have observed people for so long. The man is, I perceive, a man of some importance and by this I do not mean that he is self-important.

His frame is one which is suited to a physical environment, but his manner and the way he carries that frame leads me to believe that he is something other. He is not only well educated but has been trained well, or prepared in some sense, with great attention to the fine details of living. It is only an instinctive impression, but gestures and expressions can hint at certain possibilities. Perhaps he is a man with a calling. He has purpose, yes, but his humour around his partner indicates another side to what is probably a serious aspect of his profession.

He is no doubt a self-made man, a director of his own life and most probably a leader too. I noticed they are married and from their body language together and buoyant spirits a honeymoon of sorts is perhaps in the air. Maybe they are embarking on some new business venture together. I am not often wrong about these things.

I will enjoy very much making this suit. Perhaps I will enquire from the gentleman as to the purpose it will be put, when I see him for his fitting. I am a little curious."

- 47 -

THE IMPOSSIBILITY OF FATE

Leaving the apartment for the reasonably short walk to the Citizen's Centre, the concept turning itself over in EZee's mind was that of luck. He felt its fiendish power all the time, endlessly going about calculations at a speed that would make a human mind spin. But luck seemed for him something more than mere probability.

To accept that luck, both good and bad, had a significant impact on every person's life was to accept that there was really nothing one could do about it. This was especially true if one believed in fate.

There was his earliest memory, a nightmarish scene of animalistic fear in an environment which he couldn't fathom. How had he come to be there? If this was his birth, as he suspected, why had it been so black and vicious and painful for him? He'd spoken to other Synths, especially those who were on REM since day one, and their memories of entry into the world were calm and full of light. Some even talked of it in spiritual terms with music playing and an all-encompassing feeling of contentment. Were the conditions of his birth fated. Was his experience just bad luck?

Then there was the matter of his time in the monastery with the monks. To have been discovered, rescued and saved in every way, and to have lived and learned in their peaceful community. Was this just good luck? Was it good fortunate, balancing the bad luck he'd had previously?

Dismissing vital elements of one's life as just lucky or unlucky was to EZee no better than showing indifference about the beauty of a flower or the ugliness of weed. It was just too easy.

Fate compounded this problem. That horrible idea that everything that happens and everything that will happen is already decided. EZee thought of Zhang and the moment in which he'd said with some sadness that his own life was already written on the parchments which he studied. But who had made the words on the parchments? How were they able to predict the lives of others, and who in turn had given them such a gift?

The problem he had in this moment was that he'd been lucky for quite some time now, and, save for losing her REM, nothing unfortunate had happened to either of them. Things had been fine, nothing had gone wrong. Luck had been on their side for quite a while now and as the day for their departure came closer this was making him nervous.

A million things could go wrong at any second, statistically it was quite likely, and to live in hope that everything was just perfect, and would stay that way, was a fool's paradise. He found himself crossing his fingers, never having done such a thing before. Where had this superstition come from? He quickly uncrossed them, not knowing how or why he had done this for the first time in his life. For many minutes afterwards he couldn't concentrate, and couldn't remove the feeling associated with the action he'd so surreptitiously just performed.

Nearing the Citizen's centre he looked up at the clear afternoon sky. The moon was hanging there. The light it reflected from the sun, its grey-white ghostly presence an almost perfect circle, defying the light blue around it. He felt it belonged at midnight amongst the stars, but here in the daylight, he felt it was an imposter, spying on the city from its heavenly hide out.

Was this moon an omen of good luck, or bad luck? Was it a reminder that our lives are presided over by the determined motion of forces outside of our control? Or did it signify the lunacy which defied all luck and all logic?

Few people looked up here, and even when they did their eyes usually came to rest upon the sky-scraping towers, scattered all around like giant chopsticks stuck in the ground. EZee sometimes thought he could see through the daylight blue above. He knew the stars were right there, hidden, waiting for their turn to come out.

He'd begun to imagine a story to himself of the Future People whom he believed were hiding up there too. In his mind they were just like him, but he imagined the incredible power they possessed to take flight to the heavens, would also enable them to look back from whence they came. Even now they could be looking into his eyes as he scoped the skies for their craft.

- *48* -

REMOTE SENSING

Toto had noticed some strange things going on lately. She woke one day and had great trouble finding the other two, until she worked out there was only one place they could be, namely Pod Six, which didn't even have a camera within it. She actually had to call them up on the intercom. They were both in there alright, but it took Kristina a while to answer and when she did she was out of breath. Apparently they were checking on the visual condition of the battery seals, that portal being the only place you could observe them from. It didn't take two to do that.

At this point in time, she was at one of the computer terminals, when a small red alert flag came up for JJ. She took a quick peek, and mentioned it too him a few minutes later.

"There's a flag for you JJ, it's about the EZ1 unit. Are you still monitoring that screw up? I don't see what you'll learn. Kristina said he's not even hooked up, no feedback, what's the point?"

"I know what you're saying but, it's become kind of a hobby now. What's the alert?"

"I don't know, I didn't read it, I don't know why you bother really. Haven't you got something better to do?"

"Can you tell Kristina I'll be in the Console room."

"It's ok, I'm here. I can hear you."

"There's an alert on the EZ1 unit, do you want to check it out?"

"Yep. What's he up to now?"

"Honestly you two are like a couple of kids with a new toy."

Kristina and JJ moved to the Console room and JJ brought up the alert.

> 12:14:2049
>21:21:37 UTC
>AUTOMATIC ALERT UPDATE
> SUBJECT EZ1:613
>UNIT REGISTERED WITH HONG KONG CITIZEN CENTRE PASSPORT
AUTHORITY DATE 12:13:2049 AT 13:01:09 LOCAL TIME. PASSPORT
APPLICATION IN PROCESS. APPLICATION STATUS : BLOCKED
PENDING REVIEW.
>AUTOMATIC ALERT UPDATE FOR SUBJECT EZ1:613 CURRENT
>CENTRAL AI SERVICE
>CLOSE

"So our man registered as a citizen," JJ looked up with something approaching pride. "I knew that update would do the trick, give him a kick in the right direction."

Kristina wasn't so positive. "Yeah but he wants a passport too, must be thinking of going somewhere."

"Maybe he's got holiday plans, a little windsurfing in Thailand, volcano climbing in Fiji, maybe he's going to take a fly-drive through Australia."

"He could just need the I.D., must be hard getting a mortgage or life insurance or whatever without one."

"It'll be an automatic block. CyBex will have him registered as a missing person or persona non grata. I'll see to that."

"You're going to unblock him? Are you authorised to do that?"

"Look around you Kristina, we're in charge around here."

"Still, I mean we did that firmware update and everything, I know you didn't get authorisation for that, but this, you'll be giving him the means to go wherever he wants, assuming he's got some money, which I doubt. Ok, I can see you're just gonna go ahead and do it, don't mind me, I just work here."

JJ typed away for a few minutes. "There, his application should sail through. When he checks out of the city, he'll pop up, and when he does, he ours."

"You make him sound like a fugitive, or a convict or something."

"He's a company asset, an employee, and you know CYBEX always takes care of its own. We can bring our boy home, run a thorough diagnostic on him and give him the full work up. He'll be as he's supposed to be, perfect, zero defects and ready to take on the world."

"Well I think he's already taking on the world. He has to be, the way we pushed him into it. Anyway what if he doesn't want to come in? He's got rights."

"I'm not so sure about that, he was never signed off as complete, it might be he doesn't qualify for full Synth status. I mean he'll get his passport, and I'm sure he thinks he's perfectly complete but if you look at the letter of the law, he's probably not... legitimate, for want of a better word."

"But you think you can call him in under the protection of the company, like a recall for faulty goods. I hope he doesn't have any of this residual stuff running around his system, it wouldn't feel good for anyone."

"He doesn't really have a choice. He has a command structure, there's top down orders going on all the time."

"But who's giving those orders? It's not the company, and except for our little Laser intervention, we're not calling the shots, he's got no owner to speak of. Really, who's he listening to when it comes to doing... whatever it is he's doing?"

"There is free will Kristina, I'm sure you're aware of that."

"Yes, I know, I'm just not so sure he'd be… capable of handling himself or… responsible for his actions."

JJ was far more confident, largely by virtue of his own self-knowledge.

"He'll know what the right thing to do is. When he's connected to the Ultra-Net, to all other Synths, he'll have the Hive Mind they all have. He'll be a tiny working part in a huge machine, one element of a whole, like a bee in a colony."

"Might be quite nice, being that connected. What about his individuality though, his personal identity? He must have built up a whole stack of that."

"Well our recent blast from up here might have wiped out a lot of that already. He'll keep what he needs, that's the most important thing. When he's connected he'll probably get it all back anyway."

"Doesn't sound very scientific."

JJ became a little cross.

"Well it isn't! Anyone who thinks Synth technology is perfect in some way is living in the past, sure it was meant to be, but things didn't quite work out did they! It's the Synths that are suffering."

Kristina hadn't seen him like this before.

"Hey, it's ok. He'll be ok. You know, bottom line, he'll do what he wants to do. He's already taken a big step entering the system, he'll actually be more free when he's tied in deeper. He'll feel free, and he'll feel… complete. It'll be like removing a blind prisoner's chains and then restoring his sight. This is of special interest to you isn't it? I mean you really care about it."

JJ looked a little unsettled. "I, er… it's interesting to me, the Synth psychology, their philosophy. It's ah, something to wonder at, the differences between them and us I mean."

"Do you have many Synth friends?"

"A few."

"You can't tell can you, whether they're, what they are?"

"No, that you can't."

"So I could be one of them and you wouldn't have a clue." Kristina was becoming playful in the way she led this conversation.

"Ah, that's how it works, in most situations."

"I could just be stringing you along, every day and you'd be totally in the dark."

"That would be terrible, you wouldn't do something like that though would you?" Now JJ was playing too.

"Well, it might be exactly the kind of thing I would do. I mean I'm already a woman, I have my wiles. It's not too much of a stretch of the imagination for me to want to maintain a hidden advantage is it?"

"It would be a crafty trick." JJ felt he had the upper hand.

"But then, if you were, one of them that is, I wouldn't know, would I?"

"You'd have no idea." He felt on top of his game now.

"Just as well."

"What do you mean, just as well?" He was suddenly confused.

"Just as well that I know."

"You know. You know what?" Here he was beginning to perspire.

"That you're, a one hundred percent hot-blooded man."

"Oh that, yeah." And relief.

There was a long pause. During this time JJ had been frantically making utilitarian emotional calculations before coming to the most logical conclusion which would benefit the greatest number of people, himself and Kristina foremost among them.

"Kristina?" She'd been distracted for a moment, looking through one of the portals at Earth, the craft now being above The Antarctic.

"Yes, what is it?"

"I have something to say."

She turns and looks at him close up in the eyes. "Oh, ok, I'm listening."

"I'm a Synthetic person."

"I know, aren't we all these days?" Kristina's remark was casual.

"No, Kristina, I really am, I'm a Synth." JJ was insistent.

Kristina put both her hands on his face and kissed him. "I know."

"How, what do you mean? How do you know?"

"I was told, by the Company, before we came up."

JJ was totally bemused, for several long seconds, then he flapped his arms around.

"So you've known all this time?"

"Yep, I was assigned to you. You're my little hobby, it's just that somewhere along the line, it got a little personal, and er… intimate."

JJ found himself blushing. "So what do we do now?"

"We keep it quiet, we keep it just us, and when I submit my report, I keep it very objective and very professional."

"Like nothing ever happened?"

"Exactly."

"But when we get back to Earth we…"

"We play it by ear, personally I'm thinking of a log cabin by a lake."

"Well, I like the sound of that."

- *49* -

ANOTHER IDENTITY

EZee roamed the streets buoyant with a strength of renewed optimism filling his heart. It was a long walk but the warm air seemed clear and fresh. Walking was something he'd begun to enjoy more recently, subtly altering his gait to maximise efficiency and more greatly appreciate the feeling of the muscular mechanics of ambulation. He found a hidden rhythm. Heading for the Citizens Centre he had the codes to pick up both their documents.

They were dispensed by a machine, and came in separate, slim plastic sleeves. Not containing any hard copies, their passports were electronic, these were just the confirmations. When travelling, an eye scan, thumbprint and facial recognition were all that was required to cross international boundaries. EZee pocketed the documents.

Next he made another much shorter walk towards the tailor's shop. The tailor greeted him warmly. During the fitting the suit felt light and snug when he tried it on.

"Obviously I have yet to finish the garment, but is this the suit you imagined it would be?"

"It's incredible, really." EZee looked at the Orange Silk lining inside and ran his hands over it, smiling with the smooth sensation.

"I only needed to use half of the Silk material, and naturally I've saved the remaining cloth for you." After handing EZee the piece of unused Silk, the tailor made his last few adjustments and told EZee the finished suit would be ready for collection in three days. He would have to pick it up the morning they left the country.

Leaving the shop and strolling now with a purpose through the melee, it was just a question of hooking up with one of his colleagues to gain the necessary REM for Viola. It wasn't hard to find Felix, a thin, young Synth who was always peddling his wares at a particular location.

"Yo! My EZee man, how are you feeling my friend?"

"Fine, just fine."

"Word has it you may be doing a little globetrotting in the very near future."

"Well, yes, how'd you hear about that?"

"Word gets around."

"Cool, listen can you hit me with some Ten, as much as you've got?"

"No deal dude, Ten is a no-go, in very limited supply."

"You haven't got any?"

"Not a bean."

"Who might be holding some?"

"Like I say, you'll have no luck. It's dried up, along with Three, it's a dessert. Don't ask me why. You know these things happen from time to time. Supply and demand, and then more demand."

"Ah. Robbie'll have some. Look Felix, thanks anyway, take it easy."

"Yes Sir, nice and easy."

EZee walked away a little annoyed but it was no big deal. He'd go to the hangar and get some direct from Robbie, who was always manning the station. It felt like a longer walk back to the apartment. Thinking about going in to tell Viola what he was doing, he decided instead to jump straight on the The Plasma and head to the Hangar, get it taken care of.

He opened up the bike, having no thoughts to speak of until he arrived, parked up and saw Robbie sitting there. None of the usual entourage were around him, instead he was reclining alone in the sunshine, not seeing EZee until he was right nearby.

"Robbie, you look rushed off your feet."

"Ah, man it's been a hard day."

"I need you to help me out. Viola's all out of Ten, can I score some from you?"

"No dice amigo. No Ten, or Three or Five for that matter."

EZee was annoyed, but still untroubled

"Well then can we break open some of the consignment from inside the hangar? I'm in a bit of a hurry"

"I'm afraid I can't do that."

"Hey Robbie, it won't be a problem, just open the hangar, let me in, I'll take a couple of boxes then be on my way. You can say some kids broke in."

"It's not that brother. There is no cargo inside the hangar. It was all moved last night. They took it to the harbour and loaded it all aboard the hold of some cruise ship. Hey, I hear you're going away for a while, right?"

But EZee was already gone. He rode back to the apartment in a real state. This was important, no REM for Viola would mean a rapid deterioration in her memory. The withdrawal alone would put her in a bad way, and she'd be really hurting in a couple of days. Ok to miss one here and there, but if you'd been taking it for a long time and had built up steady state, sudden withdrawal could be a nasty experience.

Arriving at the apartment he hadn't worked out a real solution to rectify the situation but held the two passport confirmation documents in his hand.

"Hey, honey! Where are you?"

"I'm in here." She was sitting listening to some music. "How'd you get on with the REM?"

EZee was neutral. "I couldn't get any, not yet. There's no Ten around, for love nor money. Don't worry about it, I'll get it for you. Meanwhile…"

EZee waved the packages in one hand.

Viola looked serious, but then perked up. "Is that what I think it is?"

"These, yep."

"Come on then, let's take a look. You first."

EZee opened it up. But Viola was interested in only one thing, "What name did you get?"

"Er…Kyle Meeks."

"Hah! That's excellent, Mister Meeks, I love it."

"Don't leave me hanging, who I am going to be travelling with?"

Viola opened hers and her face dropped. Her heart sank, she'd been secretly afraid of this but hadn't let on.

"Due to a block on your ID, your application for both Citizenship and Passport have been denied. Please do not attempt to reapply."

EZee was lost and speechless and in a frozen state, but whilst Viola was down, she seemed immediately more accepting. "I thought this might happen."

"I don't understand."

"My owner, the one I ran away from, he probably put a legal block on me. I'm outside of the system, with all its benefits and drawbacks, and I always will be." She threw the document down, disappointment flaring up into a flash of anger. EZee couldn't rationalise the situation. All he could do was look as his own document.

"Why was I accepted?"

"You don't know who you belonged to. It could have been anyone, you've got other things going on as well as memory glitches, and you can't go back far enough, even with all the REM in the world, to find out who you were."

"I was a monk."

"Don't be stupid. No Synth is a monk, you must have been something else before. The monks must have just picked you up from somewhere, like a stray dog or… sorry."

"If you can't come then I won't go either."

There was a long pause before Viola hung her head. It was with a kind of dispassionate insistence, which belied the pain in her heart, that she delivered her conclusion.

"I think you've got to go."

"I don't need to, I'll stay here with you."

"You don't know what you need."

"Oh, right and you're going to tell me." EZee felt himself rise into an undirected anger, there was a hatred inside of him which was not human. Viola could see his distress, it was part of the problem she was trying to show to him. She wanted him to know he could never be at peace in the city. She knew he loved her but she knew he had to go.

"You don't just need to remember who you were, you need to discover who you are."

"I know… who I am." EZee had felt this before, he could feel the memory now. Zhang had told him he must leave and look what had happened, it would have been better if he had stayed in the monastery and remained a simple gardener.

"You don't know who you are, you think you do but you don't. I've known it since I met you. You have an identity number, but you don't have a real identity, a personal identity, something that makes you, something that defines you."

"Not everyone needs such a thing, it's just as good to be defined by who I was."

"You may find out who that person is, you just might, but you have grown, changed and grown into this, this person you are now. You have to keep evolving, and keep changing. Maybe you won't ever be able to rest in this search, but you must keep searching."

EZee had heard such similar reasoning from Zhang, he had accepted it then and with the strength of Viola's imploring, personal argument, he felt that against his own will, he would have to accept it again.

"You're asking me to leave you for a reason like that?"

"I'm asking that you choose to complete your journey, answer your questions, because I don't think the answers which will fill your soul can be found here, in this city. They're somewhere out there… away and over the seas."

"Why are you doing this to me Viola?"

"Because I love you."

With Viola's words, EZee forced himself to think as she did. He was deeply distressed but Viola began to succeed in showing him what was good. If he stayed he would die from the pain in his soul and if he left he had the chance to be at one. By the end of the day, a day spent with a heavy heart, he had resigned himself to it and had sent word to the Minister. In the message he confirmed that he was now in possession of a passport and was ready to travel, but that he would be travelling alone.

Know the white, yet keep to the black: be a pattern for the world.

There was still the problem of Viola's REM, EZee went out into the night on The Plasma to find some, looking for the dealers whom he knew of who might have some. The memory of leaving the monastery and the pain associated with it came back to him as the lights of the city at night streamed through his visor into in his wrap-around vision. The speed and mania coursing through his caused him to stream more memory segments. They came faster than usual and blended together with the realities of his vision, but they were nonetheless as clear as the day they had been formed.

- 50 -

LEAVING FOR LIFE

The day chosen to be my last at the monastery was full of many emotions, so many in fact that I had to begin assigning them new names. The morning was spent with Zhang who prepared me for my journey.

A journey of a thousand miles begins with the ground beneath your feet.

I washed and shaved my head and beard. Looking in the mirror I saw a handsome, clean man with the future ahead of him but somewhere deep in my eyes I felt another person lived.

Awareness of myself had grown in an expansive way, I felt I knew who I was and indeed who I could become. However there was a feeling, black as the night sky which threatened to consume my identity like a maggot eating the inside of fruit. I wanted to share the knowledge of this uncomfortable condition with Zhang. When I was clean and dressed we had tea and I felt this was an appropriate time to broach the subject.

"Without trying to create it, I have a dark space in my soul Zhang, I would like for you to tell me how to fill it with light."

"Ah, I have sensed this with you too. It is in all things and it is not to be afraid of. Where there is light there is also the dark. It is the way the Universe exists."

"But it is of such blackness, it is as black as the night sky and it is always inside me."

"The night sky is full of stars. If you have cause to look into the blackness, just remember to look for the stars too. One of them is looking at you."

This was of great help and I thought nothing more of it.

The rest of the morning we spent checking the bicycle. Zhang showed me how to pump up the tyres and he gave me the pump and a small tool kit to use, should the bicycle break. I had begun to see this machine in a particular way, its purpose was to take me all the way to the city. In order to fulfil its purpose and Zhang's promise that it would do so, all I had to do was move my legs, at a steady rate for an adequate duration of time. It would be a wonderful machine if it could live up to this potential and deliver. I had faith in it.

Special food, which would last a week had been prepared and I put it in a bag to wear on my back. I was careful to place my Orange Silk inside the bag also, it being my only possession and according to Zhang, the fabric of my soul. A large container of water was strapped to the back of the bicycle and with the addition of a sleeping mat, I was nearly ready.

As I wheeled the bicycle into the main courtyard there was an incredible sight before me. All the monks of the monastery lined the path which ran around the edge. I walked along this path around the courtyard saying my farewells to each in turn. I knew all their faces and many of their names. As I said my words of goodbye, each bowed to me and I felt both honoured and moved as I bowed in return. This send off had not been expected.

Finally I came to the main doorway, where Zhang stood. We embraced and stood facing each other for a good time. It was no surprise he'd carefully prepared his speech.

"Go safely and seek happiness. You must fulfil the essence of your bird spirit, be with your people, and write your life into your soul. That is the way to become who you really are."

I was lost for words, but managed to find some all the same.

"Thank you for your kindness Zhang. You have given me life and purpose. Goodbye."

"Good bye Silk King."

And with that I mounted my bicycle and rode away down the dusty road, with the sounds of the monks shouting propelling me onwards. Soon it became quieter, with only the squeaky sound of one of the wheels for company. With the warm sunshine on my back, and with my robes blowing around in the wind, I looked forward, to the far away city.

I cycled for a very long time at a good rate of revolutions of the wheels, and I covered a great distance. Stopping only to drink water and sometimes to eat food, I saw the world scrolling by me in a seamless flow of life as I moved forward through it. Some people waved, some people bowed.

There were children playing with balls, beasts of burden pulling carts, men and women working the fields on either side of the road, and occasionally people on loud motorised bicycles and motorised cars with several people inside them.

Zhang had told me to look out for these, and not to be afraid of them. In fact I thought they were rather incredible and wondered why it was not one of these that I was riding in as my legs ached with the exertion. I imagined that it would take many pieces of paper to exchange for one of the motorised bicycles. I only had a few of these, in a small bundle, which had been gathered together by everyone at the monastery who had given those which they could find.

I also saw babies, very small people, usually carried by women. I could only imagine that when they ate more food they would grow into a size comparable to children. These were of interest largely because I could not remember being a baby or even a child. Zhang had told me that my lack of such memories was due to having an exceptional skill at emptying my mind, and that I was an un-carved block. I wasn't sure whether this was a good thing or a bad thing but it was definitely a thing of some sort.

I kept cycling all of the day. When the Earth had spun around, and the sun had disappeared I took my bicycle off the road and found a comfortable place to rest for the night, resting my bicycle against the trunk of a tree I'd chosen for shelter.

Having eaten and drunk some water I began to think about sleep. Unrolling a thin sleeping mat, I lay down upon it, looking up through the branches and leaves of the tree into the night.

As the sky transformed from a dark blue to an intense black, the stars appeared one by one. Suddenly there were too many to count, although I did try. I wanted to know which one was mine, there were so many and how one knew one from the other seemed an impossible job. And then I saw the one.

It was the home of the Future People whom Zhang had told me about, and it was incredible. I watched intently as their craft flew in a straight line in-between all of the other stars. It missed some by only tiny distances. I wondered how they had managed to climb up so high, and then I thought that perhaps they had always lived up there. Maybe it was as big as the monastery and full of all kinds of different people from all over the world. It was too much to think about. I watched traverse the sky until it disappeared on the horizon behind a hill in the distance.

I had another long hard day's travelling ahead of me so I closed my eyes. There was only the sound of the leaves moving in a light breeze, and this was plenty enough to lull me into a peaceful sleep.

- 51 -

CHANGE IN MOTION

EZee rode, caught in a mood which was transforming every second into harsher and more bare realities. This was a journey through the city that was surrounding him, closing in around him and threatening him in subliminal ways which gripped his mind in ever tightening circles.

The mood, usually free-flowing on The Plasma, was settling in for the long haul and it was solidifying into ugly forms that were hard to shake off. The imperative was to keep moving, to the extent that he found himself winding and weaving between other vehicles in ever more dangerous manoeuvres, simply to avoid coming to a halt. When he did stop, the space around him contracted, he wanted to remove his helmet, give his psyche room to breathe.

When in motion it was easier to flow into a train of thought more conducive to his situation. There were questions, as always, and answers were thin on the ground. To find the REM, to seek and to acquire. The map of the city, scrolling through his glitchy memory, was slightly unreliable, locations on it disappearing then reappearing in unexpected places.

Speed was a solution, to accelerate for short bursts, enabling higher goals to be achieved in fast forward leaps. Here, adrenaline had a role in achieving the otherwise unobtainable. Pushing onwards, driven by the deeper search for the ultimate meaning of all this.

Yet to be defined, in the profound way he needed, were his identity, his flaw, and his purpose. Fractal infinities, processing the possibilities, coming up short on the truth. Reapplication and reiteration the only methods available. Non-linear dynamics, fractured data of possible pasts scrambling through fuzzy logic search engines, offering up new ways in the now.

Always searching. Then he was off the bike and walking, eyes hunting. Artificial nature blending with self-taught nurture. Weight transference, pressure on feet, heels, soles, toes. Breaking into a sprint, running, at full speed through human traffic.

———————

As a chauffeured passenger, The Minister sat cocooned in the back of his official transport. The style was questionable however, the luxury machine of a suitable size and grandeur, but details gave away poor choices in taste. The colour, an off white, matte grey, cool and young for some, but on this vehicle out of place and suspect. He reclined with the classical music soothing his troubles away.

There were no enemies here, no need for worries or troubled fears. His was a sublime life, surely. It had no space for the irregular or discordant. He could afford to relax and feel the goodness that was his.

Alone with his thoughts, well maintained as they were, this was his kind of contentment.

The vehicle moved quietly and smoothly, its driver a seasoned Synth, took no risks in his driving style, his boss being of the highest value.

The Minister adjusted his clothing. His manicured hands moving over the cloth to appreciate its expense. His gestures slow, he could afford to be laid back.

Glancing through the window he saw his fellow citizens ambling, hurrying, rushing about, in modes of being which he understood. He knew his people, his customers. He knew their needs, their wants and their dreams and he gave them exactly what they desired. He allowed them to remember, he facilitated the evolution of their lives by giving them the memories they rightly deserved. Humans could do their own thing, but Synths needed his help, they were his children and he looked after them in his own personal way. That they strayed on occasion and required disciplining was an unfortunate truth.

The car arrived at the building and the driver pulled up. The Minister stepped out of his transport onto the sidewalk in his handmade shoes. As he walked the short distance to the entrance of the second highest building in the city, he tilted his head back, glancing up, and was momentarily dizzy at its overpowering presence.

JJ's frame of reference was as a goldfish in a bowl, but the bowl in question was one of the most expensive pieces of commercial technology in Space, and the fish inside represented the creative zenith of mankind.

He stared out through the portal, feeling it was the eye, the lens of this vessel. Its elite vantage point brought Earth into a zone of magical focus. He was high, he was fast, but he was somehow moving without moving. He had to pinch himself sometimes, so dreamlike an image one couldn't prepare for. The Holo simulations and three dimensional realities he'd inhabited beforehand, had little impact in a truly experiential way. On arrival here he'd spent several days in stunned wonderment, a state which refused to assimilate the scale of the beauty below.

The Earth appeared still, changes taking place at rates too fast or too slow to be detected. One had to look with educated eyes, the information, the knowledge, the data and the facts were the only way to get one's head around the planet. But then it took only ninety minutes to get one's entire self to travel completely around it.

It was an extreme environment, dedicated to the advancement of CYBEX and in turn, the benefit of the human race, and synthetic humans too of course. This was a paid job for JJ, but more so than just about any other calling, it was a way of life. It was impossible to be an astronaut and be normal in any sense. Even after all these years exploring Space, the life of astronauts was so separate from the truly natural order of the world, they were simply other worldly. But then JJ wasn't fully natural, and in the history of Earth, artificial life had only just arrived. He was as new to the world as it was to him.

So he did this job, and did it quite well too, he thought, and perhaps one day he would be recognised as one of the first Synths in Space. This felt good, for sure, but in his more melancholy moments he viewed Earth in a less favourable light. What had humans done with their reign? Kings and queens of an almost impossibly bountiful realm, they had squandered, warred and destroyed rare and precious resources and plants, animals, and whole societies of humans themselves had been wiped clean from its surface.

The climate had taken a beating at the hands of their consumption, greed and ignorance and only now was the preciously thin atmosphere showing some signs of recovery. What was their problem? Why did they kill everything essential to their own life?

Now humans had recreated themselves. Synths were a growing community, a subculture, but still a minority, and really at this point in time nothing more than a freakish sideshow, a fascinating distraction, cooked up at inconceivable cost. Some said humans had made a colossal mess of this endeavour too, Synth memory being what it was. It was always rumoured that the solution to the memory anomaly was just around the corner, prototypes showing promising improvements over earlier designs. But this was certainly CYBEX leading the world on. A breakthrough, some new model which would revolutionise the Synth condition was a distant dream.

Kristina's weightless yoga was being streamed live to huge sections of avid fans down on Earth. She knew the appeal; attractive, athletic Russian cosmonaut in every bendy position conceivable and some new ones she'd created in the micro gravity conditions to which she was perfectly adapted.

However, there were only a few people following her routine who could be considered interactive participants. A handful of astronauts in other orbital space stations were taking the opportunity to join in, but this was mainly a huge CYBEX publicity stunt. It made the news but then the company often did.

The accompanying music, some cheesy retro House tunes from days gone by, was hypnotic and catchy. Kristina was suitably elastic and her moves well-choreographed, and rehearsed in advance. With the world watching it had to be perfect, and it was.

When the show wrapped and Kristina had signed off, she had the slightest imagination that she'd been chosen for this mission purely for this glamorous, media friendly side to her character. She dismissed the idea quickly, remembering her training and the many highly scientific qualities at her command. She had duties and obligations too, not only for the company but for her colleagues who depended on her professionalism and skills. CYBEX wouldn't be so crass would they?

Her thoughts of JJ that came to mind. The boundaries between their working life and their personal relationship were blurring to the extent where really there were none. Up here, the psychologies of people merge, and the unit formed, although highly efficient, is unrecognisable as any team one might encounter on Earth. The vacuum outside provided a surrounding abyss, enveloping the pressurised interior and its isolated crew. Their lives depended purely upon technology.

Kristina thought of Synths on Earth, how their lives were effectively defined by the technologies within their own bodies. She questioned sometimes whether it was better to be a human or a Synth. Indeed, she wondered whether there really was any meaningful difference at all.

———————

Viola's frantic, almost manic attempts to organise herself were failing. She had tried carefully to prioritise her activities, but it was of no use. The bottom had fallen out of her life and she knew it was a pressing problem. She could handle the REM situation. Once she was back onto her regular dosing she would be on track with that, but EZee's departure and her insistence that he should go was tearing her into tiny little pieces, impossible to keep track of and pointless trying to reassemble. Time flows only in one direction and once the piece of glass had been shattered, there was no putting it back together again.

Shards of her life lay about her in the apartment. Everywhere she looked a broken life appeared before her, and it was her life. When EZee had gone, the splintered chaos would be all she would have. It was a dire situation, her emotions were bare and she was full of hopelessness. She could hardly ask him not to go now, could she?

She was moving about in an erratic mayhem. Her random actions containing no discernible patterns for her to recognise, she couldn't explain why this was happening to her. She'd forgotten herself and there was no way she could tell herself this.

Searching for items, a shoe, a paint brush, a mirror, finding them, only to have no recollection as to the purpose of the search. There were brief interludes of clarity appeared where everything seemed fine, and incredible even. Then she would snap out of this delusional state, and retreat once more into a mode of being lost inside her own mind.

It would have been an horrific thing to watch, her descent into forgetting, but there was no one there to see, much less to intervene. Her delicate and fragile constitution was no match for the storm which currently waged war within her neurochemistry. Fortunately she managed to catch herself for a moment and realising her fate was able to lie down to sleep.

She is detached from all things; that is why she is one with them. Because she has let go of herself she is perfectly fulfilled.

Zhang was in the garden, tending to some rare flowers. His happiness was not so rare, in fact he knew of few other states of mind. Perhaps he was just lucky in this respect, or perhaps it was years of dedication to meditation and a way of life which effectively allowed for little else.

Simplicity was the thread running through his life, a life which was the only life he'd ever known. He remembered being a young boy, the feelings and the wonder of his childhood, he was still a boy and that was really the best way for him. To be a man meant to be a part of the world of men, and this was a way he would never know, would never want to know.

His slow, careful inspection of the plants looked for new growth as well as any sign of disease. He was fond of the patterns he saw in nature, and studied in his own fashion the paths which nature chose to take. He was after all a part of nature too, he had his own patterns and his ways of growing, it was simple to see all as part of one.

The spirit he nurtured had its passions but its failings too. His was not a perfect soul by any means, but he cherished it. It was his and he alone could care for it.

He missed the man who had passed through here those several months ago. Feeling he had gained from the friendship as much as he had been able to give to it, there had been a symmetry to the arrangement. But he knew the ephemeral nature of such happenings, the transience of friendships and the natural way that one thing is replaced by another.

He had been a special project though. To have stumbled across a man who was a blank page, yet to be written on, but who was able to laugh and learn and become himself so quickly. Perhaps he had been a spirit of a man, or a reincarnated child or a god even. It was hard to tell these things.

The members of the monastery often talked of him, always in kind words. They remembered him; his appearance, his manner, his style, his way. But when he had left they were happy too, because they knew that through his words and deeds, his soul would have the chance to become itself, and to be free.

- 52 -

WITHDRAWAL INTO DARKNESS

Viola had really messed up. She'd forgotten to hand The Minister a report, some detailed accounts on the running of MTR at the highest level. She'd simply forgotten, and it was more than likely due to the problematic REM situation.

Usually so efficient and reliable she'd been forgetting many things, only some of which she was aware of, and now it was too late for her to get the report to The Minister on time. She knew it wasn't a minor problem, she knew because of the contents of the file. She'd finally sent it, but it was going to be late. She might just as well have thrown it away.

Errors and mistakes seemed to multiply with the hasty preparations for EZee's departure, as he was leaving the very next day. It was getting intense for both of them as rationale and logic just weren't adequate to explain what they were going through.

When he came back to the apartment, unsuccessful again in his attempts to find Ten for her, she was in pieces. She was displaying all the signs of sudden REM withdrawal, which many Synths were familiar with in theory, if not by personal experience. EZee had seen it before. It was ugly to watch and painful to go through.

First of all she was crying, continuously, this was as a result of the real pain shooting through her body, but also because of her knowledge and fear of what was yet to come. The splitting headache, the tensioning of all muscles, the increased heart rate and the panting to get more oxygen to lungs, contracted as they were by a stiffening rib cage.

When these symptoms arrived in full they went on for hour after hour, and there was little EZee could do for her. There wasn't even anyone to get angry with for what was happening, the loss of her personal supply compounded by the city-wide shortage of her dose.

Calling a doctor would be futile, the only medical solution was to induce a coma and hope that the body would see it through. It was that serious but EZee knew from early days on the street that plenty of people survived this. Viola was young and fit and stood a fighting chance.

No hospital would accept someone in this condition, it being exclusively a Synth problem, and one to which doctors had learned to turn a blind eye.

Synth deaths from REM deprivation were common. It was one reason why the black market existed, indeed the operation of MTR was designed to reduce the chances of this happening. But MTR was not perfect, the supply chain was easily broken by many circumstances. And if you were a conspiracy theorist you'd believe this was the way humans kept Synth numbers down to an acceptable level. They'd created Synths with the faulty memory in the first place and they did a lousy job of making up for it. They cut you deep then gave you a temporary solution.

Viola seemed to improve in the evening. She told EZee about the report she'd forgotten to file with The Minister and how worried she was about it. She kept repeating, in her delirium, that he didn't know how dangerous The Minister was, how errors were unacceptable, how only perfection was sufficient. He tried to calm her telling her not to worry about these things, but she continued expressing her fears. The twisted look on her face was often more one of horror than anxiety, she tried to hide the worst of her feelings.

EZee knew full well that the rumours concerning The Minister were more than just hearsay. He knew of two Synths who'd come to physical harm because of a perceived limitation in their service. One had simply disappeared never to be heard from again and those close to him had heard rumours of murder.

Certainly there was some truth in this talk, but Synths liked to make up stories sometimes. However, EZee had kept as close as possible to The Minister, in all his dealings with him, precisely because of the doubts surrounding his methods.

Again, there was little he could do except comfort Viola and give her water and food, some of which she was able to keep down. The struggle went through the night until the sun rose. As the light came through the windows EZee started to have more hope that she would pull through. The muscle spasms and fits had ceased, and she said her headache was resolving itself. Still, she now needed REM, otherwise the condition would certainly worsen.

During these hours of Viola's suffering EZee made the decision that he would stay in Hong Kong. He simply couldn't leave her like this, and in fact he couldn't really believe he'd decided to leave her at all. To be separate, to never see her again was too painful for him now. He would let The Minister know that he would have to find someone else, as the alternative no longer made sense. He felt much better having come to this conclusion. They were together now and that's the way it would stay.

However, he knew he would have to leave her alone for again, at this time, in order to search for the REM again. Giving her a dose of a different type than her own was madness, but it was something he had considered, a quick dose of Seven might improve her chances, but at huge risk. Better to continue trying all around town from the old contacts in his database people to whom he'd already put out the word he was in dire need. He knew that everyone would have heard about the shortage, no one would be selling their precious personal stock, at any price. Wondering to how many others this very same thing was happening all over the city, he said goodbye to Viola, who assured him she would be alright.

On the bike he motored through the city in the morning heat. Everywhere he went, the same story. Then, by chance, he caught out of the corner of his eye a particularly wealthy teenager whose clothing he recognised, and whom he remembered had bought some Ten from him a long time ago. He pulled up alongside him on the bike.

"Hey, excuse me. I wonder if you can help me, I sold you some REM, some Ten, a while ago, you don't still have any do you?" They locked eyes. EZee knew immediately there was something up with him.

"I remember you. Yeah sure I've got some, my cousin doesn't need it anymore, she died last week. I was looking to offload it anyways."

The neutral character of the guy's report on his own story was a killer. EZee stared at him with sympathy as a grey feeling swept over him.

"I'm sorry to hear that, really I am, what happened?"

"She couldn't live the life anymore, got tired of the place I guess. It said in the note that all she wanted was someone to take her far away from here. Someone to give her soul a new home. It was bad."

"I'm really sorry what was her name?"

"Hanna."

"Look, you might be able to help me save someone who I really care about. I'm sorry to rush you, but can we go and get the Tens, I have a very sick friend that needs it very badly."

"Hey, it's ok, I have it right here."

The young man withdrew a container from his bag. "I've got fifteen Tens. Do you want all of them? One Holo a shot right?"

"Well you wouldn't believe what's happened to the demand for this in the current market. I can give you this for all of them." EZee produced over five hundred Holo's and pressed them into the guy's hands."

"Man, are you sure about this? There must be, hundreds here."

The guy gave EZee the Tens and stared at the cash.

"I'm positive, look after yourself my friend. Thank you so much, I've got to go, I'm sorry, I've just got to go."

"Ok, dude, you take care too. What's your name?"

"EZee, and you?"

"I'm YoYo."

"You just saved a life YoYo."

"That's cool. Take it easy, EZee."

EZee sped back to the apartment, making a few more mistakes than usual along the way. He felt certain that everything was going to be fine with Viola. Her recovery was virtually assured.

- *53* -

Superior Powers

The Minister stood in a huge circular studio office, every wall of which was constructed from twenty feet high glass. The panoramic view out across the city was breathtaking. A Chinese man of medium build, wearing a plain grey suit was standing nearby. He spoke in Mandarin.

"I see you are admiring the view. Quite something isn't it. For me the perspective it gives is one of great insight. It is as though one is looking down, whilst walking on a map. It is the point of view of a king, wouldn't you agree?"

The Minister was obviously quite taken. "Oh yes, certainly. I imagine surveying the world from here makes a great deal of sense."

"It has been very rewarding, to look at people from this vantage, and I have been able to make many successful decisions and plans with the clarity it brings. But I could talk all day of the increasing benefits of an elevated point of view. Now, Minister, our venture in The United States. How are things progressing?"

"Very well, Sir. The cargo is already aboard the ship that we will be using. A cruise liner makes for perfect cover."

"Good, good. Now, my man in Miami is suitably well prepared. He is a good man. We studied together here in China, and he was then educated at an American business school. His trustworthiness is beyond question."

"Will he be handling the distribution From the East Coast to the West?"

"Yes, I have seen his business model, it is quite… revolutionary. We are predicted to have the lion's share of REM supply within a year, if all goes to plan, as I'm sure it will. What of the person you have chosen to accompany the delivery?"

"He has proven himself many times over. He is a very able and logical man, and knows the business from the street up."

"I see. Is he human, or… other?"

"He is a Synthetic."

"Pity. But so hard to find real people these days who know only how to take orders."

"He is my first choice."

"Well that is one for which you are responsible, and for which you will be accountable, should there be any… imperfections."

"He is perfect for the job."

"I hope he is."

"I know little of the contact in St. Lucia, please could you enlighten me?"

"He is an entrepreneur, an art dealer as a matter of fact. I have bought much of my art through him and his contacts. Do you enjoy fine art, Minister?"

"I'm afraid I don't know a great deal about it, I like classical music."

"Ah, music, so easily carried away by a strong wind. These pieces are by Rothko. I favour such work for its power. He refused to copy nature you know, and I admire him so for it. Art is human, and to be an artist one must be human also, anything else is well… artificial. Synthetics have no… soul. Wouldn't you agree?"

"This is correct."

"We could talk all day of such matters. I think we are ready to proceed. There is one more detail I would like you to attend to."

"Yes, sir."

"The annual MTR report has not been submitted to me on time. I need clarification as to the reason for this."

"I have not received it yet myself, Sir."

"And who is responsible for this omission, in addition to yourself of course."

"The accountant is usually very reliable with these things. There must have been a complication of sorts."

"Complications can be simplified, omissions however are countable as errors. This particular error has recently caused me some considerable embarrassment, as the state of MTR business has an effect on my other interests."

"I'll make sure you receive the report as soon as possible."

"It's rather too late for that Minister. This accountant, is he a synthetic?"

"Yes, I believe so. I do not know them personally."

"Well then the mistake can easily be corrected. See to it that they are not able to make another mistake, of any kind, in the future."

"What, would you have me do?"

"Put an end to their life, my good friend. And make sure your entire workforce is well aware of the fact it has been done. Examples have to be made. It is the only language these artificial people understand, and it's the only way they will ever learn the value of perfection, flawed as they are."

"Are you sure that you…"

"Don't question me, Minister! Not on these finer points of asset management."

"I will make sure it is done."

"Do it today. I would like to inform my partners that the embarrassment has been taken care of."

"Yes Sir, will there be anything else?"

"No, Minister, you may go."

The Minister left the room and descended the building in a glass elevator at great speed from the top floor of the skyscraper all the way to the ground floor. He left through a vast atrium and exited onto the street where he climbed into his car, which then drove him away.

Arriving at The Studio, he climbed to the top floor, his premises seeming to have lost any grandeur or air of importance. In fact this space appeared to him now as a run down and shabby set up, not in line with his status. But then his status also felt somehow cheapened. He would have to start making some changes, improvements and alterations to the organisation. It would start with the need for a punishment to be carried out, an example had to be made.

He stopped at the entrance where a security detail stood large and impressive by the door.

"Stealer, I'd like you to see to this immediately." He handed the man a small piece of paper which Stealer read in a glance.

"Are you sure about this Sir? Hasn't there been some kind of a mistake here?"

"There's no mistake. Just do it and do it now! I'm sick of you people questioning my authority."

Stealer looked at him with a blank expression, "Yes, Sir." He turned and left.

The Minister was already beginning to feel better, he felt the meeting had gone well and once the stolen consignment of REM was away to its new home and these other details had been taken care of he would be able to sit back and relax. In fact a little music would be good right now.

Stealer drove a car to Viola's apartment. He parked up outside and buzzed at the intercom to be let in. There was quite a long delay before an answer came.

"Hello, EZee, did you forget your key?"

"No, it's Stealer, from the Studio. I need to talk to you about something."

"Ok, come on up." She buzzed and Stealer went in.

The lethal act was silent and clinical. In this mode Stealer was no more than an automated tool, utilised at a distance by the actual killer who had never performed any such deed in person himself.

A minute later Stealer came out, having reluctantly obeyed his orders. He could only think in one way. The boss was the boss, a human who gave instructions with which he complied. The rules were not open to interpretation anymore than the laws which governed the motion of the planets. However, there was no rule saying that he couldn't feel profoundly saddened by the horrible thing he had just done.

There was no logical exclusion for a Synth to take the life of another Synth. Synths would soon be fighting human wars for them and in the future such military models, would be able to kill any enemy, whether they be Synth or human, it wouldn't make any difference. But such military hardware was under close wraps and certainly not yet in the civilian population.

Stealer drove back to the Studio with a heavy heart, he hated his job. He always drew the short straw when it came to tasks such as this.

He had no choice in life. Then there was the matter of EZee. He knew him as a face at The Studio, and he knew that he and Viola had been coupled together. When he found out about this, the only thing he would be able to do as a Synth would be to accept it. The fact that the guy was leaving the city was the only good thing in this. At least he'd be able to put the whole foul thing in his past.

- *54* -

THE MURDER OF AN ANGEL

When EZee returned with his hard found re-supply of REM, Viola was no longer alive.

She was so young and vibrant, but now she just lay there on the floor, so still. It wasn't right that she should die like this here. He hadn't been quick enough, holding the REM that he'd bought, tightly in his hands, he let it drop. He cried out, and cried, and tears hit the ground. He remembered feeling like this before but not from where or when.

The whole world is grateful to her. Because she competes with no one, no one can compete with her.

For an age he suffered with his dead lover in his arms. Then he began to sense that something was wrong, he felt it more than anything else. Then he knew what it was, a smell, a faint but distinctive smell which he recognised but couldn't place. It was a male scent and it wasn't his, and in that moment he was convinced that someone else had been there and recently too.

There was a bruising on Viola's neck, it was light, hardly visible but it was set in his mind that she had been killed, strangled around her perfect delicate neck. He looked at Viola's lifeless body lying in front of him, and closed her eyes. In a loving way he put a cushion under her head, trying to make it look as if she was just asleep. So confused by her death but now so focused on the quality of his suspicions.

He stood up, his head not able to integrate any of this. Then looking at the thick rug which covered this part of the floor he saw the large imprint of a boot, which clearly wasn't his. A rage began filling the void in his heart and threatened to cloud his judgement, but digging deep, he brought himself into some sort of functional capacity and he began to make a plan.

Viola was gone and it was an impossibility of both reason and intellect that he must accept this. But accept it he must. There was no such acceptance that her killer should remain at large, and the immediate accessibility of this fact made it easy to act upon. Before he even knew it, he had run from the dead body, surrounded as it was by so much art and creativity. He was on The Plasma at high speed through heavy traffic. His mind raced through all possibilities, all scenarios but he couldn't be certain of anything.

Robbie was the man he needed to see. Robbie was wired in tight to the whole organisation and was bound to know something. Why would someone murder Viola? It didn't make sense. He could only think that it had something to do with the REM. Hangar 8 approached fast. EZee drove straight through the open doors to find Robbie with a couple of friends.

"Robbie. Viola is dead, she's dead man."

Robbie didn't say anything, he just stared into EZee's eyes, eyes which had now lost something vital. EZee was panicked at the lack of Robbie's response, or indeed of the other two.

"Someone came into the apartment and killed her. She's just lying there. She's dead…"

Robbie hung his head, as did the two people he was with. "We know."

"You know? How do you know? What do you mean you know? It just happened, what are you talking about?"

"It's over brother, sit down. There was nothing we could do."

EZee was now confused and furious. He didn't understand this, this knowledge and passivity. How did they know, what were they hiding?

"Listen carefully to me, start explaining yourselves, or I'm going to start…"

Robbie stayed calm. "You don't know this stuff EZee. You're not connected. It's The Ultra-Net dude. We've always known it, right from the start, right from when you appeared on the scene. You're missing it, you're not connected. You're not wired up right man. I don't know how it happened to you, maybe you got in some kind of accident or something."

EZee was processing this information in a controlled manner, in spite of his hyper-manic state. Things were dawning on him, his problems being highlighted, his deficiencies were being made clear to him, and it was in his interest to know his limitations. He slowed down, giving the impression that he was as calm as Robbie wished him to be.

"This Ultra-Net, what is it?"

"It's everything man, all Synths have it, it's what weaves us together as one whole. Our minds we share, we think and feel as a single entity, and when one of us dies we feel that too. But you, you're outside of it, you can't feel this, you can't feel our soul. You're not really all there man, it's a tragedy but it's true. And there's nothing you or I can do about it."

At the mention of the word soul, EZee's mind sparked. He was incomplete, he was deficient of something primary, whatever this Ultra-Net was, it explained his profound angst, and now his growing anger. He could feel something snap inside of him, yet still his anger was tempered by reasoning.

"Why didn't you tell me about this before Robbie?"

"We'd never seen it before, sure we talked about it, all of us. But there was nothing we could do for you so we left you… I'm sorry brother, you're not really one of us. You're not integrated. I can't help you anymore than that I…"

EZee had a focused rage to concentrate on, his fire within was contained and heating the killer instinct deeply hidden in some remote corner of his architecture.

"Who killed Viola?"

Robbie looked at him hard without saying anything.

"Look EZee, it's not going to help you… the best thing you can do right now is…"

"Who? Tell me!"

Robbie caved in, with a meek voice he hung his head in shame.

"It was The Minister who ordered it, Stealer did the deed. He didn't want to, he had to. Human orders EZee, human orders, you know that."

"Why was it done? Just tell me that. Why?"

"Apparently she really screwed up at work, made a mess of some report she was supposed to be working on."

"A report? A report! This is about some damn report!… Do you hear what you are saying?!"

There was a long pause, the silence around them all was a tense stretch of time where Viola's spirit seemed destined to leave them all. EZee was calm in the formation of his next resolution.

"I need a weapon."

"Whoa, slow down EZee, that ain't no good. You don't want to kill Stealer. He's just a weapon himself."

"I don't want to kill Stealer, I want to kill The Minister."

"Now you're talking crazy, I know you're not connected but with this that doesn't mean a thing. No Synth can wipe out a human, it can't be done, it's never been done before, never."

"Well, we'll see about that. Robbie, for Viola, can you get me a gun or not?"

"No, no I can't."

"Robbie, you can't do anything about this, but I can. Get me a gun!"

"Ok, ok. You know the mad thing is, the only person I know who's got a gun is Stealer. And what's even more insane, he just might give it to you, specially if he knows what you want to do with it. But I don't think any of this is possible man."

"This isn't right."

"I know it's not."

"The Ultra-Net, can this help me?"

"The Ultra-Net, EZee, you can't possibly imagine it. It's like an Artificial Intelligence made up of cells, and we're the cells. What the majority wants, effects every cell. I'm thinking… We're thinking. If you say you can do this, it may well be not just a belief, it may be that you can, you can do it. If you have the authority of the Synth community behind you, then it can be done."

"I can do it."

"How do you know you can do this EZee? Can you see, it's hard for me to believe?"

"I know it, that's all I can tell you, I have a deep sense of it."

"You can kill The Minster? Because if you can there's a lot of Synths would like to see him go, me being one of them."

The wheel had turned, in fact it was the will of the Synth consciousness which had made it turn.

"So you can get me the gun?"

"When do you need it by?"

"It has to be today, before 4pm."

"That's pretty short notice EZee."

"Robbie!"

"Ok. If I can work it for you, make the connections, it will be with Stealer, at the Studio, by 4pm."

"I'll be there, make it happen. This is for Viola, Robbie, nothing more, nothing less. Look, I might not see you again, however this turns out. You come good with this you'll understand. I've got to go, I've something important I have to do."

EZee got on The Plasma and drove away at speed.

Weapons are the tools of fear; a decent man will avoid them except in the direst necessity and, if compelled, will use them only with the utmost restraint. Peace is his highest value.

Robbie was shaking his head. "That madman is going to get himself killed. A whole lot of other folks might get killed too. Not sure if we're ready for a revolution, but that seems like a sure fire way to kick one off."

EZee's past, present and future were fusing now. Less aware of his memories they still flooded his mind stream. Fixed in the now, with his future approaching at a rapid speed, his past played through his visual cortex. His recall accompanied his consciousness the way the sound of ocean waves, crashing on a the shore of a beach, might provide the background to a lover's embrace.

- 55 -

Truth Revealed

Two days of continuous cycling, my legs were seemingly able to go on forever. The path became more of a substantial road and it was a smoother surface on which to ride. I was in a sort of daydream, caught beautifully in the present moment, my experience being one of tranquil contemplation of the things I saw, riding through villages of varied size. Then disaster struck.

I had occasion to look up, there was the sound of birdsong but I could not quite place where it was coming from. As I stared into the light blue sky I could see not one, but two trails of aeroplanes and they appeared to be heading towards one another. It was a frightful thought that they should crash into each other and fall to the ground from such a height, all the people inside would be killed. They grew closer still, but missed each other thankfully, instead making a huge white 'X' way up high. My distraction was such that I failed to see there was a large open pothole in the road ahead and I crashed my bicycle into it.

I was flung from my transport, hurtling through the air at quite a rate, I came down heavily on my arms. They scraped deeply into the road surface which was rough here and I came to a rest in shock and in pain.

This was a new sensation, as much as I could remember, but I felt that a long time ago there were the seeds of this feeling at the beginning of time. I sat on the road recovering.

Thick red blood was oozing from the muscular tissue along both my forearms, it tasted metallic and bitter, as I tried to lick it clean. The damage wasn't too great though, I turned back to collect my bicycle but it was in an even poorer state than me.

The front wheel was buckled, twisted and completely out of shape, obviously I couldn't continue riding it. I picked it up, put it on my shoulder and began walking. After two hours I became tired, thinking it would take me much longer now to arrive at the city. Turning around to look back along the road I saw a vehicle approaching, it slowed and pulled up next to me. The driver, a short and sweaty man, got out and walked up to me. We spoke in Mandarin, naturally.

"Looks like you need some help."

"I do. I became unseated from my transport when I rode into a hole. I am alright but unfortunately the bicycle is no longer functional, as you can see."

"Throw it in the back, I have a spare wheel at home that might fit. It's only a short drive from here."

With great appreciation, I put the bike in the truck, climbed in and we set off.

As we drove the man couldn't stop talking, and he reminded me of Zhang in this respect. In order to make a living he bought and sold second hand cars, only very good ones he said, and he told me all about his wife and children. They had another child on the way, it wasn't clear what this meant but I didn't ask for an explanation as he was in mid-flow. He asked where I was going,

"The city," I replied.

"Hong Kong?"

"Yes."

He was impressed when I told him how far I'd already come but advised me there was much further to go and that perhaps I should consider buying a car. We soon arrived at his house which was certainly large.

Fixing the bike was simple and quick. With my tools we removed the old wheel and his replacement was a good fit. I was very happy and thinking of Zhang, proud that the bicycle now had a new lease of life. The car salesman was perfectly pleasant and perhaps had helped me because of my status as a monk. He asked if I would like to have a drink and some food and so I went inside his house with him.

We sat down at a table and ate a meal of stewed beef and vegetables, it was a little difficult to swallow, knowing it had come from a dead animal. His two children were beautiful, as was his wife. I was fascinated by her as she had a very large bulge in her stomach as though she had swallowed a watermelon whole. It soon became obvious to me, after some embarrassing questions that this was the baby that was 'on the way,' and pieces of a bigger picture started dropping into place. No sooner had they done so than other questions began creating further spaces.

Who was my mother? Where was she? Why did I not know her?

The contemplation of this revelation and the following questions was interrupted by a compound shock and these two circumstances occurring so closely together defined much of my thinking thereafter.

Another man entered the eating area and sat down next to me. We looked at each other, our eyes locking together for several seconds. Suddenly I felt deeply disturbed, he was quite bright and cheerful however.

"Hello brother."

"I am not your brother," I said, feeling only that I had only just met him and that brotherhood could not be won so quickly. "I am a monk, I have brothers, but I have left them all in the monastery."

"I am sorry, I feel from your tone that I may I have offended you in some way. I merely wished to express my solidarity with an equal."

Once again I was severely taken aback by this rude man but my host intervened. "This is Wulan, our synthetic person, please forgive his approach, he is quite an early model, but was purchased at a very reasonable value. He seems to like you."

Wulan said, "It's not often that I meet someone on the same wavelength, someone who's the same as me."

This was beginning to give me a headache. "We are not the same, I don't know what you are but I'm not like you."

"But Sir, we have exchanged data. You are EZ1:613, I am TX3:712, we are brothers."

Whatever he had seen in me, I had also seen in him and it gave me knowledge of self. A myriad matrix of numbers, letters, symbols, codes and an infinitely repeating pattern of swirling mathematical algorithms, had fired between us. It was not our minds that we exchanged for that I knew was something else, but it was a registration, a recognition and an awakening.

My host was speechless, as was his wife and the two children who stared at me. I was in a uncomfortable state where there was a pressure in my head and it was surely due to the circumstance of holding onto several conflicting beliefs about my very existence at the same time. These beliefs did not harmonise, they did not cohere to form a complete truth, and they did not correspond to any reality of which I was currently aware. I stood up suddenly, physicality being a default protocol, and left the house without saying a word. I picked up my bag, cycling away as fast as I possibly could and I didn't look back.

To have left like this didn't make much sense to me and I couldn't formulate in my thoughts the reasons why I had. I knew only that it was better to leave than to stay.

I cycled until I arrived at the ocean, immediately recognising it as such from Zhang's beautiful descriptions. In normal circumstances I'm sure I would have taken a long time to create my own impression of this vast body of water but I was deeply preoccupied.

The effort to simplify the questions which had been racing through my mind had been accompanied by a high pitched note in my ears since I had left the man and his family. The encounter with Wulan, their 'synthetic person' as he had been called had forced me to launch the most basic of investigations into my very existence. These were the questions of my life; What am I? Who am I? And Where am I from?

All streams flow to the sea because it is lower than they are. Humility gives it its power.

I stood on the cliff edge looking out at these sprawling fields of waves seemingly in perpetual motion. It was not the peaceful pool of cool, calm water I had imagined, instead its chaos and anger seethed beneath a slate grey and green surface. I quickly came to an understanding with it. This was my mother, and my father, and I was the child of its razor sharp horizon. I adopted its power and its form to be my own, in a fearful denial that I was not of nature, but of something else.

Looking down at the rocks some fifty metres below me, I thought that had I fallen I would cease to be, of that I was sure. I was made of flesh and blood and whatever else was within me could not prevent my death.

Without memory or identity it would have been easy to end it there, but instead I sat down and cried. Pulling the Orange Silk from my bag I held it to my face and wept into it, until my soul felt empty of tears, the Silk now dark with my anguish.

The realisations of my true nature were at this time impossible to understand. I was in no state of mind to come to any conclusions..

I walked back to my bicycle and continued my journey, there was nothing else for me to do, and to be in motion was to be alive.

- 56 -

Suspension Of Self

Hanging in the balance, EZee's mind was somewhere in tension between several types of dilemmas. His programming and experiences to date were not capable of reaching solid ground. His footing was unsure, his position was untenable and his mental space uncertain.

Thought preceding action was a fairly distinct notion for him, but instincts and activity which bypass the brain - animal reflexes, were taking control. The transition was similar to a survival instinct but here he was no longer running for his life. He was running for someone else's. He was calm but focused, on edge but strong, overcome with emotion but clear as to the task in hand.

Such states were brought about by the novel oscillation between other states. He had heard of a question from an intelligent Synth, whom he'd met once on the street when he was dealing REM, it was simple and perplexing; "To be or not to be?" He hadn't understood it at the time but in this heightened state he found meaning in it, purely for himself in these specific conditions. It was a question of existence, of life, and indeed of death.

The same Synth had recited another quote, which had made immediate sense to EZee, but it now came back to him with greater force and further meaning. He remembered it word for word; "Man is nothing else but what he purposes, he exists only in so far as he realises himself, he is therefore nothing else but the sum of his actions, nothing else but what his life is." It was French and currently it meant everything to him. He held its impact in his mind for a long time before he began to live its essence and plan his future actions.

A strategic element came into his thinking, it felt foreign initially but grew in the power of its logic and indeed the intensity of its power. His was, unknown to him, a military insight; a study of one's enemy and a cold emotionless stratagem to carry out the necessary actions. This was the all pervading philosophy within him now. He was beginning to feel more like the machine he was intended to be. Not knowing this intention, he only knew that this came naturally to him and so felt no need to question why it was so.

Still inhabiting a grey zone, or at least an area which refused to be defined, he was in unchartered territory. Morally his algorithms were in turmoil. The mathematics of 'why' and 'should' were in dynamic completion with 'how' and 'when.' But morality was a backdrop to his chosen direction. Morals were a conversation taking place in a crowd nearby whilst he was sharpening his mental blade.

Far from shunning the uncertainties of the unknown, he welcomed them. To live in between positions of comfortable understanding was to remain static. Venturing into the wasteland, the no-man's land, was to enter a proving ground, and required constant movement, a kinetic exploration of the self which was evolving with rapid acceleration.

Accompanying the actuality of these internal shifts in perspective was a new sound. Any music of the spheres, which might have otherwise played throughout the Synth's mind was replaced by a single note. A high pitched whine, a taught tightrope of indiscernible source. At a low volume, the pitch wavered slightly, weaving amidst any vestigial confusion. This was not a distracting hum, it was a Synth call to arms, and a fine tuning of the killer soul.

Where EZee had troubles in these rapidly unfurling processes was with the pure feminine touch of the lover he'd lost. Her beauty and passion, her gentle grace tempered his mind. It was, he felt, a human feeling, the best of humanity, something soft and kind and warm. It pulled him in another direction, a most fluid and pensive force, asking him to bring all he was feeling into the equations he was trying to solve. Her voice echoed inside and encouraged him to integrate his emotions in new ways.

She was everything he was fighting for. That she was no longer alive carried no weight. Her spirit was alive and the ideals she stood for were still singing in his heart. He listened to her as he prepared himself.

Another voice pulled him further away from his determination. The voice of Zhang, gentle and quiet, teaching and easing his consciousness into the world. It was hard now to remember his words, they had become faint as though their powers were waning. He tried so hard to recall the lessons of these verses and the imperatives of their wisdom but it became harder. Even the vision of the monk in his mind was fading.

The memories that he had worked so hard to gain were rapidly receding, as though a higher power was pushing them into the background. EZee hated this movement, not knowing whether the rearrangements within his psyche were temporary or permanent. However, he didn't fight what seemed to be his mind preparing him for something vital. He began to enter into an acceptance of these changes. Like a child putting away its toys, or a soldier putting on his armour, he was readying himself now, consciously acting out his plans.

The words of Zhang, even his feelings for Viola could not hold him back from his undertaking. He managed to grasp a verse, before it was swept away.

He doesn't think about his actions; they flow from the core of his being. He holds nothing back from life; therefore he is ready for death.

These alterations to his conscious mind occurred at the fierce speeds of The Plasma. As EZee brought it to rest outside the apartment, all required internal modifications had been made to his mind, to his body and to his soul. He was ready.

- 57 -

NO LOGIC FOR THIS GRIEF

As he entered their home, Viola was the only person he wanted to see, and the only person he had held in his mind during the last few hours. The manner in which he had vacated the scene didn't make him proud but his action had been motivated by a deep and dark force, driving him to think in a way which was as painful as it was unfamiliar. There was no way he could leave her as she was now. He wanted to make it right for her, and to be with her one last time.

He picked her up gently in his arms, carrying her to the bedroom and laying her on the bed, arranged her so that she looked comfortable. This wasn't a ritual or a strange act for him, it was to do with dignity, peace and respect. She looked serene somehow and no longer in pain which gave him the feeling that she was asleep.

He put one of the suitcases they had chosen together at the bottom of the bed.

"We're going on a voyage now, a holiday of a lifetime. Our honeymoon will last forever." Then he took the remaining piece of Orange Silk that he had kept, and laying it over the length of her body, kissed her on her forehead. "Bye bye my Queen." Turning, he left the room, closing the door behind him.

He went to work. He showered and shaved his head, but not his beard. Playing some of Viola's music, he put on his suit, the one that Viola had given him when he'd first moved in with her. He was simply going through the motions of his routine. Then he put all the clothes they had bought into the remaining suitcases and carried them towards the door, stopping as he opened it.

"I'm just going out for a bit, I'll be back in a while."

He walked through the door, carrying the cases, then closed it behind him. By the side of the road he waited, calmly, peacefully, for a taxi, eventually flagging one down and locking eyes with the driver.

"Do you know the concrete underpass, down by water, near that giant clothes store?"

"Oh, you mean The Cathedral."

"That's it."

"No trouble brother."

EZee put the bags in the back. They drove and very soon they arrived. He paid the driver.

"Take it easy brother."

Unloading the bags he carried them towards the group of homeless Synths, gathered as a congregation under the great concrete structure above. A woman recognised him.

"Well if isn't EZee One!"

"You remember me."

"Got a good memory for faces, never forget a face, forget everything else though."

"I've got some clothes for you."

"Lovely, lovely and some shiny bags. Put them down just here. Will you stay for a while have some food with us."

"No, I've got to be going."

"Oh well, be seeing you."

EZee left and walked slowly back to the flat, giving himself this time and taking in the views of the city for the last time. He arrived and went to the bedroom, opened the door slightly and standing in the doorway he whispered to Viola.

"Something's come up that I have to take care of, it's just a business thing. I'm going to have to meet you at the ship. We're in cabin 243. I love you baby."

If you open yourself to loss, you are at one with loss and you can accept it completely.

Taking only his bike helmet, he left the apartment. The Plasma sped at an elevated rate into the heart of the city, where he had an appointment to keep.

- *58* -

VERY SUITABLE

He took a moment outside the tailor's shop. Last here with Viola the memory was still fresh in his mind. The feelings he encountered then were now no longer present, indeed there was an emptiness were they had once been. With no rationale, he felt that to enter this establishment would be to leave a particular world behind him and to accept that there was only a new world ahead. This was a 'before' moment, there would be an 'after' moment, what came between was currently of little concern. It was with this slight degree of numb disinterest that he entered the shop.

The tailor greeted him warmly. "Ah Mister EZee. Welcome back."

"Good day to you."

"Is Mrs. EZee not with you today Sir?"

"No, she was unable to make it. If we could get down to business."

"Certainly. Will Sir be taking the garment straight away or would you prefer to try it on first. Just to check the measurements."

"Thank you. I would like to see myself in the suit, see how it looks on me, see how it makes me feel."

"Perfect."

The man took a few steps and lifted the suit from a hanger nearby. EZee put the suit on in a large changing room. Wearing a new pair of shoes, the ones carefully chosen with Viola, he walked out of the changing room to the tailor who was waiting patiently.

"Ah yes, just the ticket, Sir. If you please."

The tailor ushered EZee to stand in front of a long, broad mirror, in which EZee could see himself clearly. The tailor began pulling out some minor creases and they spoke as he did so. EZee was slightly fascinated with his image, seeing something, and someone, whom he had not seen before.

"Is this a suit for your place of work, Sir? I only ask as I like to have a picture in my mind of my clothes as they are being utilised in the field, so to speak."

EZee spoke with a kind of detachment which he wasn't used to himself.

"I'm actually just starting out in a new job, it's my first day."

"Congratulations, a very special day then."

"And the nature of your profession, Sir, if I'm not being too forward."

"No, not at all. I used to be in sales, then an opening came up in distribution. I imagine you make suits for many different types of people here."

"Oh, I can safely say my clientele come from all walks of life. So it's distribution then?"

"Well, in a way, due to forces outside of my control I've felt obliged to accept another position."

"I'm sorry to hear that Sir."

"It's not a problem. The new role simply requires a slight shift of perspective. It necessitates the adoption of a different skill set, an alternative mind set, that's all."

"And what is the title of your new role, Sir?"

EZee stepped away from the mirror, seeming to have had enough. He began walking around the shop, looking at the various rolls of fabric. But he quickly began talking again, apparently enjoying this opportunity for conversation with the curious tailor.

"I'm a Systems Analyst."

"My goodness Sir, that is quite an occupation, it must be fascinating job."

"I specialise in malfunctioning systems."

"There are certainly many of those in this day and age."

"Fault diagnosis is the key concept to be mastered."

"Well, yes I imagine it would be."

"If you can find the root cause of a problematic system, that's half the work done, right there."

"So that you can correct it…"

"No. Not always. Sometimes, yes. It may be a simple case of removing or destroying, an unwanted element of the system to regain system integrity. But occasionally you might need to make the addition of a particular element in order to restore the balance to the system."

"That makes perfect sense Sir."

"Sometimes though, there is very little that one can do. Fortunately just knowing the nature of the fault, and its location, is enough to enable the health of the system."

"I imagine with such knowledge one could… work around certain problematic areas."

"Yes. You are right about that. But whatever the strategy, there are always consequences."

"Naturally."

"Using a specific solution may prove to be a success but often there are knock on effects, there are always unwanted side effects to any alteration in a system."

"It is the case with tailoring too, Sir. If one changes a seam in one place, a subsequent alteration may be required at another."

"Of course, sometimes one cannot predict the next link in a chain of cause and effect with any degree of accuracy. Particularly in a chaotic system."

"Oh no Sir. It is more of an art than a science."

"I think you just have to have faith that you have identified the fault, at it's most primary level, and then act appropriately."

"One needs the courage of one's convictions and then one must act decisively."

"Once done, many actions cannot be undone."

"Precisely Sir. You can only cut a piece of cloth once."

"It's important to appreciate that."

"Well yes, especially if there is only a finite amount of a particularly rare cloth. Is the suit to your liking, Sir?"

The suit was a perfect fit, close but with free movement. The warmth of the wool was apparent and, opening the jacket, the Orange Silk lining was flawlessly stitched in. In front of the mirror once more, he put his head to one side, gazing at his reflection. He saw the suit, his head, his face and he saw his hands. As he looked deeper he could see himself as one whole person. He thought that perhaps he was a handsome person, just as Viola was a beautiful woman. He thought that they were a beautiful couple together. He had a perfect image of himself now, as a man with a task to perform.

"Excellent. I'll wear it now."

"As you wish Sir."

He paid.

"Your other clothes, Sir, shall I put them in a bag for you?"

"No, I won't be needing them, if you'll dispose of them for me I'd be grateful."

"Certainly. If you have any issues with the performance of the garment please don't hesitate to pop in, I'm always here."

"I'm sure that won't be necessary."

"And, of course, if Sir has any further tailoring requirements I am here to serve."

"Thank you."

EZee left the shop, thinking how helpful some humans were, and was quickly on the bike again, the suit giving him more than ample room for manoeuvre. His next appointment he was not looking forward to so much, but it demanded his total focus.

There is no greater illusion than fear, no greater wrong than preparing to defend yourself, no greater misfortune than having an enemy.

- 59 -

STRICTLY BUSINESS

He left The Plasma just moments away from The Studio entrance and walking in through the front door, climbed the metal staircase.

Careful as someone crossing an iced-over stream. Alert as a warrior in enemy territory. Courteous as a guest. Fluid as melting ice.

The usual faces were there, and on one floor, Stealer stood motionless, with fixed expression.

EZee had nothing to say to him. They squared off, for more than was comfortable for Stealer as he saw the intent in EZee's eyes. Without talking Stealer took a gun from an inner holster and handed it to EZee who took it firmly in his hands, feeling its weight and its cold machined metal touch.

"Loaded?"

"Yep."

"Better be." EZee then pointed it directly at Stealer's right eye and quietly whispered, "Bang!"

Stealer flinched and EZee put the gun inside his jacket pocket. He walked up the remaining steps and emerged into the open space of the upper storey.

He thinks of his enemy as the shadow that he himself casts.

The Minister was sitting in a large chair but stood up and walked over to EZee with some degree of happiness.

"EZee, come in, have a seat. I thought we could have a drink to celebrate our arrangement, toast your journey."

"Actually, I have rather a nasty headache currently and I must be getting along. The ship and everything."

"Ah yes, what time does she weigh anchor?"

"Just a couple of hours from now."

"Good, good. Are you all packed?"

"I have everything I need."

"I was sorry to hear your partner was not able to join you, the journey would have passed so much more quickly with a companion. It seems passports aren't so easy to come by these days. It's a shame."

"I hate bureaucracy. Viola really wanted me to do this though, she said it was the only way for me to grow. We said our goodbyes earlier."

The Minister had a nervous tick over one eye which twitched slightly.

"I hope you won't miss each other too much. I would have liked to have met her."

"I'm afraid that won't be possible now."

"Well look, we'll keep in regular contact, as your journey progresses. I think that's the key to good business. Regular updates on progress."

"Communication is everything. I just have a quick question. The REM is all loaded, yes?"

"Ah yes, of course, I almost forgot, it's all aboard. You'll have no trouble. It's hidden within the subframe of one of the cruise liner's tourist coaches. They have three in the cargo bay. I have the registration number of our rather special one here, it's B126 583W. It's all in the folder." He handed over a brown folder which EZee took.

"That's all I need to know. I'm ready now."

"So. I'd like to shake your hand EZee, to formally seal our deal, and wish you all the best for your future."

The Minister came forward and extended his hand. EZee hesitated at first and then took it in his. From the weight of the rather puffy palm, he made a quick calculation as to the human's weight. They shook.

"Well I imagine you're keen to get underway. It was good of you to come in, to say goodbye."

"It was nothing."

"Is there anything else we can do for each other? I think we've covered most everything, as I said everything else in the folder."

"There was one other thing."

"Oh, yes, how can I help?"

"Well maybe I can help you. It's a matter of memory."

"Right, well that's our business." The Minister laughed nervously.

"I understand that recently you had cause to discipline a Synth, someone as important as an accountant I understand."

"Unfortunately that happens all too often."

"This one was very special to me. Her name was Viola."

The Minister's face sank, and bordered somewhere between panic and confusion.

"That's a terrible coincidence, the names I mean."

"Yes it is."

"I'm sorry EZee, I don't see what this has got to do with me, or you for that matter."

"It's come to my attention that she was killed for a minor misconduct."

"Quite frankly, this is not a conversation I'm prepared to continue, I think you…"

EZee removed the gun from his inner pocket.

"Do you remember her, Sir, an accountant by the name of Viola?"

"No, I can't say that I…"

"Viola, do you remember the name?"

"Yes, yes I recall someone of that name but you… put that thing away, we both know that you're not going to use it."

"Do you remember her number?"

"What?"

"Her identity number can you remember that?"

"Well, if I had to remember all the ID numbers of my employees, I'd have to…"

"I can remember all of them. You don't have one do you?"

"This is stupid, give me the gun and let's forget about this."

The Minister began walking towards EZee, holding out his hand for the gun, but EZee simply lowered it slightly.

"Why did you kill her?"

"Look, this is all rather academic, it's just a question of hierarchy and orders from above. You're not going to shoot me, you can't you're a Synth."

"Well I'm kind of curious about that, it doesn't feel like it's something I can't do. What happens if I…?"

EZee shot The Minister in the leg. He fell to the ground crying out in instant pain.

"Ah, interesting, expression of pain. Why did you kill her?"

"She, she… forgot a report, my superiors were angry, an example had to be made."

"Mmm, doesn't sound like a very good reason to take another life, or maybe you think her life wasn't worth very much, not as much as a real person for example."

"You're a Synth, you work for me, you can't do this."

"What's your name, who do you work for?"

"I'm, I'm, my name is, it's Phillips, Jordan Phillips."

"Is that your full identity?"

"Jordan Richard Phillips, that's my name. What do you want?"

"And who do you work for?"

"What do you care?"

"Who?"

"Chang, Kino Chang, he's, he's in the Government."

"Ah, now I understand, you work for the government. You have no soul Mister Phillips, has anyone ever told you that?"

"Who, who are you?"

"I'm… The Silk King."

EZee pulled the trigger for a second time. It didn't feel like he was killing anyone, he was just moving his finger slightly. It was the bullet passing through The Minister's head that had killed him. The killing had come easily to him though, he was surprised by that. It was as if he were born to it.

The world is sacred. It can't be improved. If you tamper with it, you'll ruin it. If you treat it like an object, you'll lose it.

EZee left the room and walked down the steps, stopping in front of Stealer to hand the gun back to him.

"Someone else can run the show from now on, someone suitably… synthetic."

"Yes boss."

"And you'll be keeping this to yourself of course."

"Naturally boss. Not a word. We're all in this together."

"You haven't seen me."

"You weren't ever here, and I haven't ever seen you before."

"Do you think the same can be said of the others?"

"Their memories are very unreliable boss, they probably can't remember who they used to work for."

"Which person was that?"

"The one who you just removed from the equation."

"He doesn't exist. However, I've created a considerable mass of inanimate organic matter upstairs, and it needs to be disposed of immediately. Will you see to it?"

"Personally."

"Would you also make sure this building is thoroughly sanitised, before vacating it yourself?"

"There will be no trace of any kind life here within the hour, animal or vegetable."

"Good. Stealer, now about that thing you did. You didn't do it, do you understand, that was someone else."

"I don't know that person."

"You don't know me either."

"Who are you?"

"You don't know."

That was enough, leaving the building some of the other Synths bowed to him as he left, good news travels fast thought EZee, as though they were all reading the same text, at the same time. 'We're all in this together,' Stealer had said.

Soon EZee was back on The Plasma, blasting through the city at full tilt, heading for the cruise ship and his departure from the city he would try to forget. Memory fragments flashed through his mind, a fractured fast-forward recall from his first impressions of the manic metropolis to his present status quo.

- 60 -

PASSPORT CONTROL

I arrived in Hong Kong wearing the plain red robes of a simple monk. I'd ridden on a bicycle for hundreds of miles to get here and I spoke only a smattering of Mandarin.

Within days I was run down and ragged. Everything around me was disturbing. I walked the streets in a heavy daze of both awe and nausea, the wealth and the poverty living so close to each other.

It was an immersion into extremes, and it was my memory that was the first attribute to be degraded by the environment.

The drug I found to help me remember who I was, was a hateful pill in many respects, but one that propped up a whole subculture. In hindsight perhaps I should have been better off without it all together. Its miraculous effects being mixed inexorably with the darkest of flaws made it a double edged sword of the most lethal kind. The problem with necessary evils, is not that they're evil but that they're necessary. I had lost my only love, and it was the grip of REM with its fiendish backlash which was ultimately to blame.

As I handed over my Plasma to the cruise liner staff for it to be loaded into cargo, I glimpsed the tourist bus with the identifying registration plate being driven through the great doors of the ship. These great steel hinged plates were like a gaping mouth, ready to receive the millions of tiny coloured capsules within the bus. My Neon Green Thirteen bike would follow into storage for safe passage.

I was going where they were going. It was rather a lot of REM for just one person, I know, and I wasn't sure exactly what I was going to do with it, but I knew I would have decisions to make regarding this, at some point.

A spark of an idea burned brightly at the front of my mind for a few seconds. An impulse to turn back in this moment took a strong grip on my emotions and threatened to arrest me in my tracks. There was a revolution to be ignited here, that I might lead it with a fiery revenge still in my heart was a passionate temptation. The Synths minds united in their shared consciousness with me, the outsider, the crazed loner as their murderous leader. But I checked my fire.

With a freshly formed coherence I felt in my core, there was a unique individuality within, which demanded to be explored, and I needed to be solo to explore it. Having paused for just a few moments, I reassumed my personal direction, momentum being with me.

I went through customs. This was a first of course and I assumed it would be a formality. I was only curious to see if there would be any interest in my shiny new identity. I had no fears of being flagged and apprehended for my crime. There was no danger of Stealer or any other Synth having reported my deed. I was certain of that in a way that I couldn't explain to myself. But would there be some initialisation procedure when scanning my codes for the first time?

As I expected the process was swift. Officials went through the voice, retina and voice imprints and without much more than a cursory glance they waved me through. Couldn't this be fully automated? What was this personal involvement in such a rudimentary basic identity check? I didn't care.

That was it, I out of there. Behind me now was a digital wall, which separated me from the city. I was effectively already in an another country.

- *61* -

Cybex Orbital Space Hub

Authentication

JJ was half asleep. It was easy to doze off when you're in Zero-G and he found himself to be in a meditative state where not even his weight was a distraction to his mind.

Somewhere, a long way away it seemed, a tiny quiet beeping sound was chirping away like a solitary bird in a tree. JJ knew it was there, on some level, he sensed its presence but still it failed to soak into his awareness sufficiently to command attention. It wasn't relevant to him. He felt he was sitting under that tree, slightly drowsy and tipsy, with Kristina, by a river in North Carolina and the bird was only one wonderful element in his sensory mind-scape.

Then it became an electronic bird and it was a digital river and the sunlight was artificial and Kristina was whispering in his ear.

"Hey Cowboy, what are you dreaming about?"

And JJ knew he wasn't dreaming, the beeping was constant and repetitive and seemed to be getter louder and more insistent, so he opened his eyes.

There was Kristina alright, but he wasn't on Earth, certainly not in his home State. He was in the Media Module and Kristina was floating in front of him, right up close, looking him in the eyes. There was a lag however, before his reality overwhelmed his dream.

"Where's my beer gone?"

"No beer honey, in-flight cabin staff are only serving fruit juice or water."

EZee shook his head and looked around, suddenly the beeping seemed more pressing.

"What's that… that beeping?"

"I think something flagged must have come up. Do you want to get out of bed and check it out?"

"Er… yeah. How are you? Are you, are you…?"

"Awake? Doing my job? Responsible for a space craft?"

"Ok, Ok."

They manoeuvred themselves over to the nearest terminal and sure enough a small icon was blinking softly in time to the beeps. JJ touched it, entered the alert page and was quickly fully alert.

"Whoa. Look Kristina, it's our boy, the EZ1 unit, what do you know!"

Kristina was locked on too. "He must have used his I.D. registration somewhere."

"At the port. He's got on a boat!"

"Well I never. Where's he going?"

"Hold on, let me just look. Ok, Ok, Ok… there. He's going to St. Lucia, via the Panama Canal, on some cruise ship."

"Well what's the point in that?!" Kristina was incredulous.

But JJ was flummoxed. "I don't know. Maybe he's on holiday."

"Why doesn't he fly?"

"I'm sure he's got his reasons, maybe it was cheaper. We've go to call this in."

"You mean grass our guy up?!"

"What do you mean grass him up? He hasn't done anything wrong! Command will want to know about it, that's all."

"Do you think we should tell them about your little laser show too?"

"That was different, we were just helping him out. Now we need to report his current status to Command, and they can take over. We're remote sensing not remote control."

"And you're saying the laser wasn't a type of control?"

EZee's face was blank. "You wouldn't do that."

"What grass you up?" The question hung in the air.

"Well what do you suggest then?"

"We help him out again."

"And how are we supposed to do that? What sort of help? Does he need any help?"

"Well precisely. Why don't we just leave him alone, give him some time to do whatever he's doing, go wherever he's going?" Again Kristina's question created some air.

"We could do that. You know it doesn't make much difference. I mean what are CYBEX going to do anyway?"

Kristina knew she had got her way. "They could send a company launch or a helicopter to intercept this… cruise ship… pick up their faulty product for analysis."

"It's hardly likely is it. But they're sure to find out. The link to our system will download the data, and probably sooner rather than later."

"Well then they'll find out, but our guy will be home free by then, he's already away. Has he been assimilated yet? I mean Ultra Net connection, is he connected?"

"I don't know, let me check." JJ busied himself at the terminal for a while and then looked up, disappointed. "No, not yet."

"Well, when will he be?"

"Hard to say, as soon as he picks up the local system and locks on. Could by any time, soonish probably."

"Why don't we come back and check up on him in a bit?"

"Mmm, yeah, I guess that's the best thing to do."

"Pod Six?"

"Pod Six."

- 62 -

ALONE AMONG EQUALS

Without any forewarning I was subjected to a powerful transformation beyond my understanding. Just after I boarded the ship, whilst walking through a passageway on deck, a momentous wave of energy came upon me, and passed through me. Something was filling my core with a trillion pieces of information. This, I later found out, was the Ultra-Net, the Hive Mind of the Synth.

By methods unknown to me at the time, I had been interconnected sublimely, profoundly, now and forever, with my kindred spirits. I felt their feelings, I thought their thoughts and I could see Viola mixed up in all of them in some hazy hologram, warm and fuzzy around the edges.

Its net covers the whole universe. And though its meshes are wide, it doesn't let a thing slip through.

I had slumped to the floor and lay there, blacked out, for how long I don't know. I was a man out for the count, floored by a digital uppercut in the first few seconds of the first round.

A friendly soul helped me up off the deck of the ship where I had fallen.

"Are you ok, brother?"

I looked him in the eyes and I knew. "Yes, I'll be just fine."

The man smiled "I'll see you around."

That night, around midnight, as the ship moved gracefully through the waters I stood on the uppermost deck of the ship and looked out to the horizon. The indigo blue of the sky met the black mass of sea in an impossible line. The moon was a slim crescent and the stars were out to play. Every moment was infused with Viola's soul.

Things arise and she lets them come; things disappear and she lets them go. She has but doesn't possess, acts but doesn't expect. When her work is done, she forgets it. That is why it lasts forever.

I had decided to wean myself off the REM, I knew it could be done, and I knew I didn't want to be making any new memories, not for the foreseeable future anyway. The memories I'd made in my short life, and the connections between them, had some kind of permanence now, as if they had been banked on my behalf.

In these moments, millions upon millions of atoms were rearranging themselves in threads, to weave fantastic patterns in the folds of my soul. A complete immersion in the greater synthetic world, formed ripples and waves of understanding. I was with my kind, all of them. I had new paths to walk down but I was no longer alone.

With a slight movement somewhere above me, I suddenly became alert, caught by something in my peripheral vision. There it was, moving through the night's sky once more, the point of light starship flying through Space, straight and true, racing around the world at some kind of crazy speed. And I felt connected to it too, as though I was flying with the Future People who lived within. Surely they were up there, looking down on me in this very instant, looking out for me as I sailed in another, different kind of ship far below them.

That which has no substance enters where there is no space.

As for my identity, I know who I am, and it isn't some number or code. Through the awareness revealed to me by assimilation into the unity of Synth consciousness, I understand my original intended purpose to be no more than that of a simple soldier.

I will always be Viola's work-in-progress, and perhaps in time, I will become an artist of sorts myself too. I turn the ring on my finger and I realise she is a permanent part of my soul.

As the ship moves away from land I watch the lights of the city recede into the distance and their hold over me diminishes with every new second. I am not much more than a fugitive and a thief, and my freedom is fragile, but I have left few tracks and I rate my chances. I relax as the hunt for answers is over. I know I will always remember, but for now I must forget. As for my home, it will remain for now a place within.

When there is no desire, all things are at peace.

A gentle gust of wind blows my jacket open and with it rippling in the breeze my eye catches a flash of its Orange Silk lining. Sliding my fingertips over the natural material I feel strangely at one with myself. My ever changing inner world merges with the outer world forming a new reality of existence. I happen to wonder about where I'm going, and hear the words of the monk echoing within.

Each separate being in the universe returns to the common source. Returning to the source is serenity.

Deep in my psyche I sense a strong and steady wave of vibrant natural energy flowing through me with a constant force. Its quality feels unique to the person I've now become and in this moment my future is revealed as a journey towards the origin of my life. I seek serenity. I seek the source.

EZEE'S JOURNEY CONTINUES…

Printed in Great Britain
by Amazon